MRS. OCTOBER WAS HERE

We are aware that a civilization has the same fragility as a life.

—PAUL VALÉRY

The duration of the universe must therefore be one with the latitude of creation which can find place in it.

—HENRI BERGSON, *L'Evolution creatrice*

MRS. OCTOBER WAS HERE

by coleman dowell

A NEW DIRECTIONS BOOK

Manufactured in the United States of America
First published clothbound (ISBN: 0–8112–0518–5) and as New Directions Paperbook 368 (ISBN: 0–8112–0519–3) in 1974
Published simultaneously in Canada by McClelland & Stewart, Inc.

New Directions Books are published for James Laughlin
by New Directions Publishing Corporation,
333 Sixth Avenue, New York 10014

For Bert and Tam and Mickey and Frances

MRS. OCTOBER WAS HERE

FOREWORD

Somewhere, out beyond the limits of the twentieth century, there is an outpost called Tasmania, Ohio. It is not so cold as Cleveland, nor so drab as Cincinnati, nor so mean-spirited as Columbus. It is not nearly so large as any of those three rather ghastly Ohioan Fates (Cincinnati spins; Cleveland measures; Columbus bites with mad yellow teeth), having had the good sense to stop at natural barriers, knowing that if you climb every mountain and ford every stream, chances are you'll wind up with a wet hernia.

Tasmania lies, like an English pudding, rather heavily in its basin, which is formed of a ring of pretty hills that are called locally 'mountains'; The Tasmanian Mountains. However, if you should look for this ring of hills on a map you would not find it; so much for fame. Or, perhaps, one man's mountain is another man's gap.

But in the sense of being true barriers, allowing to if not indeed forcing upon the Tasmanians privacy, the hills did function for a great many years as effectively as Himalayas or Andes. So effectively were they barriers that Tasmania itself has appeared on American maps only since the Revolution. On account of the intrepidity of one eighteenth-century French traveler and cartographer, Tasmania, prettily colored, wearing the ribbons of her two little rivers and the tufted cloak of her hills, can be found on a few maps drawn up during that period. One such, a gift by the author to the town, hangs on the southeast wall of the Curio Room in the Tasmania Museum and Library; the remaining three hand-colored samples, remarkably like the paper money of Latin countries, are to be found in Paris, Dresden, Madrid.

Of rivers, as noted, there are two: the Tasman, source unknown, inclined to languor and silt; and the Demon, which springs in green foaming rage out of the hills in springtime, grows to maturity and dry death each August, and in-between times behaves more or less as does any normal river. In passing, it should be speculated that Demon could be a shortening of Van Diemen['s Land], which could have been the original name of Tasmania, as in the case of the island off Australia. But speculation here leads to the edge of the metaphysical, having Tasmania, Ohio, anticipate by at least a hundred years the island's name change which occurred in 1855; the Frenchman's map of Tasmania, Ohio, was drawn up in 1753. Metaphysics and Ohio make ludicrous twins, as though one tried to couple Boeotia or Columbus with acuity.

That the Tasmanians were aware of their middling position, of , in short, their normalcy, was evidenced by their self-styling as The Heart City: TASMANIA, THE HEART CITY, OHIO, still greets one via signs at the four possible points of ingression to the place. Great Bend, Kansas, and a few other places had put up a fight, saying that Ohio was an eastern state, practically Eastern Seaboard, and they had set in circulation a few jokes of an unkindly nature, one having to do with the high incidence of Hard Failure in Heart City, but gradually these tapered off. The controversy had taken place in the nineteen-forties, shortly after the war, when patriotism flared for a moment before dying and some Americans believed that being the very heart of the country was an enviable, highly honorable position. The rest of the country was quickly disabused of the illusion, but Tasmania, exhausted by its day under the arc lights of publicity, had fallen once again into refreshing slumber and so did not know that to be an American was to be belled as a leper.

In its happy somnolence, like a child fed but not exercised, Tasmania burgeoned in the only way that it could without climbing the mountains, which would have woken it up: its

American-ness grew apace, vice and virtue neck-and-neck like equally matched race horses. Bigotry and generosity clicked cannons; xenophobia and neighborliness bumped stifles; sexual repression and adultery rubbed gaskins; and the avaricious and the naïf laid cheek by muzzle and trotted quietly together down Splendor Street.

The following is Tasmania as it was before the Revolutionist, Mrs. Septimus October, and an extraordinary collection of the worldly transformed it forevermore, a term of relativity taken nowadays to mean vaguely until the year 2000:

A town built on the shape of an X. The business street, Splendor, runs SE to NW and its appropriate sections are called South and North Splendor. The rougher businesses—bars and so on—are contained on the northern stretch. The southern half features—tucked among hardware, dry goods and chemists—the library and museum, post office, firehouse, church and school, elementary and high occupying the same building. Running from SW to NE is Marvel, The Street of Mansions. The houses there are big and old, with more character than beauty. The rest of the town proper is divided into twenty streets, alleys, and rues, five within each wedge formed by the X, with such names as Rue Flambeau and Powhatan. These streets, alleys, rues, form concentric squares and are accessible only from those points at which they touch Splendor and Marvel, with the exceptions of the four outlying streets which form the borders of the town and are given over to railroad buildings, granaries, warehouses. Inconvenient; Ohioan; American.

(On the Frenchman's map the view is from the north; that is, the map is drawn up with N in the position usually accorded to S, and it is upon this eccentric map that these descriptions are based.)

From the hills to the west comes boiling in the springtime the Demon River which circumnavigates the town's south end. The Tasman enters the basin through a gap in the hills to the NW; at a position of due north, or six o'clock on the dial of the town, it begins a swing away from the town heading

3

NE; this continues until, on the town's dial at 7 o'clock, it cuts abruptly south and, for a quarter mile of its greatest activity, makes rapids and threatening noises as it approaches conjunction with the Demon. They come together due east like long-separated lovers, flinging the red and white foam of their union into the air there, and then move off side by side, the green and the earth-colored, compatible but unassimilable, eventually to the sea.

As pretty as the foregoing description may be, it could be dispensed with except for one factor: where the Tasman swings northward away from the town, then swerves abruptly south, it has cut from the earth a rounded point of land in the shape of a vulpine nose. Like the object it resembles, especially when worn by those of Semitic cast, this point of land is a focus for the dislike of the mainly Protestant Tasmanians, for it is where the wretched, the poor, and in a few cases, the rebellious, have been forced, or have chosen, to gather. It is Tasmania's slum and borgo and is called The Wolf. (There is an Australian marsupial, a carnivore, named the Tasman or Tasmanian Wolf; perhaps this is the derivation; if so it brings us perilously close to the exotic, and gentleman-corn normalcy and such exotica are as unacceptable in tandem as, say, literacy and the average Columbus Ohioan).

To find the location of Tasmania on a modern map, turn the map so that the line separating Indiana and Ohio runs parallel to your mouth. With this image, think of a beast crouching upon the map, drinking from Lake Erie at Cleveland—a firewater drinker. Its forepaws rest upon Toledo, its hindfeet—the animal is in bas-relief—lightly touch Springfield. That little round hole, or anus, is Columbus. If you will now make a mark centrally between front and hindfeet, and from there draw a line to about where (it is a female beast) the second pair of teats counting from the hindquarters would hang . . . on the other hand, it might be simpler to take a reading of 83° longitude and 35° latitude . . . or, simpler still, you could go there.

It has no slums now; The Wolf is dead. Bigotry is unknown;

people are polite. Everyone has about the same amount of income and the average age will soon be eighteen. And so on.

There is, too, a Curiosity as befits a monument to a Revolution, which is what Tasmania is: A man, not young and not old but aging, stands on a ladder each early morning and polishes the air. Then he climbs down and polishes brass plaques, four set at intervals along a low wall, hauling his polish and rags and ladders in a little stripe-painted jeep like those you see running around Acapulco. Each morning, rain or sun, snow or tornado. Curious, yes; but more curious is that he does not know, nor do the Tasmanians, nor do any of those bright and terrible people who poured into the town during the stay there of Mrs. Septimus October and her revolutionary crew—none of them know why he performs this task. It is like the empty, atavistic gestures of some animals, especially the human one, especially in the area of religion: all but the ritual has vanished and still the cloth is spread and the bells rung; Christ is forgotten.

But despite bishops and the officious; despite fire, disorders, laws; despite indifference and forgetfulness—records of even the lowliest events somehow survive, however fragmentary, and those fragments abound with answers. These are the records of those events. There are some answers here.

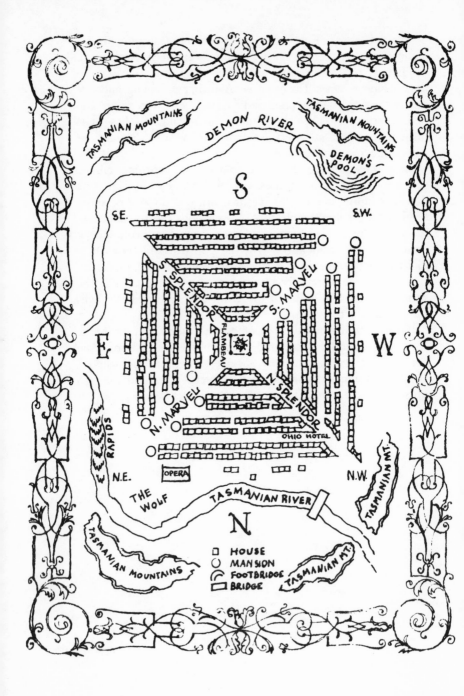

PART I
Tasmania

UNTIL MRS. OCTOBER came to Tasmania and began many things that, like most mortal leaders, she was unable to see through due to extenuating circumstances—among which a thoughtful person must give high precedence to deaths of a bizarre nature—Cecil (ne Buck) Jones was just another decorator trying vainly, in a town addicted to the shabbily familiar, to effect a bamboo renaissance.

That is not innuendo; he was not Red, or Pink: chinoiserie as a noun for decorative style or politics was unthinkable to him because he did not know of the existence of the word, and had barely heard of China. He worked in bamboo because he had been able to buy dirt cheap a shipment mysteriously left on a railway siding, and he proceeded to 'do' one bamboo showcase, his sister's basement, which he christened The Game Room. But as it was empty of game, or games, and was sweltering in winter because of the antiquated coal furnace and stank weirdly of jungle spoor in summer, nobody ever went down there if it could be avoided.

Bucky had corresponded with Mrs. October for some time before her arrival in Tasmania. He had answered an ad in a magazine to which he subscribed, which read:

CONFEDERATE WANTED
Lady w/ unlmtd wlth, hby rdcrating ctys,
twns, cntrys, desrs crrspdnce w/ prson owng,
n chg of, or ntrstd n same.

Bucky had been told often enough by friends, "Boy, you've got this town sewed up. Decoratorwise, you own this town, literally." Bucky sometimes recognized a figure of speech when he heard it, and if in this case he had not, his bank account would have told him the difference between literal and actual: his balance was $14.60. He had spent all but the last money saved from his job as gas-meter inspector on the showcase: the fanciful bird cages, lion cages, and the like, had cost more than he had imagined they could, for in the eventuality they ever came to be filled with game, each piece of bamboo had been reinforced with slender steel rods up the center holes.

Bucky's sister's husband, who traveled, told Wanda that if she ever needed immediate cash for tiding her over between his visits, all she had to do was advertise winter quarters for the circus. He exaggerated, as usual; the game room was smallish—no bigger than two nice-sized bomb shelters, though he may have forgotten its size because nobody went down there, including the owners. In fact, that it existed at all came to be taken on uneasy faith alone after the child of one of Wanda's friends wandered down and came screaming up the stairs babbling "people in the cages." Bucky, who was paying a call at the time, was bothered and spoke frankly to the child's mother.

"No sibling of the premature age of six, which I personally don't care he's not mine, shouldn't be allowed to look at the TV so much, which he's too young." He added gently, drawing on his yellow chamois gloves—a post-gas-company affectation—"Honest, Marie Louise, you'll traumarize that kid."

Marie Louise's nostrils dilated but she waited until Bucky was out of the house before she began, priming herself with a long pull at her Presbyterian highball.

"Like I believe you know, Wanda honey, I don't speak French personally . . ." Her pause was ominous and as always it made Wanda nervous, though she was wearying of such attacks upon her in lieu of her brother. Marie Louise continued.

"My personal education has been such that the French language as spoken by the persons of France is not known to me personally. However, my good friend, Myra Little, whom, you may recall, came to us from New Orleans, Louisiana . . ." Again she paused to heighten the effect but Wanda spoiled it by going on record about Myra.

"That bitch."

"True," said Marie Louise, caught off balance by the open attack, which she immediately turned to advantage by stressing the found word, "*but* Myra Little does speak French like a native to the manner born and furthermore she keeps her ears open . . ."

"Among other things," said Wanda, her eyes snapping. She was nothing if not a moralist, at that time, and she knew what she knew about Myra Little. Marie Louise, whose bond with Myra was their—separate, of course—indulgence in extra-marital sex, felt a twinge of worry. Consequently she adopted a tone of voice that for sheer righteousness put Wanda's in the shade.

"Wanda Phelps, do you want my advice or don't you?"

"No," said Wanda promptly, "but a fat lot of good may it do me."

"O.K." said Marie Louise, rising and pulling her child against her knees so abruptly that it belched Patio Cola. "I just thought you should know that the entire city of Tasmania is laughing out loud at your brother. Cee-cil. Huh."

Wanda, when driven to it, occasionally mined a vein of satire deep within herself. She now felt so driven. Cocking an ear toward the street she said, "Hark. I hear Tasmania laughing." Marie Louise was so angered by the way her words were turned to her disadvantage that she gave her child a rough push in the direction of the basement door.

"Go play with the people cages, sugar," she said, and ignoring the child's terrified wail, she held her empty glass out to Wanda with a peremptory gesture of her other hand, long index finger pointing dramatically at the bar. Wanda, impressed, still was able to notice that the fingernail needed cleaning.

"Now you're going to listen whether you want to or not, Mrs. Phelps. No best friend of mine's brother is going to get away with telling me how to raise my kid which he mangles the French language in the English Grill at the top of his lungs and my friend Myra Little said she's never heard the

like before wherever French is spoken. *Credenza. Huh.*"
Wanda meekly poured drinks while Marie Louise recovered
her breath.

"All right, dear. What did he say that was so untoward?"
Her mildness disarmed Marie Louise so that she spluttered
a bit at first, trying to recover her indignation.

"Well," she said finally, "he was talking about Louise Quints
and Myra said that was screamingly funny and a disgrace, too."

"That's a strange combination," Wanda observed.

"What is?" Marie Louise was genuinely interested. She
hadn't dared question Myra too closely about the matter, and
besides, when Myra told her what Bucky had said, Marie
Louise automatically laughed so hard that she could not have
heard an explanation if one were offered. But once again she
was doomed to disappointment. Wanda only said, in the same
mild tone:

" 'Funny' and 'disgrace.' "

"Oh."

"Now, what should poor old Bucky have said, so I can tell
him?"

Marie Louise stalled for time by drinking her fourth Presbyterian chug-a-lug, trying desperately the while to recall one or
two of Myra's words.

"Well, it's Louie, not Louise."

"And . . . ?" Wanda's insistence was like a mosquito repeatedly stinging the same bump.

"I told you, Wanda; I prefaced my remark by stating that
I don't speak French personally, but then I don't pretend to
be a decorator and go around spouting about foreign things,
or anything whatsoever which I can't pronounce."

Wanda, who had been standing, sat down with such sudden
ease that it came belatedly to Marie Louise that her friend had
actually been, in spite of her deceptively mild tone of inquiry,
as tense as a cat. Marie Louise cursed this bit of hindsight as
she waited for the counterattack.

"Who was it, dear, said she liked the singing voice of Gladys
Swathouse, pray?"

"Oh, really, now! I was ten years old when I said that!" Which was not true; she was considerably older—twenty-five, to be horribly exact, and she knew that Wanda had a memory for such tiresome details. She strove, therefore, to regain the upper hand by pointing out to Wanda a possible (Marie Louise was an optimist) irrelevance: "Besides, Swarthout's not a French name and we were discussing French . . ." When Wanda was silent, Marie Louise feared that she had exposed a more damaging ignorance. Somewhat piteously she asked, "It is? A French name?" Wanda, who had thought for a moment that her friend had her, drew an imperceptible breath of relief. Still, rather than risk falling into what could be a trap set to catch what she thought of as her 'lack of information,' and the consequent exhibit of said lack of information to a hard world by her suddenly ruthless friend, she merely smiled superiorly and the smile was successful enough to effect the humiliation feared by Marie Louise. Wanda could feel her friend's humiliation and would have changed the subject then and there if Marie Louise's hardhearted use of Miss Little's name to subdue her anger did not continue to rankle. She pressed on.

"Foreigners to one side, or back where they came from, name me one person in the city of Tasmania that talks French like a native to the manor born. Name me one."

"How would I know whether they did or didn't!" Marie Louise was touching in her total surrender.

"Then how do you know that Myra Little does?"

"Everybody knows . . ."

"Everybody? How can they, if they don't speak it themselves?"

Marie Louise, confronted by the need to think, could only shake her head. For some reason beyond her, Wanda could not stop even there. She felt that she had to draw from Marie Louise a verbal retraction of her, and Myra Little's, insinuations about Bucky, as well as an admission that all of Tasmania shared the same 'lack of information' as the two of them, Wanda and Marie Louise; if Marie Louise would do that, then Wanda would willingly concede that Myra Little spoke French so perfectly that she stuck out like a sore thumb in Tasmania. Her need made her voice authoritative.

"I am waiting for the name of a French-speaking person who can verify Myra Little's great gift for languages."

At the words "I am waiting" Marie Louise was afflicted by a headache of such flashing white light that she could read by it a fact almost obscured by the rush of time and events. Her mother had taught piano—years and years of piano lessons before senility came in paradox bearing great age in one hand and extreme youth in the other and said to Mrs. Hackett, "Here . . ." No, no! What it said was "Ici . . ." and that was as French as Louie Quints, and the reason it said "Ici" instead of "Here" was because those yellow sheets of music on the square grand piano bore, as often as not, French titles . . . Lost in the past, reading, despite her pain, the legend of her mother's brilliance, Marie Louise forgot momentarily the awful present and immediate past.

"Mother," she said, eyes closed, lips pursed to receive the redeeming nourishment she had never before wanted, before she found the old teat dry and remembered everything and stiffened, too late. Wanda's laugh tinkled; the tinkle was followed by:

"Oh? Who was it asked for Miss Clara de Lune's latest recording in Stewart's Record Shop—if memory serves, only last week?"

"I'll thank you to leave my old mother out of this, Wanda. You know damn well she's enjoying her second childhood."

"I certainly hope so," said Wanda.

That anyone should wish for anyone else's mother to be senile seemed to Marie Louise, in her confusion which tended to becloud her own attitudes, to be dirtily below the belt. She reached figuratively for the most effective object at hand with which to quell her friend, and though in the split second before launch the thought came that Wanda had meant she hoped Mrs. Hackett was *enjoying* her peculiar state, the weapon had already been set in flight and could not be recalled.

"Being senile is not quite the same thing as being bone-stupid!" Now, Wanda thought, detached, does she mean Bucky, or me, or both of us?

Feeling as pale as a white rose on Mother's Day, she drifted upward from her chair like smoke from a softly burning cushion. She stood with hands tenuously connected, head slightly inclined, thinking of Geraldine Fitzgerald.

"Good day. You will excuse me if I do not show you to the door. I must beg a previous appointment." She glided from the room and her silent supplication that she be allowed to do so without knocking anything over—a table or a lamp were her usual fellow travelers in dramatic exits—was answered for once by a sympathetic Deity.

Climbing the stairs, hearing below her the infuriated sobs of her erstwhile best friend, Wanda tried with all her might, so she thought, to curse her brother for a troublemaker, but each way she turned in her mind she encountered her dead mother's shrouded image, large and bulky as a dust-sheeted sofa from which there issued a hollow-voiced admonition: Look after little Bucky, now. Wanda had promised; the promise had been extracted as the mother lay dying; from such a promise there was no escape . . . not, thought Wanda in trembling superstition, throwing herself across the foot of her bed, not that she wished to escape. Bucky *was* her little brother, blood was thicker than water, or Presbyterian highballs for that matter, and Marie Louise could go to the devil, though Wanda certainly hoped she wouldn't actually go to the devil; it was just an expression.

Thus, equalizing all sides, mentally smoothing Bucky's path, soothing Marie Louise, forgiving Myra Little, obeying Mama, Wanda took their imagined turmoil into her own breast and enclosed it in little cells and snugly wrapped the cells in protective tissue, as she had been doing all her life. Sometimes she imagined—usually when the flatness and weight of night lay above her like earth—that the contents of the cells were gnawing through the tissue; that the whole mass was not unlike a bright fleshy flower that would, when it bloomed fully, tear her breast open and cause her such pain that it would be all right, at last, for her to scream. Dwelling on the effect, sometimes she longed for the cause.

Still, she had her methods whereby a measure of relief could be obtained. She could, for time-honored instance, look forward to Friday when her traveling salesman husband would return to her. Anticipating the sick headache through which she would keep him at a distance when he tried to press upon her his reeky needs, she felt a little joy with a speck of savagery on it, like a highly peppered crumb of steak—but how much pepper can a crumb hold? The taste, to a mouth starving in blandness, was maddening. She gave herself another crumb of seasoned meat, thinking for one brief moment in madness of a time when she should be able to gorge and engorge and disgorge in a continual chain reaction: she thought of the canasta game last night, specifically of her guests whose company she had been reduced to seeking because of Bucky's transforming her home into a chamber of horrors, among other things (even as she sought relief her old dead mother started looming up before her, forcing Wanda to rush at her satisfaction and barely sideswipe it). Her companions in the game were foreigners; she suspected that they were Jews; they had only recently moved from a squalid house in The Wolf to a fairly decent apartment on a back street, from which they hoped to move—so they told her quite openly—onto Marvel Street someday! Addressing them in her mind as she would have liked to have done last night, she said, "You will never make Marvel Street your home, for all your stupid talk about Democracy and opportunity and America. If nobody else stops you, I will." As her mother obtruded and began to blot the dear scene from her mind, Wanda imagined herself spread-eagle over the doorway of a gorgeous old house on Marvel, stopping the Levinskys with her body, saying to them, "Avaunt, Jewish persons; avaunt!"

But here was Mama; and "Yes, Mama," she said, and got herself in hand, but she thought that she and Mama were certainly not at odds on the subject of the Levinskys, and if she could just keep from connecting them with Bucky in her mind she could hate them as much as she wished, with Mama's approval. It was a small pleasure but a pleasure nonetheless and because of it Wanda resolved to stand by her brother, whatever he did, even though that 'whatever' already included writing to and getting from a foreigner some very peculiar mail indeed. Wanda had read all of Mrs. October's letters to Bucky and as many of his to her as she could divert him from, in the midst of writing, long enough to allow her to read them.

"Oh, Tasmania," she sighed, "your troubles all lie before you," and she smiled . . . with sympathy, or so she later said when she related the foregoing to a company of several hundred persons, from the stage of the Opera House, in line of her duty as a militant Revolutionist.

Bucky's face proved to the town's satisfaction that he was capable of trust. Not by wide-eyed openness that made people snap their fingers and come up with the name Ron McAllister, but because his left eye was squinched and the cheek below it delicately puckered. The disfigurement was the result of a wood brand thrust into his face by his mother when he was seven years old, part of a ritual of primitive dentistry in which a string was tied to the tooth with the other end secured to something immovable—mantelpiece or bedpost—and the fire thrust into the child's face was meant to cause him to leap back in alarm, leaving his tooth—and the mercenary dentist downtown—dangling. Bucky was unable to imagine that his mother would actually burn him and so stood his ground, grinning. Later, through the bandages, he apologized.

"Gee, Mom, I thought it was a game—I mean, like proving I wasn't a sissy, or something." His mother, who thought that he *was* a sissy, went into a decline of sorts and died a few years later—seven or eight—still thinking it. Her efforts at a deathbed change of heart, an old family tradition, were futile. Counting the decelerating beats of her heart all she could manage to think was, 'Like father, like son,' and the only image that she could conjure of the Beyond and the Waiting Beloved (her husband had died shortly after Bucky's birth; she had thought of him as Two-Shot Sam) was that the Beloved would probably be waiting in one of her own nightgowns which he had, in fact, preferred to wear. Unable to do anything dramatic with her last breath, knowing full well that she would not be able to bring herself to watch over Bucky from on high, she had handed the ball to Wanda: "Look after little Bucky, now," and feeling anticlimactic, had passed on.

Still, she had left Bucky with a legacy, for women found his squinch-eye and puckered cheek attractive and they felt that he was, further and unlike most men, trustworthy. "He has been through the fire," they would say, "and knows what it's like," and after he had read their gas meters they would detain him with coffee in the kitchen while they poured out their life stories, accent on the married or sexual part. Many would gladly have extended the camaraderie in the kitchen to coyness in the parlor to lubricity in the bedroom, but there was something, a feeling of innocence, that kept them from the attempt. This led to sublimation and a sort of sister act.

"Whaddaya think of my new curtains, Bucky?" the lady would ask. "Snappy, huh?" Bucky would agree wholeheartedly with the snappy, and then over a second cup he would squint at the curtains while the lady of the house implied her husband's lack of understanding of her taste, using the curtains as illustration.

"Well, *he* said they looked like a chippy's drawers, meaning the ruffles and all." Bucky would consider it carefully, spooning sugar into his cup until his coffee resembled mocha cream.

"Well," he would say finally, "husbands say a lot of things" —and would leave it hanging there, including the doubt that the husband was entirely wrong, until the lady would ask, "Whadda you think, seriously?" at which point Bucky would turn to her the disarming side of his face and tell her, "Yellow, now, that'd do it, Mrs. Hendricks. See what I mean? It'd pick up the yellow in that cushion and . . ." —bypassing the yellow dried egg on the breakfast plates—"and the table top, and—say, did you know that more packages in stores are yellow than any other color?"

The question seemed to that particular lady to be loaded, as though not to be able to answer affirmatively would be a worse breach of taste than hanging chippies' drawers at one's kitchen windows, for by that time it was apparent, through Bucky's indirection, that he must be in agreement with the husband. Mrs. Hendricks thought about it after Bucky had gone and with a 'what the hell' attitude she had gone downtown and bought new curtains, yellow, without ruffles. She also stocked her kitchen with yellow boxes, a trifle puzzled that they were a bit hard to find until common sense told her that of course most people used more sugar and cornstarch than any other products. Having arranged the boxes and the cushion and the plain yellow curtains just so, and having got rid of the dried egg at the last minute, she settled down to wait for her husband's verdict.

Mr. Hendricks, who in twenty years of marriage had never noticed a new hairdo or dress, commented on the result.

"Hey," he said, hoisting an appetite-sharpening drink (in some cases the drink would be appetite-dulling, depending on whether the wife cooked like his mom or hers), "Hey, kid, now you hadn't ought to've done all this just because I said . . ." and tactfully he broke off and tendered a little kiss, gratified to have his kitchen apertures resemble something other than those through which he peered on poker nights.

It happened that Mrs. Hendricks had been planning a modest change in the color scheme of her living room. Bucky's esoteric knowledge of the colors of packages in stores, and Mr. Hendricks's reaction, gave the lady the idea that Bucky might be filled with other lore that could be equally if mysteriously helpful. Before they knew it, the next time Bucky came around to read the meter, they found themselves deep in a discussion of decorating that was so original on Bucky's part that Mrs. Hendricks was tempted to tie him in the cellar until the job was completed lest the marvelous ideas leak out to the other ladies of the town.

In a fever of creativity, they had upholstered the parlor chairs in shaggy cotton rugs and wall-papered the upright piano. Floors were stripped and spatter-painted; bamboo replaced walls and indirect lighting buried in the floors made reading impossible, which was no problem at all.

Most diabolical stroke of all was the conversion of the little Birthing Room into a chartreuse and silver bar with a touch so clever that Mrs. Hendricks predicted it would put Bucky on the map as far away as Columbus. She told him, "You gotta have a gimmick, and boy, you have got it!"

As they visualized it, guests would enter the bar and grope their way to the high stools and perch there and name their poison. (Mr. Hendricks, tending bar, would have to be in on it, which dimmed Mrs. Hendricks's anticipation; she could see him grinning and winking and spoiling the whole delicious thing.) Envy and a slight case of nerves would make the guests drink rather more rapidly than usual; they would become aware that they were being watched by their hosts, who would seem to be waiting for SOMETHING; their eyes would roam. Over the door, dimly lighted, they would see— think they saw—a place setting for a dinner party: plate, two forks, knife, two spoons, napkin, wineglass—over the door, attached to the ceiling, upside down—as unnerving as Poe's Raven.

That, at least, was the way Bucky and Mrs. Hendricks visualized it, but by the time it was completed there were so many versions of the Raven Surprise in town that the only ones to be stricken with fear of the d.t.'s were the husbands. Still, the ladies could not really blame Bucky for using his gimmick to the fullest, for it was done in irrepressible high spirits, and by the time of the practically simultaneous unveilings, Bucky was a new star in Tasmania and they were all glad to share in his light.

Long before he became a star Bucky had enjoyed acceptance among the men of Tasmania, an acceptance which
amounted to a kind of popularity grown, though he did
not suspect it, from the twin roots of contempt and relief,
for which his squinch-eye and puckered cheek were responsible. Stretching their imaginations to the fullest, husbands
could not fancy their wives in sensual comportance with the
half-man that they naturally believed Bucky to be. It was
not the idea of ugliness which gave them their assurance, for
ugliness, as many of them personally knew, was a masculine
attribute; instead, it was their rejection of the possibility
that a man could be *partially* destroyed by his mother and still
be a man, which would have made them all suspect. All or
nothing, they argued, needing to believe it. Most of them had
had mothers who had tried unceasingly to make steers of
them and more than one had been pinked by the shears, but
that was all (thank God) and the narrow escapes had rein-
forced, they believed, their masculinity. Only their mothers
knew, and their wives sensed, the resultant alloy; making
assessment by sound alone, the men who sat in judgment on
Bucky clanked their pendulous accouterments and pronounced the tone pure and remembered Mom on Mother's
Day and got choked up about her when they heard Irish
songs and had had a few. On the other hand, Bucky's mother
had not only branded him in a place he could not hide or
forget; she had also, obviously, got to him in earnest where it
mattered most because he was about as aggressive as a canary
and as easily frightened.

When he left the Gas Company and went into Interior
Designs, the men saw it as being what they had suspected was
a bird proving them right by sprouting wings. Bucky's voice
was soft and his movements, while not really sis, were lacking
in a particular harsh angularity. He moved, in short, at least in
their eyes, as though he lacked certain leg-separating impedi-
menta and so was accorded by all the sultans free access to
their harems. Within those portals he was recipient of the
stories of failed or failing marriages, due, according to the

wives, mostly to too little use of the bed for other than sleep; and he received financial, political, and ideological secrets which made him a walking cross-reference index to the town's ills.

Thus, however unwittingly, he divulged those secrets to Mrs. October in the lengthy correspondence that preceded her arrival in Tasmania and proved beyond a doubt to be what she had sought and in her own way prayed for when she wrote her final Ad to the World: the potential fool general, idiot-savant, and perfect accomplice for her last attempt at revolution on earth, and the salvaging, in her own special way, of mankind.

When Mrs. October chose Bucky's letter from the many that she received in answer to her ad, and decided to nourish it as she would a delicate plant until she could intuit the kind of bloom it would bear, she decided at the same time to re-sume her favorite name out of the dozens she had worn over the span of half a century. In addition to the touching near-illiteracy of the letter there was a quality of dogged romanticism which reawakened in her the thing that had both caused her to be a revolutionist and to have chosen the name October originally. The letter, with its individualistic grammar and spelling, made Mrs. October think of a little child, which was how, in the bloom of her admitted Savior complex, she had thought of all mankind. Such a person, she thought, would be trusting too (as mankind had turned out not to be en masse) and she began to indulge herself in fan-tasies of long talks about Santa, the Easter Bunny, America the Beautiful, God, and other myths.

The choice of Bucky's letter and the consequent fantasies were the result of a fact perhaps not simple: after fifty years of wanderings, agitations and exiles, Mrs. October was tired. There was, she imagined, a connection between her tiredness and the homesickness (if it could be called that, considering that she had no actual home) that afflicted her more and more frequently at dusk. At other times of the day or night she would think with amusement of yesterday's nostalgic longing but when the limbo hour once again arrived she found herself helpless before the onslaught of its melancholy. Reading Bucky's letter for the tenth, or twentieth time, she came to feel that she had willed it; that she had invented this young man in Ohio, who wrote so childishly, for the express purpose of giving her an excuse to return to America after thirty years.

Bucky's letter read:

> Dear Box 000,
>
> Your letter interested me, which I read in City and County, the magazine that is like my House Organ if I had a house (ha). Seriously, I am a Designer of Interior Designs and as the one such in this town (Tasmania, Ohio) I can pretty much write my own ticket, not to brag. I would be especially intrested in extending my field of endevor to exteriors and working with architects to acheve a harmony of both facades, in and out. I am acquanted with exterior materials, bamboo ex cetera and have some amusing ideas of interchanging said materials, such as bamboo inside, wallpaper outside ex cetera.
>
> Please do not judge me to exentric on this matter. In line of my work I have experimented with cabbage-rose wallpaper on a board fence which is like a flower garden when the light is not too bright.
>
> This city is old-fashioned, as they say 'square,' but with many possibilities. Due to its many homes of Revolutionary Times which a modren minded architect would view as a challenge, not to change but to fix up.
>
> Hoping to hear from you at your earliest convenience with a view toward working out something to our mutual advantage, with best wishes for the coming Holiday season, I remain.

After nearly two weeks of keeping the letter to herself, Mrs. October called a conference of those traveling companions she most trusted: four people at the moment, out of a flexible cadre that could range in number from ten to eighteen, the minimum and maximum personnel for the accomplishment of her mission. Due to recent defections and one death, the number stood currently at a baker's dozen, and the four she called in for consultation knew that whatever was in the wind, one of them would be expected to triple, or two of them to double, in certain roles.

The most likely candidate for the extra work was Aurelie Angelique, who was the first to arrive. She and Mrs. October actually were seldom apart; that Mrs. October had kept the letter from her for so long was the measure of its importance. AA, as she was called by friends, had seen Mrs. October poring over the letter and had wondered, and had feared. She too, was growing tired, and sometimes longed for Macon, Georgia, which was the only place—at that moment and as far as reports could be trusted—that was not in turmoil of some sort, and for her to long for the scene of early degradation in preference to taking part in a new revolution spoke to her, more than anything could, of the depredations of age, and the frailty of ideals. But she kept her fear to herself.

Sitting by the fire with a mug of rum-laced tea, retreating behind the shield of French (a long way from the cotton patch) she received what she termed 'le tableau.'

"Remplissez-moi le tableau, Madame," she said, speaking from the clouds of rum steam which isolated even more her narrow face like a dark cake, studded with raisin eyes, plum nose and prune mouth, from the rest of her. Whatever emotion inhabited her breast and animated her extremities, her face wore an expression of constant exasperation at the ineptness of the creature for which it saw, smelled, heard, and tasted, so that its efforts to maintain a separate existence had resulted in a neck of great length and maneuverability. She could do an about-face without moving anything below the clavicle; this ability, and hair of a length to walk upon (the downward-growing hair bespeaking white ancestry, never delved for; she suffered the idea) made her a handy spy. At such times she would let down her hair so that it covered her face, turn her head about and watch the suspect through the thick veil while ostensibly reading a paper, studying a building directory, or feeding forkfuls of tripe à la mode de Caen to the base of her skull. Since suspects are notoriously stupid or they would not be suspected, this ploy generally worked well . . . There had been a few instances when the observed turned observer and saw, or thought he did, a pair of eyes where none belonged. In a couple of documented cases, this had led to the straight and narrow via rehabilitation; in another, it had led to religion).

Over a second cup of rum tea, Mrs. October handed Bucky's letter to AA and watched with interest while it was read. When she had finished and sat for a moment in ritual silence, AA tapped the letter with a forefinger; her head, as though its ears were offended by the sound, tore at the mooring rope of the neck and her eyebrows, assisting the attempt at flight, flew up to her hairline.

"Une parodie?"

"No, I don't believe so."

"Ah. Quelle naïveté."

"Yes. Certainly that." Mrs. October was careless so that her wistfulness and hunger showed through the words. AA felt that it was a time for great tact.

"Ça promet bien."

Mrs. October smiled as though pleased, and said, like a partial question, "Happily . . ." AA considered it.

"Dangereux, peut-être."

"Ah," said Mrs. October, a full note, "eternally," and the ladies nodded and smiled at each other, one of them chilled. AA's smile was taken, and meant, as approval of Bucky Jones and Tasmania, for without her approval Mrs. October would not have proceeded, at least not immediately, and AA knew this and knew that without almost immediate change her friend and employer was in danger of wasting away. So long between revolutions!

The others were summoned from the anteroom and tentative plans were drawn, pending further proof from Mr. Jones that he and his town were as ideal as they appeared at first glance to be.

When all had gone from her study, Mrs. October took from a drawer her letter sent in reply to Bucky's. It was a letter like a garden. In it were planted many seeds and their locations were marked but none had yet taken root. As correspondence with Bucky proceeded, Mrs. October, in accordance with her usual protocol, would continually check his letters with her first one, marking the shoots as they poked up, until all had sprouted, which would be her cue to move. But the order of appearance of the shoots was engrossing of itself to her, telling her more about Bucky than he would ever tell her, direct, about himself; she thought about this with tenderness, not one of her accustomed emotions; and she felt even sorry to take advantage of him in the sense of knowing more about him than he could know about her; but, she thought, wasn't that generally true of mothers in relation to sons? She grimaced with self-amusement and smoothed her letter and imagined that she was checking against it the new growth of his latest letter to her—his final letter, for she imagined in a pretty little fantasy that she was going to meet him tomorrow. The urgency in her feeling made her resolve to step up her campaign. It was odd about the urgency; it was like a wildness in the air above the earth; a kind of premonition—"And yesterday the bird of night . . ." she murmured, and read what, in her light italic hand, she had written to Bucky:

Dear Mr. Jones:
   When I was much younger I spent several months in a country of gardens. It was actually a garden country to the extent that in the houses set among the gardens the citizens ate, slept and moved about amongst mounds of compost, bags of bone meal, peat moss, sand, decomposing fish, gravel, basic slag, topsoil, manure. The dwelling places functioned, in fact, as mere extensions of the gardens: as potting and tool sheds. If there was heat, it was not to warm the bones of the gardeners but rather to nourish the sprouting seedlings which were that country's major industry, the income from which went to buy more seed, and more; most of the seed in the world.
   In such a milieu, at least for a woman of my perhaps

peculiar sensibilities, cultivated verdancy on such a scale assumes the aspect of morbidity. Once I found a weed and looked upon it as a gift from heaven. 'With this weed,' I thought, 'I can perhaps begin . . .' But before the thought could grow the weed had died. I had, you understand, in my zeal pulled it up by the roots. It was prickly, fierce of demeanor, promising. Its roots, alas, were shallow. It had survived not through determination or conviction, but through oversight. A digression into sadness that I may one day explain.

I began, in my final weeks in that country, to fashion (behind drawn shades and locked doors, a most horrible enforced condition) rags and paper and splinters into flowers. I was content until I remembered the origins of my materials: plants. I was, you see, prejudiced against what that country was most preponderant in. It seemed to me, then, that my rebellious act was nothing more than indulgence, and that, having been transmuted, my materials could only feed a fire, not start one, and certainly the world abounds in all manner of fodder. You see, beyond the original change or transmutation—from plant into paper, firewood, rag—beyond the shock of survival and survival of shock at what one is and what one was—lie but two choices: action or inertia. The paper of my flowers was tractless; the rags, bannerless; the wood, fireless. I left, in my house in that garden country, a bouquet of chicken bones.

No, Mr. Jones, I do not judge you eccentric, in haste or leisure, as the foregoing may support. Cabbage-rose wallpaper, especially on a board fence (knotted with weather, perhaps despairing of paint?) elicits my most sympathetic responses, in the way that a little hammer in the knee-region causes the leg to kick; call it a proof of life, because I ask you to; and forgive my verbosity.

Hoping, indeed, that we can work out something to our mutual advantage, and with the greatest best wishes for your coming Holiday season, I remain.

Mrs. October had known intimately Henri Bergson—or, as she would say when referring to him, "I know him," because in the time-sense they shared (had shared) his death was overshadowed by his duration in the more important form of collective memory and in the experience of those to whom, like Mrs. October, the élan vital was the pedestal supporting all reality. Contradiction being the essence of revolutionary activity, Mrs. October was addicted to exact time as measured on a clock's face while in the same breath denying the existence of scientific time.

In keeping with a philosophy in whose evolution she may have been essential, and by virtue of a nature mystical in the extreme, Mrs. October practiced intuition to the extent of its being her profession, of which revolution was but a result. Her divination of Bucky's letters was both an oracular exercise and a deciphering of runes using the primary key of instinct. Her bound volumes of such exercises, at which she worked during fallow periods as well as fertile, numbered well into the hundreds. Some of their pages were given a later essayistic form; some were presented as narrative fiction. She most enjoyed the fictional disguise; as she was fond of saying, in another life she would have devoted her energies to *that* particular method of reordering the world. She confessed to an inspirational response to certain situations; some names were enough to release the Muse. For example, Bucky wrote to her:

"My sister Wanda's friend Marie Louise is mean to her mama. I hate to say this because Wan thinks the world and all of her and sometimes I think she's just about all Wan's got besides me and I'm not much (ha). But Marie Louise's mama, Mrs. Hackett, is a good old lady and is like they say here senile which means she thinks she's a little girl about nine years old. She was our piano teacher. Now the town hasn't got a piano teacher though Omerie Chad can make the piano talk and some say the organ, which makes them laugh, which I don't know not having heard him. Anyway Marie Louise some say hates her mama because of her being old enough to be senile which puts Marie Louise at an older age than she wants to say she is. Which I don't know if it's true."

This material Mrs. October transformed into her first longish 'pre-revolutionary sketch' in the volume titled TASMANIA – BEFORE.

Projection 1 — Mrs. Hackett

Marie Louise would say to inquiries about her mother's age, "Well, if I'm under thirty, Mama COULD be under fifty," and then, because her brush was uncertain even when attempting to paint lilies, she would add, "Couldn't she?"

As uncharitable as many of the townspeople longed to be with regard to that 'under thirty' clause, no one actually ever said "No" because of their regard for Marie Louise's mother, Mrs. Hackett, who, if she was under fifty, was enjoying the earliest second childhood of anybody around.

She was a tall woman, thin and flat and straight, with fingers that were like weathered bones—"artistic," as they used to say and still did out of habit, though the hands were all but useless, which may have been exactly what they meant. Her head, too, was like a skull found on a desert: equine, with long teeth the color of old piano keys and skin that bound the bones tightly as though to impede further growth. Her feet, dressed summer and winter in white kid, were narrow and lengthy. She wore leghorn hats with streamers to cover her yellow hair that had come out in patches, exposing the leached-out scalp like a glimpse of the dry earth through clouds. She wore dresses of a bygone cut and material—dimity and pongee which tended to a profusion of sashes and bows and ruching.

Dressed in white organdy with enormously puffed sleeves and dozens of stiff ruffles edged in red rickrack, wearing a floppy organdy hat and carrying a somewhat thrysoid shepherdess crook—perhaps a costume from some forgotten gala—she could slow down traffic in midtown on a winter's day.

Her friends had given up trying to make her dress sensibly for cold weather; her feet could not have been squeezed into any of the little "one size fits all" plastic booties which they favored and they all admitted that a heavy winter coat would look just silly as could be with the organdy hat. Grubbing with her through her trunks in search of a lost doll, they had found an evening cloak of transparent velvet with a wealth of passementerie, and sometimes she could be persuaded to wear it, but more often she eluded even those well-intentioned ones who liked to say that they kept an eye out for her, and in general they left her alone, taking their cue from Marie Louise. "Oh, Mama's all right," she would say, looking wistfully at the snow, thinking for no reason that she could place about death in winter, and sighing.

Mrs. Hackett had gone into second childhood unexpectedly, in the middle of a piano lesson. She was coaching, against the coming event of her yearly recital, her least promising pupil in the nuances of Percy Grainger's "Country Gardens." "No, *no*," she was saying as the child interpolated a bit of the Beatles into the most delicate section; "No, *no*"—and all at once, according to the girl's report, she had gone onto all fours to pick up the pencil she used as a pointer and had stayed that way, crawling under the piano and gurgling. The pupil told those of her own set that Mrs. Hackett had also peed.

If any of the girl's report was true, then Mrs. Hackett grew up at a rate that would have alarmed a parent because when Marie Louise dropped in on her the next day she was reading *The Wind in the Willows* and said without being asked that she was nine years old. Marie Louise thought that she said "ninety" and put her foot down hard, pointing out that if *she* was still under thirty then she could not have a ninety-year-old mother without causing talk of a highly nasty nature. Calculating rapidly, she said, "My God, Mama, assuming I'm twenty-eight years old, that would have you doing it—subtract two, carry nine months—when you were over sixty-one years of age *and daddy died when you were forty*."

She had gone on in this vein, interspersed with her mother's observations about Toad of Toad Hall, until it came to her that she had, as she told Wanda, "lost my Mama and gained a kid sister."

At first it had amused her to play paper dolls with her mother but this had soon given way to a cynicism that took the form of teaching the woman who had been famous for her prudery to say bad words. At gatherings in Mrs. Hackett's parlor—a great many gatherings in the first months of her senility; during that time she was courted as a queen by lines of Tasmanians waiting to gain admittance—Marie Louise would stand by her mother's chair and coax her, "Now darling, recite a little piece for our friends," and Mrs. Hackett would oblige with the latest pornographic limerick she had learned at her daughter's knee. But she was clever and soon caught on to the quality of the laughter. She would smile sweetly until her guests had gone and then would say, "That verse was naughty, now wasn't it," and though Marie Louise would never admit that it had been, she grew foxy and went far afield, consulting the dictionary and certain other books for words more subtly objectionable. This, too, backfired in an odd way though it did contribute to a kind of general higher education.

Beginning with the pictures in the plain-wrappered books, Marie Louise would go on to cross-indexing until she was almost certain that she had backed her quarry into a corner and if challenged could verify the word's reproachable nature. But it was certainly not as much immediate fun to have Mrs. Hackett say "fellatio," pronouncing it "fell-lot-e-o" the way she had been taught, and get no reaction except a few nervous titters. However, her audience soon took to asking how the words were spelled, knowing that something had to be up, and writing them down and looking them up at home and reacting there—surely the 'delayed take' nonpareil; and then like schoolchildren they were bringing their books with them. Ranged about her with books and paper and pencils, writing down the words and looking them up, it was as though they once again attended her opening classes for beginners in which she, with chalk and pointer and blackboard, had introduced most of them and their children to the preliminary mysteries of music, having them count out and mark with their feet—"But softly, boys and girls; this is an old, old carpet on an old, old floor"—the different time-values of the notes as she drew them on the slate. The hysterical, delayed laughter of the adults at the unearthing in their reference books of some meaning was like an echo of the chaos resulting from the teacher's slow counting out of a whole note—"Oneeeeeee Twooooooooo Threeeeeee Fooooooour"—which they were supposed to fill in with sixteenth notes, shouting and pounding their feet—"ONEtwothreefour FIVEsixseveneight NINEteneleventwelve THIRteenfourteenfifteensixteen."

Mrs. Hackett had brought the audiences to an end by getting sick. At least she had said that she was sick and had gone to bed with a pickaninny doll for comfort, and though the doctor, who had been her husband's best man and her lifelong friend, examined her with sympathy, and loathing for her daughter, but could find nothing physically wrong with her, she refused to get out of bed, which meant that Marie Louise had to pay for a full-time nurse to stay in the house and, as she said, "eat like a goddamn horse all day." Marie Louise's husband, being the one who actually paid, accused her of responsibility for her mother's condition and gave her an ultimatum: Get her out of that bed in a week or pack up and move back home.

Marie Louise was frightened at the thought of, as she told her friends, "practicing a profession for which I am not trained"—namely, nursing, and she approached her mother with a tenderness that was awful in its supplication.

"Mama . . ." she said, and meeting suspicion mingled with blankness at the address, she had for the first time called her mother by her given name, Belle, though she had tried for a diminutive and wound up calling her mother "Belly," which was a hard beginning because that was one of the words her mother knew to be naughty. She had tried again, so softly as to hide the venom with which a sharper tone would have been tipped like a poison arrow, though she was not entirely successful.

"Dear little Belle," she murmured, "tell big Marie Louise what the hell's the matter with you."

Still, she had had a week of grace and in that time her

mother had extracted from Marie Louise a promise to keep "the big people" away from her. It seemed that their laughter frightened her ("of all things!") and made her wonder ("Can you imagine!") whether she had ("The poor old thing *whispered* it . . .") soiled her dress in (shrieks of laughter) *the water closet.*

Which reminded Marie Louise unpleasantly of the horrors of her own toilet-training which, because of her mother's prudery, had not been accomplished until Marie Louise was in the second grade of school and was known as "Stinky," which was what, in nostalgic moments, she was still called by her husband.

Following her two weeks in bed Mrs. Hackett had entered a time of loneliness. When well-meaning friends called on her she would turn them away at the door, saying that her mother was not at home, after which she would wander through the house searching, wondering where her parents *were*, certain that they had told her exactly when they would return so that she wouldn't worry, and then she had to go and forget. When she got hungry she would make messes at the stove but got so she could cook a passable meal of Quaker Oats and buttered bread toasted in the oven. Once or twice a week the ugly woman who called her "little sister" when she wasn't being mean and scolding, came to see her and made her eat vegetables and tough meat and shoved *coffee*—Mama would just die!—at her in big cups. When she tried to explain about not being allowed stimulants she was either told to shut up or got stared at in a very rude manner. "Shut up" was an expression that only very vulgar people used, foreigners who lived in the bad part of town and were allowed to work for respectable persons only in the daytime. Mama would say, "I wouldn't trust one of them in my house after dark," and everyone would nod.

Belle did not honestly know why this was so, for she had been taught that nighttime is the snuggest, warmest, safest time of all. When Papa had to go out to attend an accouchement and she and Mama were left alone in the evening, Mama would tell her over and over about nighttime being so snug and safe. Over and over—standing at the window pinching the curtains peeping out. Over and over—poking up the fire and piling on big lumps of coal. When Belle got sleepy Mama would hold her on her lap in a chair with its back to the wall and croon to her about how snug and safe nighttime was, letting out little screams when a shutter banged or ice slid off the roof with a funny noise. Once in the summertime she had made Papa repeat something that he had said to her before they were married, that she said only he would know, before she would unhook the screen door and let him in. Standing in the hallway while Papa nuzzled Belle's hair and laughed, Mama had said that of course they couldn't use those words as a password ever again because *they* had heard and would use them to gain admittance and have their way. "Who with?" Papa had asked, "you or the String Bean?" which was what he called Belle because she was so skinny, and Mama had said, "Perish the thought!" and she threw up her hands and walled her eyes.

The time came when Belle stopped looking for them to come up the walk, or listening for the jingle of the harness on her father's buggy. She did not forget them but they became like the doll that she could remember but could not find anywhere, the one that was larger than she was when she got it, whose head had got broken so that the mechanism holding the movable eyes could be seen at work. She knew that she would find it eventually; to look for it each day became something as necessary as keeping herself meticulously clean; and she knew that her parents would come in one day and tell her in fine detail—her father was a famous raconteur—what it was that had detained them. She missed them, but what at first had been a strong pain became a mild ache like the feeling in an old fading bruise when you pressed it; unless you pressed it hard it did not hurt at all. Gradually she began to allow her mother's callers to come in and sit with her and then they were helping her look for the doll and pick out what clothes to wear, and after a while she was returning their visits and sitting in their parlors and eating sweet cakes and drinking lemonade. She had found, though, that she must not ask them, however discreetly, if they knew where her parents were because they would, at best, pull long faces; at worst they would sniffle. It was a peculiar reaction that she did not care to investigate.

Gradually, through such adjustments, the adult world became partly hers once again. She joined more frequently in conversations and was listened to without the unkind laughter that had puzzled her, especially after she revealed a candor that was sometimes uncomfortably on the mark. For example, when she picked a chrysanthemum bud in a friend's garden and gave it to the lady with a curtsy and a compliment, and was asked dryly and yet condescendingly if the gesture were not "premature," Belle replied in a low swift voice, "Compliments are frequently premature, but some manners never show up at all." Another time, when one of the ladies told a bald truth to another of the circle and excused her wounding frankness on the grounds of friendship, Belle observed musingly, as though recalling the words, "Friendship isn't the license to say just anything at all, but the consideration not to say it." In their confusion the ladies explained to each other that "she heard her mother say that." Part of the confusion was because it had not been in her former nature to make such remarks, and though they admitted the pungency of what she said, they felt on more comfortable grounds with their "old little girl."

As they told each other, she had always been a bit other worldly, for there was no wider chasm known to woman than that separating the old-fashioned girl (Belle) and the modern (themselves). To emphasize the gap, they gave her gifts of dolls and other discarded toys of their children and grandchildren.

Too, she discovered that although they would help her look for lost toys in her own house, when she visited them she was expected to leave alone whatever toys there were lying about and must not play with the other children. It was, she learned, not the grown-ups who minded; it was the children. As her mother would say, they were a different breed—incomprehensible, selfish, and shockingly common—and they did not want her to touch their things. She had been brought up to share her playthings, but had also been taught not to point out other people's shortcomings, so she left the children to their games and ignored their rude stares as she sat, bored but polite, in a big chair in the circle of grown-up ladies.

Speaking of rude children, there was one house to which she would never return as long as she lived because of a dance one of them did while she was visiting. The girl, who was her own age and the granddaughter of one of the ladies, was said to be a clever dancer and a disc had been put on the gramophone so that she could demonstrate her talent. The machine seemed to be broken, for the noise that came out of it was harsh and bewildering. Belle waited for someone to repair it, which would give the little girl a chance to fetch her toe shoes. Instead, the child (Belle later decided that she was a runaway circus midget) had begun a series of jerky, broken movements that were horribly as though she were poking fun at old Mr. Symes who had Saint Vitus's dance and was an object of pity. The child, or midget, had gone on to move her midsection in such a way that Belle, without having an idea why she did so, broke into tears. All she knew was that something seemed to be pulling at her mind in a way that was like a nightmare that tries to make you remember something you never knew. The motions—back and forth, side to side, round and around—filled her with a nameless terror and brought pain to the most private parts on her body. And the sound, the terrible screaming sound from the gramophone. Until she cried, the ladies had been smiling and nodding and winking at each other. Afterward they gathered around her and murmured and soothed, but the grim little dancing girl had said rudely, "What's the matter with *her*" and stared at her with eyes as hard and bold as a boy's.

Needing to confide in someone, she had told the ugly woman who sometimes fed her unpleasant food about the incident. (Belle came to accept that she and the woman probably were distant relatives but she refused to put a name to the relationship; one thing she knew for sure was that the woman was no sister of hers, being considerably older than her own mother. She got around her predicament by not calling the woman anything and thinking about her as little as possible.) The woman had screeched at her story like a parrot and slapped her legs which were encased in some kind of pantaloon and hollered out something about second childhood being brought on by the beetles, saying that now it was all clear to her because imogene had told how she had stuck some of lucy in the sky into percy grainger and mama had gone down on all fours and peed.

None of it made any sense to Belle, who smiled at the ugly woman and wished with all her heart that she would go away and never come back. From that day on she had to listen to others saying the nonsensical words—beetles and lucy in the sky and all fours and peed. Belle learned how to live with it, and how to smile, and how not to listen. Finally, because her disposition was what Mama had said was as amiable as anyone could wish, she came to enjoy her visits with the grown-ups, who were really a jolly bunch, the sole exception being the one they called Marie Louise, who was mean-spirited, kinfolk or not, and that was that.

Mrs. October was not averse to stacked cards, knowing that they were a metaphor for life's basic premise. Still, it intrigued her to see, upon emerging from her creative effort, just how large the stack against Marie Louise was, and further, just how peculiarly committed she had been, in the throes of the projection (which was how she termed her inventions) to the sympathy-arousing qualities of a woman whom she had never met, of a type she had never particularly admired. She supposed it was because of a quality of childishness in herself, best exemplified by the fact that she played the viola d'amore in duet with Aurelie Angelique on the jew's-harp and that the duets always ended as they began, in fits of schoolgirl laughter. In the writing, or projection, of Mrs. Hackett, Mrs. October had found herself including the lady in the musical romps and had sketched on the margins of her foolscap ideas of trios for the musicales to come.

Childish, yes; but without the streak of simpleton running through her Mrs. October sometimes believed that she could not have survived—flourished, indeed, on and on in the face of so much eventual defeat, the only kind worth noticing. She had had revolutions come much closer than within an ace of total success only to find herself a moment later at some country's borders, having been escorted there in a welter of vehicles as spiked with weapons as are sea urchins.

Lacking the sense of perpetual games and of the core of laughter nesting within even the darkest acts and conditions (among these, surely senility belonged) like the orange heart of the sea urchin, she would long ago, perhaps since Henri's death, have collapsed into a state of Jet Set indifference: obeisance to Bergson, even in such drastic thought, for as a Jet Setter she would have remained in perpetual motion! But she knew, as did Aurelie Angelique—their greatest, most striking, perhaps only similarity—that horror is itself a game begun with the simplest proposition, or dare: A few words that a small child (or senile woman) could utter; and that at the end of the horror, however protracted, it is possible to cut through it with intuition and faith and find the original, harmless, child's words and save oneself by recalling only *those* in the days, months, years afterward (a presampling of Mrs. Hackett's state? Preparation for senility?).

Aside from remarking such similarities, and enjoying vastly the company of preferably extreme individualists, Mrs. October did not give to any individual person very much thought. As a composer thinks in clusters of notes, so, during her revolutions, did Mrs. October think of people in groups, or even in terms of the line drawn around them which the Greeks called the moira and the Germans called the Gestalt. Which was why her growing feeling for Bucky, while amusing her, was partially distressing; and on top of that, to find herself so very drawn to the idea of Mrs. Hackett as though she, Mrs. October, were the mother of that senile lady! As of course she was, in the sense of having created her on paper by filling in with details *meant* to be fanciful whatever slight outline she had to begin with.

Her reasons for writing the projections in the preferred form of fictional narrative were complicated. Certainly high among them was the hope of, for a time, defeating the self-sobriquet of artist manquée. Another reason was one which directed some of her revolutionary activities: to make more bearable the realities of less colorful lives. Also, the stories allowed her to catch a glimpse of herself without the eternally self-conscious pose of the revolutionist-at-work, who can see himself only in the exaggerated glare of his perpetually exploding ego: heroics, pronunciamentos, 'total' concern for 'little people,' probably the most dead giveaway of all. At least Mrs. October believed that indefinitely prolonged compassion was as humanly impossible as was sexual orgasm sustained for a like period. She herself seldom made the effort to put herself in another's place (which was the meaning that 'compassion' had come to have by mid-twentieth century) except in the fictional word. By using the fictional form, she believed that she would not strain the credulity of a theoretical reader, a strain she was acutely aware of when reading the first-person accounts of 'involved' journalists. So much putting of oneself in another's place connoted a facility which was ultimately the same as being able to change hats rapidly, with just about as much meaning connected with the gesture. At most, it was a way of protecting the head (from soft cap to helmet). So much donning of other peoples' skins, outside fiction, was to allow one to thump, ostensibly, another chest; but it was still one's own bones within the strange skin that benefited from the massage.

But at the end of all reasoning and excuses and explanations there waited a phenomenon for which there was no rational explanation, and no excuse when it turned out badly:

Her projections were like a person's shadow thrown upon

the ground; when measured, it proved to be a bit larger than life but otherwise as accurate as a slightly enlarged photograph of a thumbprint. In this particular, she knew, lay the secret of others' allegiance to her. That the allegiance contained a measure, perhaps large, of fear was regrettable but she was as unable to change it as Henri had been unable to accept it as having any connection with intuition or instinct or even intellection; it violated too many conditions to fit into respectable mysticism. Once, in weakness—early in the game, when she could still be astounded—she had written of her gift: "The Desk Hive: Honey or Horror?" But she was powerless to control it, even if she had really wanted to for those whom, like Aurelie Angelique, she believed she loved.

Aurelie Angelique, after years of October's companionship —years now literally countless, obscured and confused by events—had never come anywhere near understanding the woman whom she alternately or simultaneously admired and rather disliked. She had been attracted—a mutual exchange with a common base—by Mrs. October's extreme eccentricity and by her embodiment of glamor. (AA had no trouble switching from name to name as Mrs. October donned and discarded them, thinking always and exclusively in the present.) When AA first saw her she was leading a crocodile down the steps of the Sacre Coeur, blithely deserting a raging battle of political differences which she had instigated amongst the tables of Montmartre. This information she passed on to AA as they made their way together to the revolutionist's waiting car. AA was never quite sure that she had been so simply attached by the other woman as her memory would have it. According to memory, she, AA, had stood gawking at the flamboyant woman with the grisly pet and when they drew abreast of her the woman had held out a crooked arm, saying "Come"; and AA, according to memory, had taken the arm and with no backward glance, except to determine the proximity of the crocodile, had gone to live with the woman and the crocodile, a pair of cheetahs and a monkey, and a greatly varied menagerie of humans.

Over the years there had been considerable turnover in pets, and some humans had been killed and one or two had defected, but AA had seldom wavered. It was axiomatic that she would waver on the first day of training a new cadre for revolution; part of the exchange between the two women on that first day was classical, frozen into permanence by repetition; a kind of comfort to them both in face of the otherwise unknown; but AA's loyalty was never questioned by Mrs. October and only occasionally—though she thought the frequency was stepping up—by herself.

She was held to Mrs. October by bonds of curiosity, astonishment, and disbelief. Her astonishment was at knowing someone who really professed to believe that the world THE WORLD could be rid of prejudice, hypocrisy, exploitation and slums, and above all, of hate. Her disbelief (and her dislike) was that such a person could care so shallowly for individuals.

AA had seen Mrs. October, in the throes of revolution, with a wave of her hand order the dispatchment (DEATH, AA would think, trying to believe it) of a hopelessly wounded erstwhile right-hand man or woman. The "hopelessly" came from Mrs. October; no doctor had ever been summoned to verify and to sentence. AA had never personally witnessed a dispatchment (Mrs. October's word, as though a hurt person were a letter—yes, sent to the dead-letter office) but she had heard the order, seen the airy gesture, and missed the person. And yet despite the evidence, the crux was that she could feel only disbelief in the long run—no, the short run, for she would be overcome by a dreaminess following such an incident that set it apart as though by a brief refreshing sleep and what she was left with was the dregs of a rather persistent but really harmless nightmare. The death orders, and subsequent disappearance of a person whom AA had come to know well, were less vivid to her, a day or so after the fact, than were the saliencies of her own childhood misuse, which for some reason or other were the only things she had kept back from Mrs. October. Perhaps she feared that once she had exposed her roots in all their sordid deformity, she would be given not understanding but further misuse, as was the case in the United States of her entire race.

But the strongest bond between AA and Mrs. October was that of curiosity. AA, dreaming as a child of bizarre and story-book worlds, in all her hunger could not have conjured the image of someone as strange as Mrs. October. Like the bull-diker, in a book by Carson McCullers, who fell in love with a dwarf, AA could not look at Mrs. October without her lips curving into a smile of pure enchantment. She did not think about the dispatchments and other horrors when she actually was with the woman, which was nearly constantly. She waited for each word from the woman's incredible store as though they were confections. Often there was sharpness, or a bitter aftertaste, but this did not diminish anticipation. It was true, as Mrs. October liked to say, that the two friends never ran out of surprise or surprises. About the only cut and dried thing between them, aside from their first day exchange, was the form of their endless discourse: they argued.

They could keep themselves fascinated for the length of a morning as they dueled on the following field: at what precise point, in what exact measure, does coffee with milk become the sublime café au lait? They agreed that what occurred in the cup was alchemistic, and that the hairy hands (they both favored hair on the knuckles) of a lovely youngish waiter could indeed be the philosophers' stone; but mixing the brew themselves, wasting enough coffee and milk to nourish, as AA said, all Paris, they could not agree upon the second, the instant, of transformation, though one of them poured and one of them dipped with a spoon and tasted, murmuring, "There. Oh, you passed it. Now there's too much milk. But for a moment it was perfect, really," and the other would say firmly, "Entirely too much coffee. You must be suffering some sort of deficiency. Maybe the chemist could make you up caffeine pills." And on and on, without boredom.

Sometimes AA was scalded by guilt because their private

games involved some prodigality, some enormous waste of material things the lack of which, in her growing up years as the daughter of a sharecropper, AA could not forget. Her ideas on revolution still revolved around the gaining of those things which, in the company of Mrs. October, she squandered, nor did she find reconciliation of ideology with practice in the fact that all revolutionists, no matter the diversity of their revolutionary goals, were practitioners of the same paradoxical bent. Radical young, protesting in New York world-wide hunger by rolling about in the streets on thousands of loaves of bread, so enraged AA, afflicting her with hunger pangs from thirty years ago, that all that kept her from betraying Mrs. October and thus all revolutionists, was merely the lack of opportunity; they were so seldom apart.

But thoughts of counterrevolution and betrayal were as a rule kept in a kind of mental safe with an elaborate combination too tiresome to fiddle with most of the time, along with AA's growing hatred of white people, which she looked at only at night; and a few other such gems harder than diamonds.

Excerpt from Bucky's Fourth Letter:
"Omerie Chad is a funny man with a long little dog named Madame Alexis. He is like they say very cultured and I may have wrote you he plays the piano and sings and his parties are famous which I don't know I've never been to one (haven't been asked, ha). One funny thing is where he came from nobody knows but since he's lived in Tasmania (four maybe five years) a lot of people mainly men are working for him which as they say is GOOD BUSINESS."

Tasmania — Before — Projection 5: Omerie

Self-definitions may as a rule be questionable but when Omerie Chad of Chadden, the name of his carriage house on Rue Flambeaux, called himself an aesthete nobody questioned him at all. His home, his clothes, his English accent, his opinions, were definitions of aestheticism, as were his dislikes. These included socialism, most twentieth-century prose with the exceptions of that written by Virginia Woolf and Nancy Mitford ("She understands"), and all serious music written since World War I which, he said, destroyed the Muse. *Daphnis et Chloe* was one of the aural signatures of his establishment (written nightly upon the dark), and for gayer moments there was anything by Cole Porter, especially the songs from *Kiss Me Kate*. When he was loosened up, which was usually by ten o'clock any P.M., he could do a wicked "True to You Darling" at the piano, going Lisa Kirk one better by singing two verses in French—"doubtful French," according to Myra Little, but as she was the only one to know whether she meant accent, taste, or translation, it did not detract from the enjoyment of The Regulars.

Omerie—no diminutive allowable as the only choices were Om, which smacked of hippies, and Erie, which would cut too close to the bone—was a town mystery. Where he came from nobody knew, nor even the general direction.

One ten o'clock, that being somehow his hour, the occupants of various parked and cruising cars along North Splendor were galvanized by his appearance out of thin air, so they said, in front of the Beaux Arts Bar and Grill. Although the season was midsummer and Tasmania smoldered like cigarette ends in its bowl of mountains, the figure that stood in the pale blue spill of the Beaux Arts' neon was dressed in a long motoring coat of black glove-leather with boots and gauntlets to match. What of his shirt that showed appeared to be ruffled, an odd combination with the leather and his butch haircut that was so short his head looked shaved. What they took at first to be a whip—hallucination being the tool of association—turned out to be a leash and at the end of it a little dog of unusual length and presence, the latter demonstrated by her (as it turned out) cool disdain when all the cars with one impulse sounded their horns and kept on sounding them in what could have been an effort to dispel the mass illusion.

Man and dog stood their ground—indeed, he took no more notice of the racket than she did—and shortly they were the nucleus of a curious circle of half-drunk Tasmanians; and soon after that—the reports were as chaotic as the event itself—man and dog and a select group had vanished into the night. Girls who had been heated to melting in parked cars by the hands of swains found themselves alone, frustrated, and missing intimate garments. Men whose reflexes had been slowed down by highballs and a kind of dreaming state brought on by exotica in the prosaic vicinity of the Beaux Arts, shoved elbows back to dig at familiar ribs of whosoever spouse they were with and encountered vacancy.

True, not many females were missing and not all those missing had been selected by the man and the dachshund for the orgy. One wife, at least, was found lying over a sewer grating from whence, she said, there came a breeze. Still another had reneged at the last moment and taken the opportunity to slip off home to her sleeping husband and children; and another young lady was found throwing up in a vacant lot. But the cream of all sexes had been slyly skimmed and taken off to top God knew what kind of pie, and lamentation and the calling of cops was the order of the night. Which divulged a peculiar, even an ominous, fact: the Chief, himself, was missing and his wife was frantic.

From that night on Tasmania was broken into factions: those who had attended the first party at Chadden; those who *said* they had attended it but "kept to themselves," which was why they had not been noticed; and, of course, those who had not, would not have, and would die before they *ever* would.

It became a fashionable pose among the Chadden Cognoscenti to pretend that they could not recall how they got to the carriage house on that first night, though any number of awakened sleepers along the route could have told them that they walked, and very noisy they were indeed. The truth of the matter was that the Tasmanians had been as quiet as shock; the noise came from Omerie's impersonation of Lisa Kirk and Pat Morison—especially the "I Hate Men" number when, in keeping with the original score, he would slam his fist onto any passing porch for emphasis (it was the buildings which were passing; the people stood quite still in their awe), and at each slam, Madame Alexis would bark three times perfectly on cue and in tempo as though timing the duration of the bang.

However they got there, they kept returning, and their frequent attendance led to some pretty drastic changes in the day-to-day look of Tasmania, and in some habits and tastes of a more secretive nature. The changed appearance was mostly in the sartorial category. Tasmania, being on the outskirts of the twentieth century, despite the examples set on TV, had, by the mid-Sixties, but recently become reconciled to the fashions of the Forties: ducktails etc. for its young men and the New Look for its females. Omerie, with his shaven head and Edwardian elegance, had permanently arrested his own development, tonsorially and sartorially speaking, at the modes of London in the Fifties, knowing that fashion is made by oneself knowing what is best for one, and the young men in his group followed his lead in moderation, supply in Tasmania having no relation to their particular demand. The young and not-so-young women—predominantly the latter—who became privileged Regulars, wore what Omerie told them to wear; what he, in most cases, made for them to wear, and in most cases it was godawful, which, as he explained, laughing through a mouthful of pins, was the fun thing, and fun, as an element, didn't they see it? was the sine qua non of chic (in women).

As to the secretive changes touching upon habits and tastes, it was just that Omerie made homosexuality, passive or active, a paying proposition to the boys and men of Tasmania, including the Chief of Police who was father of four and somewhat pious. It was because the Chief's alliance was an indispensable to Omerie's overall design, which did not include blackmail by others nor any variety of sex rap, that Omerie courted and won the man—it took a week—before he revealed himself dramatically in front of the Beaux Arts Bar and Grill.

Omerie was not as young as he looked, not that it mattered, the indulgence of his tastes not being based on a mutual attractiveness but rather on a bank account. Still, he was able to make himself amusing enough in the preliminaries that his company in bed was not found to be nearly as bizarre as had been imagined; or rather it had the bizarreness of a game extended either beyond or into fantasy. Boys who all their adolescence had threatened to bend others over barrels and put it to them found themselves doing just that; regular chaps who had said to each other "Kiss me, I'm coming" found their beseechments had had a ready answer, after all; and those timeless words of the street corner accompanied by a grasping of genitals: suck this—were at last seen as having been handed on to them, priceless heirlooms of hyperbole, as genuine negotiables. Their fathers had said, and the ones among them who were fathers said, "Show me an American and I'll show you a man who knows how to make a *dollar,*" and though some of them might have despaired in the past at so ignobly letting down The Motto, they now saw, truly, that You Can't Keep A Good Man Down, without paying him; and they were good men, and they came to like it, and they prospered.

For Omerie was generous. His sliding scale of payment began at $12.50 and spiraled on up, no ceiling as yet in sight for the adventuresome, and Omerie had occupied Chadden for five years now and Madame Alexis was six years old and there had been plenty of adventure, not all of it of a benign character.

Omerie's main protection, aside from having the avarice of others to his credit, was what he thought of as a prevailing stupidity but what was really a profound American-ness that could only name a fruit if it was baked in a crust—the apple pie syndrome. This was exemplified by the Chief of Police who, in the puzzled loneliness of his brand-new condition, would speak to himself, over and over as though with repetition to bore a hole through which light would pour: "That old boy pays me to let him do that with his mouth. Now, I thought I knew it all, but I'll be dadblamed . . ." and he would mentally scratch his head and chuckle at how easily he was getting off. But not with his wife, which he had to admit was probably a blessing since four children in five years of marriage had set a Tasmanian record and given him an aura he did not quite like as stud, or rather as failed stud because when the fifth year went by without a dropped kid even his brother deacons in the church had started to wonder aloud about whether he had squeezed out his last drop, which reflected on his wife as some kind of a juicer. 'He *pays* me,' he would think, and chuckle, and put his wife's cold cream on the sacred object that was buying shoes for the kiddies and all manner of extras for the home.

But deep puzzlement persisted because of the act's namelessness; and he was lonely because he did not really get that many calls from Omerie and in his sexual fantasies he gradually came to pay his obeisances to the new-found sphincter which was closer, in being truly toothed, to his original dreams and fears than the one he had found by accident nestled in the thatch between his wife's legs, rather than cleanly in view atop her belly.

With the younger men (the Chief was well into his forties) the case was similar. Their talk of perversion had been the same as other figures of speech: Kiss my foot, or I'll be damned. None of them offered a foot for kissing or expected or wanted to be damned, any more than it was believed a man could become a cross-eyed mule by saying that he would be one. And if any of the hepcats among them, on requesting a pal to give them some skin, had been offered a portion of a flayed beast they would have run away.

Though the fact that they could and did perform the acts without punishment was proof that the acts were allowable, some sense of self-protection, some underlying suspicion, kept them from comparing notes.

And yet Omerie and his direct illustration of words really having meanings led the deeper thinkers to a reassessment, or re-evaluation, of the language, for which they saw themselves to be paid researchers. Many an argument over the interpretation of metaphor led to more precise verbal abuse; challenges were given when an innocent offered to lay somebody two to one, to which the explanatory rejoinder might be, "You furnish the dolls; I'll show you who lays two to your one." Gone were the days of friends offering to "cough up" their share of a check; at the first word the air would be thick with flung gauntlets. The result was a comparative purity of usage based on caution.

Note to self: You seem to have written yourself into a hole here which may be too deep to be useful—i.e.: Revolution without sloganism is like blah blah blah too tired to unearth simile—is difficult, slogans being rallying cries blah blah blah. Point is purity of usage will not allow any slogans whatever so best break off here. Interesting, though, how this has led to eternal paradox ruling life: whether a good or comparatively good result achieved for wrong reasons—in this case, sort of double avarice—is better than the reverse: bad achieved for the best of reasons . . . some of my, alas, revolutionary projects falling tediously within the latter. Oh well; now we've got a clear-cut (if not clean-cut) homosexual in our revolution, without which a revolution is just too drab; average man when radicalized (dreadful American term) tends to lose all sense of humor which, in the homosexual, especially with danger about, becomes more pronounced; the greater the danger the fiercer the comedy. Commendable, say I, having danced on a number of graves. Who, oh who will dance on mine? Omerie—in retaliation? I have had too much fun with this projection, too cruel at the outset, a real old queer-baiting bitch. Change it before the time comes. Make note. Change it. And shut up and go to bed and dream of Bucky. Never, never project a cruel thought about Bucky; it would be self-murder (different from suicide). Speaking of tendency to self-destruction, don't forget to get in touch somehow with Roman. SOMEHOW; hah. Something at last too personal

*for the journals? Suppose he won't come? Curious; I believe
he could manage it, too. All that gravy and not a drop for
me. Tell him he is needed to lead sexual revolution; much too
tired personally and AA says positively* non. *That will do
it. It will. God bless, Bucky. Good night.*

The day came when Mrs. October snapped shut the clasp
on her Journal, summoned her staff, and, without too much
encumbrance, embarked for the target site. They were to
make one stop in a city split asunder by a curiously bloodless
revolution. There had been reported not so much as a broken
nose, although there was much violence to property. The
purpose of the stop was to witness and if possible to learn, for,
although it was not true of all the company, Mrs. October had
grown weary of the sight of blood, progressively as she felt
her own thinning within her veins. She had almost evolved a
theory that the young were bloody-minded because of an
unconscious desire to be lightened of their own weight of the
fluid. In her youth, in the springtime, tonics had been given to
"thin the blood" (her youth falling in a country and time of
tediously lengthy peace), but the practice had long ceased,
having been replaced by wars and famine, the latter perhaps
nature's own tonic.

Reports had reached her, in her comparative isolation, of an
extraordinary change in modern youth, which, if it were
true, must be seen as massive delayed mutation, occurring to
youth all over the world, simultaneously, in those years called
in America 'the teens.' According to the reports, children
developed normally—e.g., with the usual violent propensities
including cruelty to animals as well as to each other—until
just past puberty at which seemingly arbitrary point they
put down their brickbats and assumed the shields of flowers
and home-lettered signs reading LOVE and other associated
words mainly in the four-letter category. They sought change
—indeed, from the ground up, and would burn buildings with
alacrity, but only—so ran the rumors—when said buildings had
been thoroughly emptied of life, including rats. The only

animal for whose life they seemed to hold no respect was the pig, perhaps springing from the currently prevalent tendency toward the Far East and its religions, some of which were dietetically severe. Which could explain in part but not really satisfactorily the rallying cry, as reported to her, of "Kill The Pigs." Why kill them if not to eat them?

And yet, as an educator-revolutionist—not all revolutionists educated or were educated—it was incumbent upon Mrs. October to learn the answers to such questions as well as the latest methods and it was to these ends that they made their stop in the city, settling down in their private plane (one of the luxuries upon which she insisted) through a pall of smoke as thick as a bed of black feathers. All breathed deeply—"Ah, the old familiar smells!" Hearts quickened.

At a barricade of burning cars and felled trees Mrs. October was collared by an old antagonist, a long-lived bureaucrat who mysteriously turned up wherever she was and subjected her to a question and answer period, though mainly questions because his interrogations usually presupposed the answers.

They had been in town for several days without seeing him and Mrs. October had grown a bit nervous. She had come to count on him as proof of some sort that she was, as she told Aurelie Angelique, "still in the running" in the sense of maintaining her fame, though watching the felling of great old trees made her wonder if she really wanted to be included under the current terms defining revolutionist.

"Ah," her antagonist (whose name she never knew; she thought of him romantically as "X") said, and launched his first loaded question. "Tell me, Madame d'Armont . . ." The name dated both of them; she had not used it for years; how long between revolutions! "Do you still maintain that revolution is Art?"

She never had, but smiled and gave him her attention. Certainly there was an art to revolution but to twist it and make it, furthermore, upper-case was typical of him. His accent was vaguely Baltic with an American overtone as though he had been dwelling for a time in the American Middle West. He went on, "The Artist, even the New Artist, does not destroy the foundation but builds upon it. He knows that without the efforts of others he and his art would not be possible. Where would the New Comedy of Menander have been without the Old Comedy of Aristophanes?" She had no idea. They were being slowly enclosed in a circle. He gestured toward the devastation. "But look, look. They are striving to reduce to rubble, and the rubble to dust, and if possible they will disperse the dust of all but a handful of persons unless stopped." Bloodlessly? she wondered, but said nothing. He insisted, "Will you deny it?" Mrs. October said—a touch of brightness, a soupçon of irony—"A negative request, is it not? I would prefer something which asked for agreement . . ." There was palpable tension in the circle which felt peculiarly to her like a sphincter which strove to engorge or disgorge. Given a choice, she thought that disgorgement, and at once, might be a creative endeavor. She waggled her finger roguishly at X, laughed and told him, "Positive thinking, my old friend!" The near-endearment was a warning to him to go easy.

X was obviously frightened; he was also evidently determined and somewhat suicidal. He continued.

"Have you not heard the slogans out of America, my dear Madame? First there was 'Up Against The Wall'—pardon me —'Motherfucker,' and now it's 'To the Ovens'—again—'Motherfucker.' Could that be mistaken, Madame, for revolutionary rhetoric? What is it but a literal statement of intention to mass murder? To mass murder the fathers, for what else *is* a motherfucker? . . . asking your pardon once again." He was trembling and sweating but ploughed ahead. "I find the idea that this . . . statement . . . of walls and ovens was formulated and propagated primarily by those of Jewish descent frankly incomprehensible. Have not they, above all others, seen enough of walls and ovens? But no—they deny their own history; it never happened, that reign of terror. They say it quite clearly, those who have heard of Voltaire: Toute les histoires anciennes, ne sont que des fables convenues. It is one of the hundreds of slogans . . ."

"Perhaps we could have a coffee together," Mrs. October said briskly, turning and starting through the crowd. She did not care for X, but he had been so long on the scenes of her triumphs and failures that she did not relish the thought of seeing him dismembered; it would be as though a household pet to whom one paid little attention were suddenly savaged before one's eyes.

Her arm was laid hold of, not gently; just as abruptly, the grasping hand was wrenched from her and she looked down in surprise at the place where it had been and saw there Aurelie Angelique's clamping fingers in the act of returning the rough paw to its owner, a young, fierce male, a mere boy. AA muttered "Up Against The Wall!" and there was a gush of approving laughter. In the pleasant lull Mrs. October looked back at X and saw that he was being pressed between two walls like a victim in a story by Poe.

"Come," she said without emphasis as though the occasion were ordinary, "would you mind helping me clear a path, Monsieur?" She smiled as his captors automatically released him to come to the aid of a lady. But he would not take advantage, what a bother. His face was darkened with the blood of his passion. He raised his voice.

"Incomprehensible that Jews! . . . but the word here is 'descent.' 'Of Jewish descent.' The propagators of this . . . outrage . . . bear as little resemblance to their ancestors as does the iguana to the iguanodon!" He was shouting; the walls of people on either side of him were by now very thick, as thick as the walls of a prison and as hard. As there was nothing she could do she heard him out in detachment.

"No more resemblance, Madame, including the iguanodon's ability to walk upright! The Up-Against-The-Wallers-To-The-Oveners crawl on their bellies, which means they probably will prevail like the rest of the reptiles! Ah, yes, by taking to his belly, the iguana endured; so will Red, and Ruddy, and the rest of the colorful vipers. But, Madame, no matter how you view it, it is nothing more nor less than reverse-evolution and the next thing to go—going even as we watch and listen—will be the brain. For to deny history is to deny memory is to deplete the mind. Your Bergson knew this!"

All at once he was lifted like a flag and unfurled upon the wind, then furled, then thrown out again; there was a snapping sound as though he were in fact a banner streaming through brisk air. And still he persisted.

"I . . ." (furled) . . . "am . . ." (unfurled) . . . "a Jew . . ." But it was too late for such a confession if there had ever been a time for it—if, indeed, that was what he said at all. Perhaps he had only said "I am a human." As though the wind had died down, the banner drooped from its mortal pole, lifeless.

Aurelie Angelique battered and shoved and made a path, tugging Mrs. October behind her.

The next day, on the plane en route to America, they read an account of that day in that Revolution which, after dwelling endlessly on the level of sugar in the sugar bowls of the country, got around to the incident at the barricades, beginning admiringly, "The courage of these kids!"

The company shared the following feeling as they swept high above the Atlantic leaving behind them mysterious messages in jet vapor: it was as though it were the moment between the houselights' dimming and the curtain's rise; a pause during which one form of reality was willingly abandoned and another was taking hold, but for a time all commitment was let go and the ties to life were tenuous, existing solely as memory. A curious part of their feeling was in knowing that they had already taken part in the Tasmanian Revolution; in knowing that what was to take place in Tasmania had already in great part happened within the pages of the locked Journals, so that when the events unfolded they would be merely copies of what Mrs. October had written, the way a house is a copy of a blueprint. Certain details, appointments, would be new, but the structure had been so carefully thought out that it had already assumed the space it was to occupy in hard materials and existed there palpably enough to be bumped into with the mind. All that was truly unknown was the very end, for not even Mrs. October could anticipate whether or not the house, when built, would stand.

It was only a few weeks after Wanda, on Bucky's account, had fought with and relinquished her best friend, when, on account of Marie Louise's vindictively inventive powers all Tasmania *was* laughing at Bucky, Mrs. October arrived in a Silver Cloud Rolls Royce followed by a Bentley full of colored people. Beside Mrs. October, in the back seat of the car driven by a white man, there reclined an ace-black woman who moved her hands unceasingly, as though sending signals to a deaf-and-dumb populace, though the only street observers of the arrival were a few children and derelicts.

The lobby of the Ohio Hotel, however, was another matter: it was pre-Wednesday-luncheon packed, from the dining room doors to the street doors, with everyone of consequence in Tasmania, all talking at once. They were silent enough, by the time Mrs. October reached the reception desk, for one and all to hear her ask, as she signed in, where she might find a Mr. Cecil Jones. The pronunciation with a short 'e' raised Bucky, in the minds of the more impressionable, to the same exotic plane as that occupied by Mrs. October's furs, which some swore moved of their own volition, and the swart retinue which, it became numbingly clear, expected to be accommodated with quarters in Tasmania's most austere hostelry.

Bucky separated himself from the group in which he had been hiding without their knowledge (his shortness made it possible) and went to Mrs. October like a pigeon to its nest at nightfall. Thus their first meeting took place before the eyes of the town as Mrs. October had planned, according to information sent to her by Bucky. In fact, few meetings of such historic import had ever been accomplished with less secrecy. Let the town en masse recall *that*, when in future they should be tempted to cry "conspiracy"!

Mrs. October called Bucky "my dear" in front of the town; then, enveloped in clouds of blackness, or so it seemed to the townspeople, he was borne away and up to the lofty grandeur of the Ohio's Presidential Suite with its third-floor unobstructed view of The Wolf.

By the time they had got acquainted—Mrs. October, AA and Bucky; the others smiled, nodded, slept, but seldom spoke —night had fallen and lights flickered down at The Wolf, one large round fire so placed that it seemed to be the beast's eye gazing back at them. Figures moving around the bonfire and bending to it for warmth made the eye seem to wink.

"Le loup nous regard," said Aurelie Angelique. Mrs. October, waiting for melancholy to strike at her because it was dusk, then remembering that she was now where she wanted to be and that melancholy had been left behind, reached impulsively for Bucky's hand. Holding it in a reassuring clasp she answered AA by saying, "He knows that we've come to kill him, perhaps," and feeling the trembling in Bucky's hand she soothed him, murmuring, and stroked his wrist and palm. It seemed to her that the warm dark needed only a voice, a story, to become all that she had imagined it would be with Bucky by her side. Musingly she said, "The Tasmanian Wolf. It's also called The Tasmanian Tiger, do you know that?" It was too good, a stroke of genius; she heard corroboration of this in AA's intaken breath; thus inspiration served her as promptly as a well-paid servant. She and AA, knowing that the core of their revolution had been so simply found, were humming at the same time and then singing, a song that heretofore had provided amusement in their duets but had been otherwise useless. Henceforth it would provide a rallying point, a musical slogan; children would sing it in the streets; adults would tremble to hear it (as Bucky was trembling, his hand in hers).

56

> Tiger, tiger,
> Dreaming in front of my fire,
> Your eyes light my room
> When the embers expire;
> In your eyes are visions of jungle wars,
> Writhing snakes, and toads big as dinosaurs,
> Tiger, tiger,
> Dreaming in front of my fire . . .

The sleeping men awoke; their hummed accompaniment was as disturbing as the sound made by the drone-box of a bagpipe.

> Tiger, tiger,
> Wakeful beside my bed,
> Wakeful, watchful, still
> When I cover my head—
> How much longer do you intend to wait?
> I'll awake some night . . . but a second late . . .
> Tiger, tiger,
> Wakeful beside my bed . . .

It was the strangest song Bucky had ever heard; he thought they all sang it awfully well, like people on the TV. He would have applauded except that Mrs. October was holding his hand, stroking his palm. He had to put from his mind the thought that when a palm was stroked in Tasmania, at least when he was in school, it meant "Give me some pussy" (the girl never did the stroking). Also, he had to put out of his mind the surge of thoughts revolving around maternity, for her tenderness to him made him want to lay his head on her bosom and, maybe, cry, though he was certain that in his state what he would do would be to throw up on her, he was feeling that babyish. Most urgently of all, he had to stop the commingling of the two thoughts—of maternity and pussy; side by side they were bad enough, but when they actually overlapped, letting him think for a second that his own mother was tickling his palm and meaning it, he was profoundly disturbed. Finally, he had to try—because he still

Tiger Tiger

Tig-er, Tig-er — Dream-ing in front of my fire

Your eyes light my Room when the em-bers ex — pire

In your eyes are vi-sions of jun-gle wars

Writh-ing snakes and toads big as din-a — saurs

Tig-er, Tig-er — Dream-ing in front of my fire —

Repeat

had not managed it—to get used to the way she looked. He had certainly imagined her as exotic; had thought that she might even be as outlandish as to resemble an actress on the TV. But the truth of her looks was so far beyond what he had allowed himself in extremity to imagine that he thought himself to be gaping not only at the mouth but at every other place able to gape, practically. She was simply . . . foreign, was the best he could do.

He thought that she was as foreign as somebody who had come from across the waters, and in shock remembered that she *had;* all day he had been coming up against this un-assailable fact, no matter the direction of his approach, and not yet had he been able to accept it. He had written only to a box number and had not known, until she told him, that an accomplice had taken his letters to her from the box and affixed more postage and sent them on to her across the waters—his own term, and he certainly did not mean across the Tasman or the Demon or even the Ohio or Mississippi or . . . Lord, what he meant, and what was true, was across the *ocean.* And that woman who had *come across the ocean* to be with him . . . oh no, he could not believe that she had come for that reason, no matter what she said . . . but that traveler of great distances was holding his hand, stroking it, calling him "dear" and *Cecil* with an odd pronunciation, though she did keep slipping into calling him Bucky, which she seemed to prefer.

She had talked all day long in a way that seemed to take for granted that he knew what she was talking about, but he had understood practically nothing. All day she had re-ferred to his letters, and her letters, and smiled various kinds of smiles, too many of them secret—that is, seeming to share with him a secret that he did not share with those smiles at all, as much as he would have liked obliging her. She even knew his letters by heart, saying that on page two of letter three, for instance, he had given her thus and such a *cue,* and wasn't it clever of him to put it just that way et cetera. And then there were those remarks by Aurelie Angelique—

never had he seen such a long neck on anything but a goose
—spoken in another tongue, and there were Mrs. October's
remarks, such as when she took his hand and said "he
knows we've come to kill him" and the way he knew that she
did not mean him, though he didn't know who she did mean.

It had been and still was the most confusing day of his life,
putting into the shade completely the other two amazing days
which shone mysteriously in his mind: the day his mother
burned him and the day he had decided just like that to leave
the Gas Company and go in business for himself. The day of
the burning he had always thought as somehow purging him,
though he did not know of what, feeling that that was his
mother's business and someday he too would know; and the
day of leaving the Gas Company was illuminated by the
thought he had had of a sign—not neon or anything flashy,
but a hand-painted (beautifully painted) sign, maybe Olde
English, or tall letters like on the name of a College, saying
THE HOUSE OF JONES. His own place of business, THE
HOUSE OF JONES, dignified and affirmative. And now,
added to those, a third day of astonishment, and wasn't the
third time the charm? Special days had been when he heard
from her, but even then he had known that they were only
parts of what would be the occasion of their meeting, and
so had not marked them in his mind as special on their own,
as were the other two days. Thinking of the charm of the
third time, he thought that perhaps he must bear a charmed
life, the way a turtle was compensated for slowness by the
extra safety of his shell. Feeling invulnerable and—actually!—
loved, he turned to Mrs. October in the dusk and told her
that she seemed to him like an institution.

"I like institutions," he said. "America, you know; and
Oberlin College. I guess things which have capital letters in
front of them, which I love."

"Proper names . . ." She was once again saying and asking
but he did not mind. That was just her way, was all, so he
nodded and she said, "The People, then. You like The People.
As we do . . ." and her arm embraced the room in a sweep.

The room was full of night but Bucky could see the shine of her teeth as she smiled and he smiled back.

The assistants sprawling in their chairs gaped as though joining in the community smile. To Aurelie Angelique it seemed that the smiles floated, detached, upon the night; the room seemed to her to be filled with teeth.

Bucky; what was he? already hurt in some way, what was he? What had October projected for him in those Journals, already marked by somebody's attempted slaughter, what had she made of him that you might run into even now, rounding a corner, and cry out to see? Why should she, AA, care? having met up with many a sacrificial lamb in her time; having been, herself, one, she still chose to think, who had got away. But already the disguise behind which she had made her escape was slipping. The eyes in the lobby had seen through to her and called her by name: nigger. Not noire exotique; not even Noble Savage. The down-home generic name of her roots: nigger. She had been a woman for so many years that she had forgot that she was really just a nigger; ah, the therapy of coming home, that she could not tell October about except as a joke (which it was, oh yes; a joke with as many possible variations as a fountain flowing for four hundred years with polluted water has got possible diseases, a different one for everybody who drinks there but it's the same fountain).

His hurt face on top of my strange neck: that ought to satisfy even the Medusa-hunters.

The lights had been lit, waiters had arranged a round table for easy discussion, curtains had been pulled against The Tiger-Wolf; all without AA noticing. She returned from inner space and saw that her flight had been observed, was being observed: she was the cynosure of their collective gaze. Looking at Bucky enthroned in puzzled honor on Mrs. October's right, AA for an intense moment wanted to snatch him away and run to safety, nursemaid and charge, and hide among the stars, somewhere in Ursa Minor.

Roman Chainey, the future Nobellist in reportage, had, because he wrote mainly about himself and Company, come to be known, in what should probably be called the Above-ground, as Roman à Clef. A part of his peculiar success was due to opportunism, which might be defined as "to take credit, by force if necessary," and soon after the sobriquet leaked down to his natural habitat he announced to a variously breathless world—those aboveground couldn't breathe; those underground found it more aesthetic not to—that the (his designation) allonym was his own invention and that henceforth he would be known by it, and he assumed it, in court on a sunny day, paying out two hundred dollars for the privilege, a small price for licking them by joining them.

The world knew him simply as "Roman" so nothing really tiresome was appended to the name change, and in a day or so, the news having been bounced off satellites and beamed on to our men in the moon, his reputation as an amusing fellow with a fine sense of self-satire had been added to. One of our men in the moon (the other was laid up with moon fever which was turning him, none too slowly, into Roquefort) gave his thanks and approval, speaking hollowly across space: "That Roman! Boy! I sure wish we had him up here with us to shoot the old bull!"

Roman was known irreverently to some as The Old Bull, so the message was open to interpretation. But Roman again got on top by shooting a bull at the corrida in Mexico City and dedicating the tail to "our human comets" via return television (later it was said he had said "our human vomits") following which he set in circulation the rumor that the ceremony had been dubbed (by someone else, he said at first; then when the matter became a cause célèbre, he seized credit) "Pinning The Tail On The Ass." News of the insult reached the moon and the surviving Moon Man, in grief at the misunderstanding, threatened to drop a bomb on Red China. The situation was getting out of control when Roman got wind of the doings in Tasmania and to everyone's relief crawled into his trusty trench coat with the decorations, some of which were food spots, on the lapels and breast and followed his nose, a substantial guide, out of town.

Like Mrs. October, whom Roman had met in line of duty in the years when she was known by the genuine allonym "Marie d'Armont," Roman was tired. He was also growing arthritic from having spent too many nights chained like Samson to pillars which, unlike Samson, he could not budge except in his highly imaginative recountals. He had lain in mud and in the debris of trains he had helped wreck, singing tunelessly and always drunkenly about overcoming. He had marched in vanguards in driving snow, rain, and downpours of red paint, protesting, when the pickings were slim, other peoples' marches. On a sliver of barrier reef lying off the coast of Long Island, he, proponent of community control, had marched on a tiny enclave of WASPS, demanding, among other things, that they eat bagels instead of toast or muffins for breakfast, asserting further that he would not rest until Soul Food was part of their daily staple. (Defending him, a critic-employee stated, "Roman's sense of honor is really quite special.") He had spent one week in jail in a Funky of Soul Brothers, hoist with his own petard because he had donned the disguise of Afro wig plus a goatee, neither of which, though the party was over, would come off. They seemed to have taken root and no amount of frantic showing of credentials could convince the police that he was who he said he was. At the end of a week of tugging he managed to free himself from the hair he had come to despise and he was let go with apologies from the officials, but by that time he was somewhat disgusted with Soul as well as hair and he emerged from the ring less a champion of the Black Cause than when he went in.

Honor compelled him to let the world in on his disillusion, and the ensuing outcry from (as he wrote) Spayed Cats was pitiful, exhausting, and, for once, frightening. He had lived partially by, but not with, threats, and as he felt his greatest, perhaps his only, protection lay in never being out of the public eye, he entered a long period of TV panel shows, marathons, hot seats, and exchanges of inanities with the man he was convinced had to be David Susskind III or IV. Even there he had to fight infiltration of the Soulful who got jobs as cameramen, lightmen, and janitors, and attempted to run him to ground, or into the stage, with the tools of their trades. He was always in huge close-up as cameras chased him around studios; no star was ever so well lighted in the history of TV as was Roman when heavy arc lights were zeroing in on him. One night he was nearly impaled on a broom handle shoved in the one place on his body that he had announced to the world was inviolable, but his virginity, or the stoutness of his British trousers, severely limited the penetration to the real dismay of his more macho literary competitors.

Roman was tired and his prose reflected him accurately. It was no satisfaction to him that the thinner his prose got, and too limp to stay on the page without the sticky adjectival exudations of his friends and those critics whom he had terrified in various ways known only to him and them, the louder the unisonant bay proclaiming him A Great Writer. No satisfaction at all, for in the dark hours, sometimes in the lavatory of a TV studio where a cot had been set up for him with a guard outside the door to protect him from Soul, he would assess the talent in the room and find that the throne was occupied by someone other than he. Old Flaubert might have crept in past the guard, or Turgenev; Grass, or Gass, might be sitting there, though generally the Champ was dead for fifty years or more. Once, in a memorable all-night brawl, he had taken on all the boys who put together the Bible and emerged victorious. But such splendor seemed to be passing him by, leapfrogging onto the shoulders of younger writers; there were so goddamn many, all of them convinced of singularity, which was half the battle. His trouble was, he no longer believed in his own.

In the midst of L'Affaire de Lune, with Red China preparing to shoot the moon down in what they termed "preparatory retaliation against imperialist aggression," Roman was handed, in a crowded elevator (crowded with bodyguards and friends and a bonded critic or two) a scrap of paper. He had been staring at a woman's back which was cloaked in hair, wondering why she was on the elevator and why he had the impression of eyes staring at him from the back of her head, when a hand shot out of the mass and delivered the scrap of paper. The hand was black and Roman screamed, which brought the elevator to a halt, fortunately not between floors, and in the confusion that followed the woman escaped.

Later, when he had been calmed down by praise and drink, he looked at the message: MRS. OCTOBER IS FOMENTING REVOLUTION IN TASMANIA OHIO. SHE NEEDS BOTH A POET TO TELL IT LIKE IT IS (here Roman shivered at the phraseology but perked up at the next clause) AND A HE MAN TO TRAIN CADRE FOR THE SEXUAL TAKEOVER. YOU ARE THAT JANUS. ATTEND THE BEGINNING. THIS IS NO PLOT. REMEMBER MARIE d'ARMONT? He remembered her as one recalls a severed limb. He had managed with difficulty after their parting, though she had taught him methods of survival, among them how to turn public disaffection to his advantage. Yet for a time he had ached at the point of severance. Marie d'Armont, murderess, but for a great cause. He was badly in need of a refresher course.

Once again the Old Pro: inflamed, fearless (comparatively), raunchy, he gave his crowd the slip and winged on a private plane to Tasmania, working out en route the shape of his opening lecture on the meaning of sex. Ah, Baudelaire! To climb in the ring with that supreme voluptuary once again! (One critic had said of him that he was more preoccupied than Norman Mailer with the scrotum; it was a jab to which he uncharacteristically paid no attention because he felt that Norman was a child with a child's slightly dirty but innocent fixation on that part of the body. As far as Roman was concerned, only Baudelaire came close to his dark monomania.) Calling on his muse, d'Armont (October; he must remember), he thought a good opening tactic would be to disarm Baudelaire with a quote and then . . . POW.

In large letters, so that he could read them later on without his glasses, he wrote on lined yellow paper: THE SUPREME PLEASURE IN LOVE LIES IN THE KNOWLEDGE OF DOING EVIL. MAN AND WOMAN KNOW, FROM BIRTH, THAT IN EVIL IS TO BE FOUND ALL VOLUPTUOUSNESS.

The pilot was a man with one eye gone West so that despite instruments and corrective readings he always landed Roman a few miles off course in the direction of the sunset. But Roman hired the handicapped—"They're Fun To Watch" —and in return for their loyalty gave them his; so that by the time the slack of the overshot had been taken up with the help of a truck and a haywagon, and he and the pilot stood in the bowl of Tasmania like two warmed-over knaedels, dawn was spilling its similes over the mountains.

As Roman said, choking on air and The Idea of Revolution, "Melvin, baby, it's . . . it's like a New Day." And Melvin nodded sagely at a spot a few degrees to the left of Roman and said, "It is."

With the fortuitous stroke of the loonie Moon Man, Mrs. October believed she had projected the final touch of urgency needed to give impetus to her final revolution. Setting up tensions that endangered the world was a time-honored tactic of Revolutionists and so bothered her not at all. She had always believed that if the hatred of the entire world could be focused on a single object, or victim, then by the act of destruction of that victim, the world would be rid, in one great magnificent act of violence, of its hate, and hatred would, while not ceasing to exist, lie dormant for a thousand years.

The trouble, as far as she had ever been able to see it, was not in hate's existence as part of Man's natural endowment, but in its diffuseness. Hate could bind together people of more disparate tastes than love ever could do. Love, on a vast scale, led to factions and the factions to a distrust more profound than hate—witness Christianity. Within that peculiar sado-masochistic form of thought, intradenominational differences based on interpretation of the Sacred Word were like ripples from a stone dropped in a pool: outward spread the distrust until, in the name of The Greatest Love known to man, all faiths were torn from within, and then turned outward, embroiling other faiths in their squabbles, so seriously as to periodically kill off half the world's population, but following the wars the schisms would be seen to have grown and into the widening gulfs Ecumenical Conferences dropped with hardly a sound. But the important point to consider was that in even its smallest unit—a family, or a denomination —one did not find the binding together of several members by Love that one found in a similar unit with hate as its flocculant. Clubs, communities, towns, groups of states, could be held together, permanently fused into a solid mass when race hatred was the chemical. She had counted upon this when she invented her Moon Man (en route even now; perhaps by now landed among the craters, and plotting).

She thought that the urgency set loose in the world from so many anxious minds would be the binding sought from the beginning of time; that if the man in the moon ever returned to earth in a lynchable form (she must see to it, or something similar) he would be the first victim of that peculiarly American form of death to have met it with the world's approval—indeed at its instigation and by its insistence. Men would be able to move within the familiar framework of tradition—i.e., hatred of their fellow man—and at the same time would be able to justify that hatred for once by calling its object "the monster from Outer Space," an opportunity that had not come along since Lucifer's headlong flight from heaven. At least she hoped, with some modesty, that what she had invented would be a new Satan, but one—because of her modesty—whose dispatchment would not take so long a time. (At this stage of advanced planning, she dropped the euphemistic 'projection' and called the act, in her mind, by its rightful name of invention, a more modest term than 'creation.')

A lover of mob scenes, she sat smiling wistfully over her blueprint, seeing the peoples of the world advancing over oceans and descending from skies and choking highways, a billion billion furious ants come to kill the Moon Man. She believed in such retribution—a theory, heretofore; for just as firmly as she believed that hate must go into a dormant state, and soon, if life was to continue, so did she believe that a killing of a single person, performed by the entire world in singular agreement, must be allowed for the satisfaction and catharsis of that world, and the more horrible and protracted the murder, the longer-lived the catharsis.

In other words, to state it as plainly as possible, both for herself and for those who would judge her in the future, she believed that if all the world could be made to hate the same thing—namely, HATE—then hate could be put aside and the millennium met with righteous hosannas (though the idea of a thousand years of peace had always put her to sleep). If the Moon Man, after his threat, could not be made to symbolize, to the agreement of all, Hate, and so be destroyed, then there was no hope and not only would her life have been wasted in all its parts but all lives would have been and there would be no more life. Because the Moon Man, now invented, would blow them all to—to use one of AA's mysterious expressions—"where the wind don't blow and the snow don't go," with, of course, the eager help of Red China, the United States, and Russia, among others. And she would have thrown the ball that opened the Terminal Ballgame. Had thrown it already. By this time extra editions were being hawked on the streets in those parts of the world where people could still read; in the remaining, major portions of the globe where illiteracy was the 'in' thing, TV cameras were aimed at average citizens, beseeching opinions, suggesting answers by the use of subliminal devices.

Yes, for once "manipulation by the media" might serve Mankind rather than betray it.

She devoutly hoped so. *For horror* (she had written it) *is itself a game begun with the simplest proposition . . . a few words that a child could utter . . .* (or write) *. . . or a senile woman . . .*

Yes. She was aware of the possible existence of *that* explanation for such an act of invention: *senility . . . in paradox bearing great age in one hand . . .* and childishness in the other. So God Himself must have been aware, when, unable to find a lost toy, and lonely, He had said "Let there be Light" and there was Light, and he observed what that Light illumined.

PART II
Tasmania—Now and Then

THE CHILDREN were singing in the streets:

> Now is the time
> To revolute
> When you're dead
> Who gives a shoot

But no one could make them say where they had learned
the song, or what the words really meant. According to dictionaries "revolute" meant a rolling backward, or downward,
which would have suited the parents just fine, but there was
a look about the singing children, a ruthlessness . . .

For days the catch phrase had been "Tasmania will never
be the same," with irrefutable facts to back it up: black
people who were obviously not servants had slept in the
Ohio Hotel, one of them, the long-necked woman, in the
Presidential Suite; strangers had come and some of them
had gone; the train, which had ignored Tasmania for twenty
years, was making unexpected stops, spewing out persons of
the most outlandish appearance whose like had been seen
(and disbelieved) only on the TV. Some arrived and left
on the same day while others stayed, and the Tasmanians
could not decide which was worse, for the one looked like
contempt for what had been briefly seen and the other
smacked of a takeover of some vague and thus terrifying
sort.

In the Beaux Arts Bar and Grill on any evening in the
week, tongues were spoken that were best described as 'unknown,' a phenomenon heretofore connected with a questionable religion practiced in The Wolf. Citizens turned to
Myra Little for reassurance, as she was the only one in town

said to know anything about the dreadful languages spoken elsewhere. Her replies were invariably indirect but she managed to suggest the origins of some of the strangers by stating that she, personally, had never learned Russian. A little puff, like that from a very small bomb, grew upward from the remark and this small mushroom cap soon spread out until it was a toadstool hanging over the city. This, then (they said) was the way it happened, as they had always known, as their parents and grandparents had known: destruction riding into town on the backs of a few strangers; and for the first time they deplored the protective hills that were now seen as barriers like those forming the sides of a common trap.

Each quiet day pulling in to its close was discussed over supper tables as having undoubtedly been the last such that they would be allowed, and tomorrow would bring the end, and everybody's words should be marked on it. When tomorrow came and went in peace (the strangers walking the streets and drinking in the bars were disappointingly subdued) the Tasmanians did not take heart or revise their beliefs that it had been the last day, and scares were plentiful.

It was set about that the strangers were a mess of intellectuals (the High School principal had said it), which was bad enough, but the rumor expanded to include their having chosen Tasmania as the site of a breeding place for more of their kind, with the humidity of the year-round climate being given as explanation, for it was said that Tasmania's weather approximated that of New York City where intellectuals bred like flies. Children reported that they had seen lady intellectuals laying eggs in alleys. Some parents were amused by such extreme exaggeration until they remembered that Tasmania had not one public rest room to its name—and why should it? Everyone, no matter where he was when the call came, was always within running distance of a friend's house.

And so one quiet day followed another, quiet at least in the sense of nothing more dramatic than arrivals and sometimes departures occurring, which began to rankle. How dared these people come here and sit about doing nothing, as though Tasmania were some kind of resort! There ought to be a law against it, and there probably was; surely there was something on the books about loitering?

Omerie Chad was the next oracle to be consulted. To the surprise and peculiar pride of the Tasmanians, neither he nor Myra Little, their two foreigners, had taken up with the infiltrators as had been expected, but seemed to make special attempts to maintain distance, which understandably led to some eventual speculation about whether the two of them might not be wanted in the outer world for criminal activity. For a time it was said that the strangers were hoovermen come to apprehend Myra and Omerie . . . (Since Hoover's death the word had gone lower-case and entered dictionaries) . . . But it did not set well with the town's admiring memory of Mr. Hoover that so many of the outlanders were colored and so the matter was dropped, helped to its end by the children's having 'arrested' Myra in the downtown area and surrounded Omerie's carriage house, demanding his surrender, just as the Chief of Police was coming out.

A delegation of respectable folk paid a call on Omerie, hoping to profit by his superior knowledge of the outside world. The delegation was made up of young fathers whose concern for the Tasmanian Way outweighed the pinochle table. The report they carried home was highly unsatisfactory as they admitted, and so other missions were necessary. It was suggested that if they went singly rather than as a group, more might be accomplished, and so it came to be, and it was not unknown for one of them to receive an excited summons to Omerie's house late at night, with impending revelation being hinted at to the wife, who agreed that of course he must go, SHE being told not to wait up and for gosh sakes not to worry if the business took a while.

So where were they to turn as the days wheeled like carted patients into the terminal wards of the weeks? Bucky had simply disappeared. Well, he was seen now and then, but always in the very center of either black people or foreigners, and usually linked as though by invisible chains to Mrs. October. Some said he was being held prisoner, and children took to bringing home notes that they said Bucky had dropped with a pleading look, notes that read HELP. But the childish hand was always exposed and sometimes slapped.

Their very children were being turned into liars and worse. What had they SEEN when the lady intellectuals squatted in the alleyways? was one smoldering question put to them by fathers. One child put a stop to that by saying he had seen her egg basket and that it was hairy.

Wanda knew nothing whatsoever about her brother's affairs, thank you; he had not chosen to call her once since that woman's arrival. She could not, would not, bring herself to tell what she knew about the correspondence that had preceded Mrs. October's appearance. To do so just might be construed as betrayal and would bring Mama undulating about the place like a dusty old sheet. No, Wanda was sorry but she knew nothing whatsoever about her brother.

Which was not true.

Wanda was dusting the Game Room, puzzled by the impulse, loathing the cages, when Bucky's feet appeared, hesitant, on the stairs, and came slowly down, turning into legs as she watched and then waist and narrow chest and finally troubled face. The face feared for her, asked her why she was here, but all he said was, "Wan . . ."

"Well, is all I can say."

"How are you, hon?"

(Look after little Bucky, now.) "I'm all right, dear." Hum hum, dust flying.

"Really?"

"What am I, some kind of liar?" (Sorry, Mama.) "Just cleaning up after the animals." Laugh.

"What animals, hon?"

"Invisible ones, dope, that live in these (goddamn) cages. Pretty cages, but they ought to have something in them and so I pretend they do, is all. For goodness sakes!"

"Oh."

"Where's your sense of humor?"

"I oftentimes wondered that, myself." They looked at each other in surprise. It was true that he had always been on the solemn side but he had never admitted it before. She had never known that he knew about his deficiency. It touched her.

"Welllll, that's not so bad. Maybe you haven't needed one. The way I have . . . Don't hang there, Bucky, like a cobweb, or I'll sweep you down before I know what I'm doing. Sit down somewhere." He sat and she cleaned, wondering how he might have changed in his time spent with niggers and worse. She was nearly certain that his smell was different. Feeling him as a stranger, when he spoke, she jumped.

"Wan, you know the kind of things I think?" She certainly did not. "When I'm washing the car, which I'm going to drive someplace, I think 'The Death Car had just been simonized, according to Sergeant Wade,' and it's Walter Cronkite that's saying it."

"Who's Sergeant Wade?"

"He's the one that found the Death Car."

"I don't know any Sergeant Wade. I don't know anybody named Wade in Tasmania, or in the county, and I've been stopped by all of them."

"Maybe he hasn't been born yet."

"Born to who, people named Smith? There aren't any Wades, is what I'm trying to tell you. Get the telephone book and see for yourself."

"Or, when I'm eating fish I think 'According to Doctor Russell, the patient choked on . . .' "

"There is no Doctor Russell in Tasmania. Get the telephone book. Call the hospital."

"That announcement is on the 'Eleven O'Clock News.' "

She was acerbic. "Are they going to bury you? Listen, if you're going to be found in a death car, or choked to kingdom come on a fishbone, it better be by somebody you know personally, or at least somebody *I* know, because who would they call about the funeral arrangements?" Her head ached. She spoke snappishly, "You're just not practical, Bucky."

She had sworn to herself, hand on the Bible in her mind, that she would not bring up his late whereabouts no matter the provocation. Against the inevitable event of his coming to see her she had practiced a remote tone of voice to use on him that Geraldine Fitzgerald, her model for all dream behavior, would have approved of. Coolly, remotely (Geraldine in white chiffon with a draped bodice, smooth-haired and hands like lilies) she said, "Coffee, dear?" She regretted that she had not asked "Tea, dear," though they did not drink it unless they were sick, because there was the lovely cool question concerning lemon that Geraldine spoke with such elegance. Wanda longed for hands fluttering over silver things, little tongs for sugar lumps—try and find lumps in Tasmania— lilacs beyond the windows, chintz and the smell of beeswax hand-rubbed into furniture in a high-ceilinged dim room. She longed for Geraldine's commiseration over the reality of her life: bamboo, the coal furnace, dust boogers moving wavelike in corners no matter how hard she worked, Bucky with the smell about him that could be darkies, talking about death cars and fishbones and policemen and doctors who did not exist, and the strangers in TV land who were trying to spoil the world. "Ah," she told her lovely Irish friend, "my life, my dear, my drab little life." For she longed unceasingly for the beautiful life of tradition and manners, a life that had never been hers; she had been born to coal furnaces that laid moving surfaces of black moss overnight upon floors that were oiled rather than waxed, and bathrooms that smelled of people instead of flowers, with toilet bowls forever stained brown, and though the stains were from the irony water they might as well have been from the other, for all the comfort the sight gave a girl who imagined that she must have been born cringing.

Yes, Bucky wanted coffee, of course, and she toiled up the stairs to warm it up, dramatizing the gulf between dream and reality by choosing the thickest cups she had. Her best china was none too thin, not by her interior standards based upon minute observation of the appointments in the rooms through which Geraldine moved, but she did have one cup, fragile as a leaf, from which she sipped neat whiskey upon returning late from a double feature. She possessed a few other items that a lady might not scorn, secretly collected in her adolescence as preparation for the life of spinsterhood that she had desired: a two-cup coffee pot, pewter napkin ring, one pillowcase edged with the finest lace, an afghan to drape over her legs as she lay on the chaise (she had never bought the chaise) through long afternoons when she gave way to her Brontëan melancholy, delicately coughing into one of the really good handkerchiefs.

But she had married the first man who asked her, and her long afternoons had been spent, until recently, in the company of women who played card games and slapped their legs for emphasis and drank highballs of rye whiskey mixed with half ginger ale, half soda. Her only escape from all of them, including Mama, was the movies, to which she would never go other than alone, not since her marriage. But an ugly reality had begun to obtrude even there; one of Geraldine's last pictures had shown her emotionally involved with a man who ran a grubby shop, who could hardly speak English, and who had some fragmented horror in his background that Wanda could not, nor did she care to, make out. But Geraldine's apartment had been pretty, thank God, or she never could have borne it.

But no one knew about that side of Wanda, any more than she knew about the side of Bucky that simonized death cars and regularly choked on fishbones, thereby gaining a curious celebrity. She was sorry that he had told her; it felt to her like some sort of violation, which was why she had resisted him by pretending to miss his point. Her imagination was at least uplifting, and while not practical, did not terminate in horrible messages delivered by persons she had never heard of.

She wondered if her failure to share her movie-going with Bucky was the reason he had gone so oppositely, in the terrible direction of the rest of the world which was striving to eliminate the very concept of foreigner, at least according to the TV, at which she could barely stand to look; if she was responsible, then she was also responsible for Tasmania's being filled with strangers bent on destruction. If it was so, and she was found out, then they would nail her to a cross. At least she could scream, then.

She took the coffee and went down to her brother, wondering what new revelations he had prepared for her in her absence. She had not long to wait to find out. As soon as she had set the tray down, Bucky said, "You won't die, Wan. I won't let anybody hurt you."

Covered with chill bumps, she said, "Nobody's trying to, that I know about. You?"

"Hurt me?"

"Well, that. Or know anybody trying to hurt ME, is what I meant there." She laughed.

"Why would anybody want to hurt you, Wan?"

"My god, Bucky, wake up or something. If nobody WAS, why would you say you wouldn't LET them?"

"I wouldn't, is all. I just wanted you to know. I mean, I never told you before and thought maybe you'd think I would. Which I wouldn't. You're my own flesh and blood, and Mama's and Papa's. We're this close-knitted little family, two of us dead, and . . ."

"You're just not making sense at all." Her sharpness must be immediately tempered lest Mama start looming up. "I never thought you'd let anybody hurt me, honey. Which is the same as never thinking you wouldn't . . . not . . . Well, it's never come up. We don't go around hurting each other in Tasmania, not where it shows, anyhow." She amused herself with a foxy feeling. "Anybody wanted to hurt me would have to be some kind of a foreign person, and foreigners just don't come to Tasmania. Now do they."

He told her simply, "Tasmania's as full as a dipper with people from all over the world, practically."

She nodded. "Ah. So they've come here to get me, then. I've been waiting for them."

To her shock, he wailed like a child. She went to him and put her arms around him and patted his poor puckered cheek. Wishing that she had the courage to scream, she thought that such a scream as she could give if Mama would let her, might be powerful enough to rearrange the atoms in that poor cheek and make it as smooth as her own. All at once, thinking of her inability to scream because of extenuating circumstances, she was overwhelmed by a feeling of pity for herself. It was like a madness long feared, for it had taken her in the presence of both Bucky and Mama (over there, lifting her old bulk up in the one corner Wanda had not cleaned, as though materializing out of the dust boogers). Wanda said, "Poor Wanda. Her head is killing her. Maybe you ought to leave her alone now." She went, surprising herself, to one of the cages and let herself in and closed the door. "They can't get me here," she said, waiting for his reaction. She had the curious feeling that her move had been dictated by someone; that she had played into someone's hands, and she did not think somehow that the someone was Bucky. When he stared at her in extreme fright but said nothing Wanda began to feel that something more was required of her; it was certainly a foolish position—locked in a cage in your own basement— but a caged thing might as well behave like a caged thing, or so the suggestion came to her from somewhere outside herself, and so she put her face close up to the bars and stared at Bucky like a tigress and said, rather feebly, "Gobble, gobble."

As though she had turned a key, a torrent of words came from him, words about the cages having been built to specification to hold assimilators and a lot more that she did not try to understand. One thought: the children know first— gave her pause but did not engage her. To her intense gratification, watching her brother's mouth working with the effort to get rid of words as ugly as worms, she began to feel rising in her a resentment of him, clean and heady as mountain air, and then an acknowledgment that not only had she loathed her mother but was wondrously glad that she was dead. She thought, Oh, I could sing the words! I could simply walk onto the middle of a stage and sing them for an audience. She had a clear picture of herself doing just that and with the picture the feeling, a twin to the sense of having her moves dictated, that it was an actual scene from the not too distant future, vouchsafed to her inner eye for a purpose not yet revealed; she must hold herself in check until the arrival of that day, or her arrival at it. A banner spread itself across her mind, white with red letters: WANDA = REVOLUTIONIST, and there was a heaviness at both foot and hip as though she were booted and wore the small arms of a girl soldier. Her exhilaration was so intense that she tried to impose a further vision of her own invention: tried to see herself lifting her pistol arm and taking aim at Mama's sheet; tried to smell the gunpowder, see the flash, watch the scorch-hole widening on that hateful old sheet . . . but though the thoughts came freely, no picture accompanied them. She felt like a radio trying to become a TV, and then there was an inward soothing, followed by sleepiness, and she left the cage and sat on the couch and then lay upon it, paying no more mind to Bucky ('He is just an instrument') than she did to the futile flappings of white in the dirty corner. With Bucky still talking nonsense, Wanda fell asleep.

The following week she was not surprised to receive a summons to a meeting with instructions on how to get there, signed MRS. OCTOBER.

Mrs. Hackett, dressed in her mother's clothes, sat with her dolls on a sofa looking through a photograph album. She nodded over the beloved pictures, studio portraits of her parents and herself taken before heavy drapes in a garden of columns and pedestals holding baskets of roses. She had never grown sleepy in such pursuit before, as she informed the dolls, pursing her mouth in imitation of a fading memory. "My favorite pastime, and me as heavy-headed as a cabbage-rose . . ." Not only heavy-headed; bored. The word came even as she gazed at Mama's face. She believed she should cry as penance but no sorrow touched her. Instead, the word repeated: bored, bored, bored, bored.

It seemed to her that she gazed down a corridor of growing-up years as static and artificial as the columns and pedestals—imitation stuff, easy to knock over. She did not see how she could bear to move down that inert avenue where the drapes eternally smelled of dust. She saw herself pressed behind glass, rice-powdered, wearing her mother's clothes, gazing from the window frozen in its frame at a world enlivened by the fresh air of change that could never touch her, never get to her and free her. Curiously like a memory she thought that such airlessness could form monsters out of the dust. She did not want to be a monster! Her head snapped forward as though forcibly to blot melancholy like a signature set at the bottom of her thoughts. Mama gazed up at her sadly, seeming to ask, "Am I a monster, Belle?" for she had been formed out of that dust and a fear of change.

Fighting confusion and disloyalty the easiest way, Belle closed the album and she and the dolls fell asleep.

The following day the post brought her an invitation from a stranger, a Mrs. October. After the first shock at such a breach of taste, Belle felt only delight and not even the diagram of how to reach the assembly, as it was called, that seemed to have an arrow pointing into the warehouse section of town which bordered on the slums, which Belle had seen only from the safety of her father's buggy, could change her delight at the invitation or her determination to accept it. "Mrs. October," she murmured, keeping the strange name from the dolls. It was the very name of change itself, of the fall when drifting leaves left the trees bare and everybody

83

could look in the windows of everybody else's house. Belle, who had nothing to hide (things hid from her!) thought that was a lovely idea.

Marie Louise lay clasped in the embrace of her Wednesday Steady, wondering where her kid was, watching over the Steady's shoulder some policemen beating some black men inside the TV set. Occasionally she would rise to heights of display, then subside, as remembrance of what she was engaged in came and went. When she thought of herself being made love to, which she did more or less constantly save during the act itself, it was neither of pleasure given nor pleasure received; it was of the picture she made, limbs threshing, hair flailing, eyes mad with a purely pictorial passion; and of the sounds—here she had to allow her partner's intrusion—of the bedroom: disembodied pantings, mutterings, cries—the slippery, slapping onomatopoeia of sex which she could not very well manage alone. Watching TV, she thought that what the policemen and black men were doing, though the sound was turned off, was for reasons of display, too; they performed for the camera the way she performed for herself. 'I am a monitor,' she thought and giggled. Her partner was making it crucial for her—oh, she enjoyed the climaxes!—and she wished generously that the men in the TV could be doing THIS instead of THAT; then, at least, there wouldn't be all that blood dripping out of the set and onto her floor.

She read her invitation to attend the assembly as her Thursday Steady was coming up the walk and would have torn it up as she did the pleas from hopeful politicians had it not been for that name: October. Well. It was high time the woman sought out her few worldly equals in Tasmania, was all Marie Louise could say.

They assembled on a clear morning, each finding his way according to the typed instructions that were delivered at

84

their homes. The instructions warned them not to be late by even a moment, stating that at the exact time printed thereon THE DOORS WILL BE CLOSED.

Some read the words with misgiving, turning back in their minds to childhood and thoughts of the mountain that opened up and swallowed all the children who followed the Piper. But misgiving proved to be a mouse which, when faced with the lion of curiosity, willingly allowed itself to be eaten.

The individual routes given in the instructions were so deviously planned that not one of the adventurers encountered another until, rounding various corners and emerging from alleyways, they found themselves en masse before a dilapidated building that looked like a warehouse, but that none of them could place as one they had seen before, or—as someone put it, raising goose flesh—at least not in Tasmania.

Mrs. October, as chipper as a kindergarten teacher on the first day, stood on the porch, or loading platform, and counted noses, ticking them off on a sheet mounted on a clipboard. She apparently recognized them by sight although no one but Bucky knew her. When all were there, and none failed to attend, Mrs. October beckoned them to follow her. Each knew that this was the time for turning back if there was to be such a time and not one of them faltered. If the warehouse had contained a sea, then they were lemmings who rushed and swarmed willingly to their fate.

When they were all inside, craning toward the crater of gloom, Mrs. October locked the doors; they heard the grating of key in rusty lock. She then walked to the railing, or barrier of some sort that separated them from the large darkness, and stood with her back against it, arms resting on it. She told them, "It's difficult to describe oneself. The best one can do is to give a sort of list of abilities—at least we know what we CAN do, if not what we can't—and name our intentions, or at least what we think our intentions are. I am a reasonable gardener . . ."—she seemed to be addressing Bucky with some amusement as she continued—"and a pretty good florist. I'll try to explain that in a moment. Mainly I put on shows—with music, and tableaux vivants, dancing and colored lights, and mirrors. And people. You. You are, or will be after today, if you return, my . . ."—she paused, then charmed them with a crooked smile—"my raw material. From you—explanation of the gardener-florist remark—I hope to fashion bouquets." She smiled openly at Bucky, who nodded and smiled in return as though he SAW; he was in fact terribly puzzled; the picture that came to his mind was of groups of people tied in the middle, their legs wired, their heads nodding outward, some of them held upright solely by pieces of green bamboo.

Mrs. October continued. "I hope to fashion bouquets of mixed varieties, colors, scents, and persuasions. With a lily and a black rose I would place a carnivorous plant," and the crowd shuddered. "A simple point to be made by such an arrangement is that the carnivore would eat neither the lily nor the black rose but would, instead, protect both of them by catching flies." The company broke into relieved laughter.

As though she were satisfied by their response and had signaled her satisfaction to an unseen assistant, lights began to bloom as softly as moonflowers. Revelation occurred so slowly that there were no unseemly reactions though all were impressed and vaguely oppressed to view the huge auditorium that none had known existed in Tasmania. It appeared to be ample enough for all Tasmania at once to fit into. There was nothing seedy or forgotten about it; nothing was new but all wore the patina of a place lovingly used and cared for. The chandeliers from which the light drifted were crystal, looped and swagged with chains of pendants. Omerie Chad said, sounding awed, "The Met," which seemed to interest Mrs. October deeply although the others could not figure out why it should.

She led them down a comfortably wide aisle toward the stage, chatting as they went but nobody with the possible exception of Omerie could later recall what she had said, because as they approached the stage the immense curtain of gold cloth parted and shimmered up and everyone gasped aloud. The stage was the largest the Tasmanians had ever seen or imagined, so deep that there was no apparent back wall. She led them up a ramp laid over the orchestra pit and onto the immensity where each felt himself to be abandoned to a flood of sensation unlike any in his previous experience.

Above them were great misty flies from which dangled a forest of sets as maddening as the grapes of Tantalus. In their craning to see more and more of what maddened and puzzled and hurt them, Mrs. October was forgotten. If she had pulled a bomb out of her bodice and told them that she was going to set it off, not one of the craners would have heard her or cared if they had.

It was as though all the majesty of America, from fruited plain to alabaster city, from Atlantic to Pacific, from river to great river, hung above their heads and to a man the sense of its weight and suspended glory was a burning pain. It was as though it had in truth been taken from them and placed far beyond their reach, bound in ropes and clamped in machinery. As mightily as they strained, they knew they could no more touch it than they could touch the stars. It burned above them, their heritage, and they, below in darkness (as the flies had grown mistily light, the stage had fallen into shadow), were little more than worms in primeval ooze. In fact, each in his own way illustrated what he was feeling by wriggling, striving for articulation, pulling to unmire his feet. As they strove a clammy cold seemed to enwrap their lower extremities. Those who tended toward arthritis and rheumatism felt the cold more acutely and tromped and stamped for warmth. Oh, they thought—as they later said when comparing notes—oh, my beloved country! a curious thought to seize upon persons who had never seen nor cared to see beyond their ring of little hills. And yet the smallest among them felt at that moment that the stolen splendor vanishing above them was the greatest the world had ever known and each would have given anything at all to be somehow party to its restoration.

When they had suffered for a while the lights altered and the heat was turned back on and they found themselves once again on a warm, bright stage gawking somewhat foolishly up at a welter of painted flats. The illusion was one of Mrs. October's greatest successes and all who had taken part in it were gratified and relaxed, feeling their revolution was off to a fine start.

As the company compared notes on what they had, or thought they had seen, the sound became like that at the foot of the Tower of Babel—supreme semantic confusion, just prior to God's setting them each adrift on little islands of separate language. It was ever thus, on the first morning; Mrs. October heard it as music from which soon a strain of purest melody would rise; this time, this time, the order, the melody, would engulf all, would cover the world, would reach the sky (though too late for the threatening man in the moon). October, hurry! she told herself, amused by the drama of the moment, which she had allowed to go on entirely too long.

She clapped her hands to gain their attention. Gradually the babble fell to a murmur and silence rolled slowly over the assemblage, engulfing them a group at a time, outward from Mrs. October, a model of stillness, toward the wings, until only Mrs. Hackett was left staring up, singing in a high voice of sharp sweetness "Oh, beautiful for spacious skies." Marie Louise hissed in humiliation, a sound so realistically snaky that women gathered in their skirts, thinking that where there had been fields and trees a moment ago there still could be black racers and copperheads. The sense of the dangling country remained with them and disquiet lay upon them as though one of the mountains had fallen, crushing their spirits. Mrs. October read their oppressiveness and signaled to the hidden pianist for soothing music, a tune of liberation, even as she gazed at Mrs. Hackett. Of all those whom she had projected in her Journals, that lady gave off the greatest sense of individual life and rebelliousness. Perhaps, thought Mrs. October, it was because Mrs. Hackett was, at least in her own mind, the youngest person there.

The pianist, recruited by Aurelie Angelique, was none other than the Imogene who had been Mrs. Hackett's last pupil. Hearing from her perch in the wings the familiar voice of her old teacher, the girl (a young mother, now, though unmarried) forgot her instructions and stumbled into "Country Gardens," which, both as a piece of music and a geographic locale, had proven to be her downfall on two notable occasions. After a moment or two more of "America the Beautiful," Mrs. Hackett fell into a reverie in which she whispered "No, no" at the girl's mistakes.

Marie Louise, watching her mother, said in sudden alarm, "My God, if Imogene sticks 'Lucy in the Sky' in there it may jar Mama back out of her second childhood!" She was overcome with the need to see that that did not happen. She simply could not lose her undemanding little sister and get back that querulous tyrant who had nagged, nagged, especially about the rumors of Marie Louise's sexual adventures.

Marie Louise ran in the direction of the music and when she found Imogene she pushed her unceremoniously from the bench and sat down and played the only piece she had ever mastered in its entirety: "Oh, Dem Golden Slippers." She threw in every hot lick she could manage, she jigged her feet as she played riffs and sang. It was an extraordinarily vulgar rifacimento which dispersed the danger and secured Mrs. Hackett firmly in her second childhood. She could not have borne the return to a world that contained such a common daughter, the one thorn on a life that otherwise had been like a long-stemmed rose rendered safe by the Master Florist.

Marie Louise returned to the stage in triumph. Passing her mother, she said to her "Glub glub," imagining Mrs. Hackett stuck in little-girlhood, covered nose and mouth as though pushed into a tub of something nasty.

AA, who had hated the tune and the performance, had

also, from first sight, hated the woman, whom she had decided to call Marie Louse, and when the woman passed her AA muttered "Clabber-faced coozie." She promised herself that if she ever decided to go berserk she would make this Ms. America the first victim of her good hatchet arm.

Rather perfunctorily, Mrs. October took them on a tour of Spartan dressing rooms—communal; there was no setting apart of the sexes, not even a door between toilets—and of spacious wardrobe rooms and showers and kitchens. The stage, it turned out, was generously trapped and the regions below contained elevators and pieces of machinery.

When the tour was over they returned to the stage and sat in folding chairs that had been put up in their absence, a half circle of rows of chairs ranged about a central one, which Mrs. October sat in. Getting right to the point she told them, "The best way to illustrate my method . . ." (method of what? They still did not know)—"is, to, well, illustrate it," and she smiled and beckoned Mrs. Hackett forward. At the same time her assistants, two faceless black men, came forth with a large cardboard box and placed it beside her. Indicating it, Mrs. October said, "The drag box." Omerie gave a laugh, or made a sound of trepidation, depending on the listener. Mrs. October suggested to him, "Perhaps you would like to explain the meaning of 'drag.'" He told her coolly, "I certainly would not," and she nodded. He was on his own now. The thought stimulated Mrs. October. (That night she wrote in her Journals: *They are quite oddly independent for this stage of the game. Even Marie Louise, my villainess, has behaved unpredictably, and Wanda actually fascinates me. Observing her growth should be great fun. Of them all, only my darling Bucky is still MINE, and ever will be. Should I say "I trust"?*)

To Mrs. Hackett she said, "Do you like to dress up?" Mrs. Hackett nodded, pleased to feel safe once more in a world of games.

Mrs. October's assistants dressed the old little girl in a gown of black silk encrusted with rhinestones, crowned her with a zircon tiara, gave her a long jeweled cigarette holder with a self-burning cigarette in it, and placed her on a chair over which a mantle of velvet trimmed with ermine had been thrown. The lights dimmed until only Mrs. Hackett was lighted, which made her a bit nervous at first, but soon there crawled out of the darkness to her feet the two assistants, transformed into vaguely South American peasants. They clutched play-money—even Mrs. Hackett could tell it was not real—and turn by turn, they 'lit' her cigarette with burning money which charred and fell in flakes onto their abject bodies.

Mrs. October whispered to Mrs. Hackett, who said, smiling at the crowd, "Who am I?" Oh, goody: charades! They called out their guesses: Mata Hari, Hannah Green, Whistler's Mother and Mrs. Hackett were a few. Mrs. October cautioned them, "Think." And they thought. The silence was deep and lengthy; Mrs. Hackett began to cough at the smoke from burning money. Marie Louise was heard to say with a snigger, "Lucky Strike Green has gone down Mama."

Someone took the cue and asked in an embarrassed voice, "Are you War?" Mrs. Hackett had not been told who she was but she did not want to be War and replied firmly, "Goodness gracious me, no," and appealed to Mrs. October with a look. Mrs. October, bemused by the burgeoning life around her, told the company briefly that the nature of the game, or inquiry, was Socratic, and they were impressed enough not to mind the lack of enlightenment and were pleased by the lack of condescension. How long—as they later said to each other—had it been since they had been forced to think, forced to delve into the dried leaves of their schooling which had been heaped into discarded piles for so long that it was fit only for burning! At least, that utterance was the form the consensus of their opinions took when it was entered permanently into the minutes of the day, so that who had said it or whether or not it had been said at all was unimportant to the Revolution. The important thing was that Mrs. October's remark was itself Socratic, making them dig into their memories for the meaning of the word; soon there arose an eager babble which became clear words grouped as questions: "Are you Wall Street?" Mrs. Hackett denied it, not taking to the idea of being walked upon. "Are you New York City?" Mrs. Hackett remembered her mother's mistrust of foreigners and said, "No, indeed." A short swarthy man that none of them had noticed before, a representative, as they later decided, from The Wolf, asked, "Are you The United Fruit Company?" Mrs. Hackett was tempted; her father liked Companies and she was fond of fruit. She encouraged the man with "Welllll . . ." The Tasmanians did not appreciate a stranger's coming so close to the answer. Those who had dimly remembered that the answer was supposed to be in *them*, forgot again in the anxiety of the time. They forgot also their embarrassment at speaking out in public and called out the names of other companies: Ford; A & P; Dupont; wondering what possible connection such respectable names could have with naked savages being brutally burned by money, but willing to accuse if accusation could lead to winning a prize. The man from The Wolf, in a hard, slightly contemptuous voice, asked Mrs. Hackett, "Are you Dow Chemical?" and she whimpered at his tone— so accusing, so rude. It appeared that The Wolf man had scored again; none of the others had made Mrs. Hackett whimper and they grew competitive, calling out any name they could think of in a pinch as having been seen on a bottle or box: Lance (a drain opener), Sure-Fire (charcoal lighter), and so on, the names being chosen for malignancy. The more sensitive ones began to feel vulnerable at the thought of going home and facing their pantries.

Marie Louise, writhing upward in the gloom from her chair to illustrate, said, "Anaconda." Mrs. Hackett's eyes glazed in horror. Omerie, staring at The Wolf man, seeming to challenge him, said, "Cox . . . ," lingered there a moment, then added "Cable Company." Mrs. Hackett connected cables with snakes and shook her head feebly.

A further bit of byplay, because it puzzled the observers, was entered into the day's minutes as it occurred between Omerie and the man from The Wolf. At the conclusion of the Cox Cable suggestion The Wolf man winked at Omerie, who then said, "Brown . . . Distilleries" and when The Wolf man raised his eyebrows Omerie unfurled his fingers one at a time—both hands, then the fingers of his right hand: fifteen. The stranger shook his head, a movement that conveyed somehow to the watchers that he was tempted but not quite convinced, and then Omerie slowly added, one at a time, five more fingers to the pot, at which The Wolf man nodded. The performance gained mystery by being performed in shadow.

To Mrs. Hackett the sign language was part of the thing that waited outside the screen door when Papa was away and Mama trembled. To comfort herself in the gloom where ugly women writhed like snakes and foreigners talked with their fingers, she began once again to sing "America, The Beautiful," but, perhaps because of overuse, the words fought back.

> Oh, beautiful for specious skies [she sang]
> For ambient waves of pain
> For purple mounting maggot sties

Shock, many discovered that day, is a cumulative thing, having lain in seed form dormant in the body, a kernel of knowledge gathering protective layers of hyperbole (an attempt to disarm through exaggeration) and euphemism, and bland fatty tissue rationed by governments and Chambers of Commerce . . .

> Above polluted plains

sang Mrs. Hackett and the words sliced like a laser beam through accumulated layers, bringing the truth closer to the surface. The place was very quiet.

Oh, beautiful for patriot's dream
That sees beyond the years
Where a la bastard cities teem
Condemned by human tears
America, America, God tend thine every flaw
Confound thy soul
With life control
Liberticidal law.

But then, like mongoose to cobra is outrage to shock, and outrage won. Someone shouted furiously, "By God, are you supposed to be this country?" Feebly at first, then stronger, a chant was set up: AMERICA, AMERICA! Feet stamped in unison, hands cracked together. They thought back, as they were meant to do, to the glory that had dangled above them in the flies. As they were expected to, they made connection between the vision and the charade of the old greedy woman and thought of money wasted by the government. They thought variously: highways; dams; airports; schools; welfare; foreign aid. But as the fervor of their chanting grew, the separate lines of their thought, stretching out to the future, came together and fused into one conviction: that change was in order and due on demand!

The phenomenon never ceased to interest Mrs. October, involving as it did both space and time: that projected far enough into the future, which is where goals must eternally lie, for an achieved goal becomes a fait accompli and so is no longer a goal, the most disparate aims come together and fuse in a process of continual assimilation, or mutual cannibalism. Instead of a collision of the worlds of reactionary, radical, conservative, there is a softening on the long journey into space so that when they touch there is accommodation and the spheres fit one within the other like the rings in a Chinese puzzle. She had given up asking herself: that, knowing this, then why Revolution?, for the answer was always the same: Because.

Even now, the tenor of the chanting had changed, had become acclamation of Mrs. Hackett as the Queen of the

Country, and she nodded and nodded, pleased to discover her importance.

The lights came on in a blaze, blinding eyes that had grown used to shadows, and an organ blared out "Pomp and Circumstance." All, despite hurting eyes, had a sense of emergence from a place too long medievally dark . . . Wanda shimmered and trembled like a candle before an open window; a tiny blaze, but she could set the house on fire if she wished; just an inch closer to the curtain, a flicker of fire running up to the ceiling, tonguing through . . . Mama had occupied the upstairs like a malevolent insect that had bored through the screen . . .

They crowded around Mrs. October with questions but she waved them aside, smiling, saying, "Go home. Think. Decide. Those who wish to continue, come back tomorrow." And like a litany, partly ironical, but reassuring, "Bless you . . . bless you . . ." Then they were gone, Mrs. Hackett in costume, for she would not part with the glitter.

Aurelie Angelique was, as usual on First Days, depressed. The delusions had once again been planted and had taken easy root but the discrepancy between October's intention and their understanding of it seemed greater than ever before. Did October really believe they would be sympathetic to her ideas of extreme reform? The virulence underlying their word-competition with Roman—who, according to the plan, had been taken for someone from The Wolf—was palpable, though they apparently had missed out on Point One of Roman's program, which was to expose them to his public sexual barter with Omerie. They would have said and done anything to get the better of him, not out of any conviction other than that they *were* better and always would be. If the game required them to hate some monopolistic or destructive company more than he, then they would, but it was just a game and words were only things you said to fill up holes in the day, a kind of rough mortar to hold a day together but not meant to last any longer than the day itself. Sufficient unto the day are the lies thereof; tomorrow there are more of the same.

But the charade had to be played out. AA had to perform, now that the others had gone, because it was one of the traditions. To be fair to October, AA did not believe she knew that AA's performance was given solely for her amusement. But the point was, it did amuse her and so AA entered the spirit of the part she thought of as The Sophisticated Mammy Doll.

She flung herself onto a stool and waved her long arms about, saying, "My Gawd, how low have we sunk, cherie."

"Simplistic," said Mrs. October, "but we are working with the simple in heart. Remember Heart City."

"The heart is the soul's pot de chambre. Heart City is full of . . ."

Mrs. October interrupted with classic severity. "When I met you, you were an optimist."

"When you met me . . ."—AA was winningly savage—"I was ten days out of Columbus, Ohio, and that's some kind of definition of optimist."

"Perhaps," Mrs. October said thoughtfully, "you need to go back for a refresher course. Your outlook seems to have become rather black . . ." But for once neither of them was amused by the mandatory recital of Black Is Beautiful, though they performed it, alternating: "Clothing; lovers; furs; caviar; truffles; licorice; wreaths; veils of a certain persuasion; a SPLENDID basic color for birds, nighttime, horses, and some cards; men look well in it, black earth is fertile . . ." Mrs. October wound it up: "But its touch upon outlook is fatal. You have become a walking, sucking, Dismal Swamp, a morass of blackness." Yes, thought AA, yes indeed, and as the litany continued she decided to give it everything she had, to tell October her last little secret.

October was drawing on her gloves—even the gestures were traditional—saying in a voice theatrically cold, "I should miss you, but my Revolution—my LAST Revolution—has not got room for dolorous Dolores; nor Deirdre of the Sorrows;

nor an Angel Dawn who rises with increasing frequency to the tune of "Marche Funèbre" and progresses from there, downward." She gave AA a look of feigned fright. "Dearest, can it be . . . do you wish to leave me to join your brothers and sisters in Motown, or someplace where it's at?"

AA, on cue, shuddered. "They'd kill me dead, darling."

"What! Why?"

"I bear the scent of too many white mothers. No mo jungle bunny-hoppin' for this black rose. They'd tear my sockets from their holes, sugar. One sniff and LAWSIE!" She banged the floor with both fists, bending low from her chair like an ape. "Merde, merde, merde! I miss the glamor of our recent past. I hate . . ." She paused; they acknowledged improvisation; she continued, "I hate this country. I hate people who might any minute say shucks. If you knew what that word did to me. I slept on a mattress stuffed with the things and then fed more of the same to the pigs. Would you like to sleep on pig vittles, Mrs. O? It don't take much imagination to move it on down the pig until you're sleeping in pig SHIT." Again she paused; she could not seem to make the woman smile. Coolly she thought, 'She's hated it as much as I have; one more delusion to chalk up,' but she was headed into truth and kept going, for the end was important to her, more so than seeing herself as a failed comic after so very long.

"Somebody, not twenty hot-damn minutes ago, to pin it down, said he'd be a cross-eyed mule. Well, dear, your best fren' use to PLOW a mother-lovin' FIEL' with a cross-eyed mule. Oh, and a trillion billion other reminders of She-who-was-called Little Tease, daughter of Big Tease, black as a racer, with a pussy that was community property. A pussy; black girls don't have vaginas or even cunts, which is sort of Britishy and smart. They have pussies, which are things with tails that rat-catch in barns and come back purring after you've kicked them out the back door. A little milk—here pussy; and here old pussy come agin, lappin' and purrin', and back she go to the barn and catch mo' rats. Did I ever

97

tell you how much I hated that hole between my legs, and was afraid of it? Here's why: think of how scared a black girl already scared of snakes would be of a WHITE snake; and white snakes lived in that hole between my legs; that's what I thought. Because when they went in I'd have my eyes closed and I wouldn't open 'em again until I felt the thing crawling out and then I'd look." AA looked; October's expression had not changed. AA said, "Oh, do I exaggerate? I don't know. On the one hand, maybe; on t'other, how in hell could I?" She got up, grinned at October. "The first white snake I had, I was eight years old. Early?"

"Yes," said Mrs. October, "Particularly so if it was against your wishes." She put her arm about Aurelie Angelique's shoulder as they walked down the aisle. "You know my position on childhood sexuality. I believe it must be only with the child's consent, and preferably with someone nearer its own age than your experience indicates. How old was he, this first lover of yours?"

If there had been a contest between them about who would amuse whom first, AA was the loser. Hearing her rapist called a 'lover' she snorted then gurgled, then got herself in hand. "He was about forty," she said and cocked her head, her startled-egret look.

"Too old," October said emphatically. "Entirely too much difference in ages, it seems to me. It's a wonder you escaped trauma." With a twist of her wrist she locked the Opera House door, transforming it with the gesture back into a drab warehouse. The women stepped into the chilly murk of a Tasmanian fall afternoon.

AA thought, 'She's not human. She really isn't human at all,' and was interested to discover her relief.

Wanda had looked for Bucky in the auditorium but had not seen him. She thought that he was either working backstage, or, because he was so short, was hidden in the crush, but when she got outside he was waiting for her. She noticed that he had regained his old eager little-boy expression and she was glad, because the memory of his anxiety-marked face as it had been when she last saw him had haunted her nights—an improvement over Mama, but still not what she wished for herself.

"How was it, Wan?"

"Stimulating," she said crisply, feeling smart as a whip, regretting that she could not punctuate by slapping riding gloves against a palm.

"Are you going back?"

"Indeed, yes." They fell into step; Wanda felt like striding but he would have been left behind.

"I'm sorry," he said, and she looked at him quickly, misunderstanding. "I meant about the last time. I felt so . . . gee, I don't know. I was kinda sick, or something."

"Traumarized?" she mocked, smiling, secretly secure, for she had looked the word up.

"I guess. I know I said some things which I don't know what they are."

"Assimilators."

"What?"

"You said the cages had been built for assimilators."

"I don't even know what that is," he said humbly.

"According to Mrs. October, it's people who eat Revolution."

"Oh." He was relieved. "She told you about the Revolution."

"No . . ." Wanda thought, she didn't say that about assimilators eating it, either, at least not in there today. But she didn't care where the words were coming from. She was changing, the world was changing, and in change there was mystery. She let the mystery course through her and took its dictation, translating for him haltingly as the words occurred: "I . . . was stretched so tight at birth . . . I was always afraid . . . when I was touched I would not break . . . but simply unravel . . ."

"That's beautiful," he said. "Just like she talks. I'm glad you're joining the Revolution, Wan. Now we're in it sort of as a family—me, you, and our . . ."

"But I won't break or unravel; I'll sing."

"I didn't know you could, Wan."

"Wait . . ." and mystery left them, a brother and sister walking together through the streets of their home town. "Good Lord, why are you wearing those dirty old clothes?" For the first time she noticed that he was dressed in mortar-bespattered coveralls.

"I'm building a foundation."

"What for?"

"I don't know. I think it's going to be a monument."

Chill, as when he had said that about not letting her be killed, touched her skin. Monuments were built for dead people. In the middle of North Splendor she stopped and put her hands on his shoulders and said, quickly, while they were still her own words, "Tell what you know, Bucky. Are they going to hurt us?"

"Mrs. October wouldn't hurt anybody. All she wants to do is kill The Wolf."

"You know what that means," she said, even while the soothing thoughts poured into her mind like sweet syrup down an inflamed throat: Good. It's high time we knocked the walls down.

Bucky did not seem to be in conflict. He said calmly. "It means there won't be any more slums in Tasmania."

A switch-over occurred so that Wanda's mind cried out 'One big slum is what we'll have,' while her lips opened and let fall a pearly "Fine."

He walked her home, unaware of the battle raging between her mind and tongue, radical utterance and reactionary thought alternating with radical thought and sophistic remark, until she was confused as to who she was. At her door, for he had to get back to his monument, it was Wanda, Eager Revolutionist, who bade him good-by in a voice vibrating with energy, while within the skull a frightened woman tried to break out and warn him that life as they had known it was coming to an end.

She entered her tacky hallway and sank onto her 'antique' bench, a forty-year-old relic given her as a wedding present. She recalled a line from a movie magazine: Jean Harlow spent her girlhood in her grandfather's ancient twenty-five-year-old house. Twenty-five-year-old houses, forty-year-old benches—American tradition. Tasmania was an old town by American standards, but the main reason the old houses still stood on Marvel was the lack of funds to tear them down and put up the new 'convenient' houses they had admired on TV. Given half a chance, the owners would fill the old houses with a clutter of Danish Modern, at best; and where tester beds had stood in master bedrooms there would be Castro Convertibles, another heavy TV advertiser, in metallic cloth that could un-ravel a real silk nightdress. Behind the façade of pride and tradition, a burgeoning plastic reality: KEEP AWAY FROM EXTREME TEMPERATURES.

She looked around at her old-fashioned wallpaper, and carpeting exposing tendons like a piece of bad veal. The two entities in her skull came together, not without despair, and said: Let it end! Look at it, it's awful! Let it end!

The stage was deep in Tasmanians. The auditorium was sparsely settled by strangers with familiar faces, some glimpsed on TV, some on book jackets, a movie star!—per-sons of lesser magnitude, as Omerie said, but their presence was taken as an augury of great days to come, and The Wolf man had turned out to be America's favorite writer, the one who had started the trouble with the moon. Since Roman's unveiling, no stranger was allowed to pass unchallenged, for the new Tasmanian pastime was Guess Who, and there was usually someone who had heard of the person, however obscure, citing, in extremity, TV talk shows emanating from Philadelphia.

The Tasmanians sat in their chairs facing outward, feeling like feeding time at the zoo but willing to rend raw flesh if called upon to do so. Each was aware of an unsuspected personality lurking within himself and was eager to bring it forth and see what it would do. Some cased the auditorium for a hidden camera, planning, when their turn came, to play to it with pretend innocence, as they had seen others do on "Candid Camera" and in the "Keyhole Kitchen," and that gasoline commercial, building to the great moment of surprise when its presence was revealed—"Oh, no!"—hands to face, peals of laughter, then the assured step forward to shake hands with the disguised celebrity or a whole panel of them, showing, with a touch of the blasé, that one was really *Aware*, too.

The games played on stage led to rehearsals at home. Old tap routines were recalled and freshened up; "The World Is Waiting for the Sunrise" pushed dropped tenors back to within hoarse screaming distance of the high F; people who had not tootled a comb for years went about blowing through tissue paper and matted hair, dandruff melodically flying; harmonicas, spoons, that ancient instrument the saw . . . in case the delighted celebrities asked them to strut their stuff.

Take By Surprise was the order of the day, and it had yet to fail. Roman fixed Wanda with a stare and asked, "Are you a frustrated chick?" Wanda paled. She had never imagined them getting to her for weeks and months, had tried to let them know this by her diffidence and introspection: a woman seriously examining her own conscience should be left alone until she was ready. But here it was, the frontal attack, the awful personal question with the world looking on. Roman told her, "You're a good-looking chick, you know that?" She was taken off base by the flattery and now occupied no position at all. She felt unmoored, floating, open at both ends. She gazed at him, lips parted; Marie Louise later told her that she looked exactly like a rabbit about to have its brains sucked by a weasel. Roman slowly licked his lips at her, the moist sound clearly heard in the well-like silence; his tongue made two revolutions in slow motion over his rather thick, sensual mouth. She did not know where to grab her body but felt that it should be taken hold of to keep it from getting away.

Sounding half asleep, he asked her, "Does Martin f . . . you enough, baby?" Even in her condition, her mind supplied the dots which allowed her not to faint just yet. In movies, when the camera wandered from the entwined bodies on the sofa and showed a blasting steam whistle on the factory where he worked, and then showed the girl dandling a baby, Wanda's mind conversely filled in the dots with a bridal shower and a double-ring ceremony. It was the way she kept going.

Still, the Opera House swung about her head as though in orbit; she caught glimpses of faces as they passed: some pale, some simpering, some of the men heavy-jowled as old hounds.

She thought: Is this really happening to Wanda? Poor Wanda, who tried so hard but had headaches. She thought: Some girl babies were more fortunate than Wanda, and heard a strain of melody but could not place it. With a pleading look, she shook her head at Roman and then walked into the wings, feeling that she had, after all, let the side down.

She heard Marie Louise butt in, bold as a brass monkey: "Well, *I* don't get enough, baby!" and her burst of raucous laughter. Some girl babies, Wanda thought, and heard again the tune, more defined. She thought, this is satori, using one of Roman's terms, and then she thought, I will share it; and with no trembling in her legs she walked to center stage and saw that they had, after all, waited for her. She folded her hands together carefully, like a singer. Yes, this was the moment—her début; it had come at last. She heard Marie Louise say with envious spite, "This oughta be good," and heard Mrs. Hackett, sounding quite grown up, say, "Shut up, you vulgar, stupid whore." *Mrs. Hackett?* But yes, she was wisdom itself; Marie Louise was vulgar and stupid and yet still more fortunate than Wanda.

She told them, "Some girl babies are born with everything." With a word she had caught them. They craned, they leaned. Their eyes said, Tell us about the mystique of girl babies, oh Wanda, do.

She told them.

"Some girl babies are pretty and pink and bubble all day

and sleep all night and Mama loves. Papa brings presents and neighbors coo and other girls like her and teachers praise her and boys follow her and she has nice babies and a paper-pretty house and her children win honors and there are a hundred cars in her funeral procession.

"Some girl babies are so hirsute their Mamas spend all of their babyhood trying to dry them after their baths, but Mama loves and Papa brings presents and neighbors coo and some girl babies are concave where they should bulge and convex where dents ought to be and Mama loves and Papa and neighbors and some girl babies grow teeth like a horse that rot and stink before they are twelve and Mama and Papa and some girl babies sprout titties that droop on the floor and Mama and some girl babies suffer blockage fore and aft and some have skin so holey oh Lord that finding the nostrils and Mama and Papa and some develop like beeves and when they pull off their girdles at night their flesh crowds the bureaus out into the hall and lays a skim of grease on the mirror and her children win honors and there are a hundred cars."

She could not stop.

"Oh, let me not dwell upon the humps, warts, beards, surplus pedal digits, cavelike nostrils, eyes at cross purposes, the unnamable concavities and convexities of some girl babies; and hairlips and bowlegs and pigeon-toes and scabby knees n' elbows and a perpetual smell of the sea; and points of ingress too big for anything this side of a Shetland pony; and hairy ears and early baldness . . ."

Wanda wept, staring and glaring at Marie Louise in particular. Then she said quietly, "Some fortunate girl babies. And some girl babies have Mamas like mine." Mrs. October's eyes seemed to be boiling at her, cloudy with warning not to add "and brothers like Bucky." How could she extricate that thorn of years cushioned in pus, if she was stopped at such a moment as this? Could there ever be another like it for her?

Alone, she thought how odd it was that her presumed laying of the ghost of Mama had turned out to be hatred for her sex, Geraldine always excepted. If sex with men was hate and evil then perhaps she should turn Lesbian and make love to an indentation. Falling asleep she giggled, thinking, 'This is the way the world ends, not with a whang but a dimple.'

She dreamed a great voice asking questions.

"Where are your husbands?"

"Traveling. They travel."

"All of them?"

"All."

"When are you in touch?"

"They write. You know it's your husband if the card is signed 'Martin,' or 'Bill'—that's Marie Louise's husband. Marie Louise used to get cards signed 'Martin,' too. She didn't know I knew."

"When do you love?"

"Don't make me laugh."

"When do you f . . .?"

"Constantly. Or never. It's all the same."

"Are you a frustrated woman?"

"I will not unravel. I will not break. This too is Zen."

She was held in Roman's naked arms, not gently. She felt for her gun. The gun went off.

She held a baby in her arms, squinch-eyed and pucker-cheeked. "Yes, Mama," she said, and the echoes rolled.

But she awoke without a headache.

On a Tuesday Wanda arrived at the Opera House wearing boots and a tightly belted coat; a felt hat dipped far over one eye; she walked with immense strides and tended to come to rest with her feet wide apart. She looked, according to her arch enemy, the nameless whore, as if she was about to take a standing-up pee. There was a moment of high drama when she removed the coat and revealed that she wore a holster with a gun in it, which she was persuaded finally to check with her coat because it made some of the others nervous.

Mrs. October thought that Wanda could be a good person on her team if she could be talked out of her obvious leaning in the direction of violence, a surprising direction, but they were on their own. She had to keep saying it, reminding herself, for their independence was always so startling in the beginning. Such women as Wanda, Mrs. October knew, upon being newly turned radical, always demanded more than more suppressed subjects. She wondered if Wanda could be appeased with the death of a small rabbit. Looking at her—the high color and burning eyes that could be, at this juncture, either from zeal or fever—the old hands at revolution knew stirrings of the blood lust that had once possessed them in their early days and their nostrils flared as though the memory were a pungent odor composed of blood, gunpowder, group urination, pot, and burning buildings. Wanda, in fact, was ablaze with charisma, which is a harnessing of fear (of one's own death; attention is at times necessarily deflected through sacrifice of others). October thought that she should immediately channel it further before more sparks were struck from her associates, some of whom had remained unregenerate killers underneath the veneer, acquired by association from her, of liberal humanism.

"Oh, God!" Wanda exclaimed dramatically, to break the monotony of having stood spraddle-legged for too long waiting for something to happen. Revolution, after all, was more than poses—which were certainly enjoyable, but there should be a series of actions to take one fluidly from one attitude to another. She would have sung "The Marseillaise" or "The Internationale" or "Blowin' In The Wind" but she did not know any of the words and next to nothing of the tunes. "We Shall Overcome," while simple, was too niggery for her.

Mrs. October read her conflict accurately and immediately assigned her to an exercise with Aurelie Angelique, to be called—horrors—"Integration." As she outlined what should be accomplished by the two actresses, which was a capsuling of female black and white relations from before the Civil War to and through the present with a projection into the near future, Wanda's zeal and fire drained from her and left her trembling, whimpering "Oh, God . . . ," for she would have to touch the negress and stay near her through rehearsal and performance. "Mama would just die," she whispered to Marie Louise, forgetting their enmity, forgetting too, that Mama was dead, for the first time since that great terminal event. She would have given anything to be able just to get her coat and her gun and head on home.

She came out of her partial trance to hear Mrs. October saying, ". . . dispense with rehearsal and play it spontaneously. Is that agreeable?" Wanda saw the black woman's ironical eyes watching her as AA agreed and everyone waited for Wanda's affirmative. She knew that she would not be able to say 'no.' It was a hurdle over which she must jump or creep if she was to feel again the headiness she had got from the others a short time before: that they would have followed her into battle—and her breath quickened.

She hated having been sucked into this thing; it was a trap which had been sprung without her knowing it was baited. But seeing Aurelie Angelique's private little smile as bitter and black as coal dust, Wanda felt an upspringing of adrenalin like jets from a fountain and thought, 'By God, I'll show that black bitch where it's at,' and she strode forward, empty holster smacking at her waist and boots going clomp clomp. She had thought that being able to hate her mother was, with the restriction placed on Bucky, liberation enough for one deprived girl, but that was nothing, she saw, no originality at all; everyone hated death. Her target had to be life, and there it was, that long black drink of swamp water. She would show them what it meant to be free, if liberation meant setting loose your hate to stalk about a stage; or if it meant, as you came to think it did from watching TV, running at the camera with fist upraised, contorting your black face and screeching (Black Is Beautiful); or if it meant kicking prone bodies or drawing blood with club in lawful or unlawful fist. As of course it did. Current words of approval, recalled from articles in magazines that defined and praised Art and just about everything else, came to her: Lacerating! Excoriating! Harshly brutal! Cuts to the quick! Draws blood!

There was one seat in the spotlight, a low stool. Who would sit on it? The mistress of the house should sit and the servant stand, but a *stool?*

"No head shall be higher than mine," said Wanda.

"Then you'd better start growing," said Aurelie Angelique.

Wanda stepped onto the stool. In the hole of light in the darkness she believed that the others had gone away, that the building had dissolved. The silence was so profound that she could hear her heart and a faint ticking like an echo from Aurelie Angelique's breast. Wanda thought, She's numbering my days, a black watch brought here to measure my life. She said, "If you'll just go back we won't have to go through all this."

"Back where?"

"Don't you know where you came from?"

"The point is, do you?"

"Why is that the point?"

"If you buy something, you ought to know where it came from in case you want to exchange it. A pair of gloves, for instance."

"Well, I usually know who sold me the gloves. I don't know who sold you. I woke up one morning and there you were, coffee on a tray and your head in a handkerchief. When I asked you something you grinned and said yes'm or no'm, but you never talked to me at all. None of you did. And sugar was always missing from the pantry."

"Why didn't you complain?"

"I was afraid to. My husband was away. He was always away. And you surrounded me. Your singing used to scare me to death. I learned how to talk like you so if you heard my voice calling for help out of a window you wouldn't know it was me. You outnumbered me three hundred to one. I ate what you gave me, when you gave it to me. And my children drank your milk."

"Why did they do that?"

"I had to keep my figure. Udders stretch. I had baby after

baby, trying to equalize. But for every baby I had, you had two."

"One for myself, and one to serve yours."

"A field nigger and a house nigger. Oh, you were a regular machine."

"The house nigger was generally your son's half-brother."

"That didn't bother me. Property wasn't at stake."

"What bothered you was that I shared your man but you couldn't share mine."

"I won't honor that suggestion with a reply."

"You had a reply. It was called rape, at the top of your lungs."

"Do you think it never happened?"

"Plant an idea, it bears fruit, like a tree."

"Which bring us, I suppose, to lynching."

"The line is straight, as Jim Crow flies."

"I think you'd better speak only when spoken to. You've got some uppity ideas since the Northerners came and went."

"Yes'm."

"Which means no'm. I knew when you started reversing your meanings, inventing, corrupting my language. When you were a slave I was afraid of you, but when you were freed I hated you. You had more nobility in chains. After the War you grew petty, sly, insolent. You mocked me. You called your music by a sex word to mock me. And me coming down from the big house to nurse you when you got sick. Well, didn't I?"

"Thanks for letting me say something. How very kind of you."

"Why, not at all! I don't know why we can't sit and talk, as long as it's in private. Go on, tell me about yourself."

"Nothing to tell, I'm afraid. Nothing."

"Now, don't be shy. You must have had experiences that I would find very interesting. Really, I mean it."

" 'Fraid not."

"Go on, I said! I want to learn about you. Now talk!"

"Je n'ai rien à vous dire."

"Ah, yes; you're all scholars now. Everywhere one goes, one hears you ask of each other, 'Is you did your Greek?'"

"The answer is generally 'I has.' It must rankle."

"Amuses. 'Black' and 'intellectual' are contradictions. We laugh."

"So do we. Remember Cleveland, and Gary, and Watts and Detroit and Newark and the city of Boston and . . ."

"Well, look; let's be reasonable. There's no reason why we can't settle this at the conference table, is there?"

"Who's going to learn whose language?"

"All I ever asked was for you to live the way I do. Use the same deodorant, toothpaste, depilatory, hairspray, sanitary napkin. Why, with the proper amount of education, housing, clothes, opportunities; with the same kinds of jobs, reading matter, sports, interests, TV—I'd be willing to have you to my house, as a guest! For dinner! Oh, mammy, stick your bosom across the line so I can cry on it!"

When the lights came up Wanda was tugging and pulling at Aurelie Angelique, weeping, begging her to "come share my stool, Sister!" When they had calmed her she confessed that she had suffered a great sense of loss and asked if they had, too? No one had.

Later, when the scene had been transcribed by the secretary, Mrs. October wrote on it: *Too literary; the voices are false, even AA's. Which may be a clue to the base of the real problem: an attempt to further ennoble a great cause with 'lofty' language; the language becomes the Cause . . . Isn't it curious to think I gave Wanda that voice because I was afraid she would otherwise cut nastily to the bone and demean my Revolution! I really must turn her loose; it's possible to learn from her, I'm sure of that. A thought occurs: Bucky was there in the auditorium. Was the fiasco my attempt to present him with a sister who would not shock him? He is so vulnerable. His 'institutions' and "things with capitals" surely begin with family, and sister. Yes, I was afraid she would indulge in epithets, blunt Anglo-Saxonisms—tools that*

*I usually encourage the use of. From now on she may; she
must. They ALL must. Step down, October (You can keep
Bucky busy on The Gift . . . No?)*

It was thus that the Revolution accelerated and became, in
AA's phrase, more "down home," and moved into the streets.

Roman and his group of volunteers—Marie Louise, Myra
Little, and two male sanitation workers of Italian origin—chose
high noon as the time for their first demonstration of the new
freedom which was to be the right and property of all. As for
the place, Marie Louise had been the only vociferous champion of midtown; the others agreed that that would be going
a bit far, for the first time around, and opted for a little
square off the Rue Flambeau where Bohemian goings-on
were not unheard of since Omerie Chad's residence there.
They did see to it, however, that word was freely circulated
among the townspeople, and the word was SCANDALE.
Myra Little's contribution was the spelling of the word and
the initial pronunciation, which became somewhat garbled in
transition and reached some ears as SCANTIES.
When the five sexual revolutionists arrived at their ren-
dezvous they found the four sides of the square packed with
several layers of humanity. A few mothers carried babes in
arms. One of the garbage men (sanitation worker was a
euphemism contributed by a well-wisher), he of darker hue,
was seen to blench; he was also seen muttering to his companion but though ears strained his words were not heard by
anyone but his friend. For the record, what he said was,
"Jeez, Rocco, I don't think I can get it up." Rocco, of stronger
fiber, replied, "I've got it up now," and began the proceedings
on a spontaneous and informal note by grabbing his own
genitals and proving himself no mere boaster. He did, indeed,
have it up and it was a not unimpressive sight, for his trousers
were so loose that he was able to lay the device out along his
palm. His friend, with the reputation of Napoli riding on
him, strained inwardly like the dark soil struggling to propel

upward a seed entrusted to it and managed therewith to, as the British say, "get a stand," which he, emulating his friend, laid out along *his* palm; together the two of them advanced to Center Square bearing themselves like heads on tilting platters.

The dictum had been to TAKE BY SURPRISE, and Marie Louise, seeing the virile rapiers thrust in her direction, quickly slipped out of her slacks and pulled her sweater over her head. Naked if not resplendently so, wearing now only wedgies and white cotton anklets, she exhorted, with many a wink, the boys to "take it off" and they did. Their disrobing was less graceful than hers. Both lowered their trousers, taking courage from each other's presence, and discovered, trousers bunched around their ankles, that their clodhopper shoes were too big to be slipped through the trouser legs, a fact that they were aware of from long experience of dressing but it had never come up before, presex; they were accustomed to a drop-pants lift-skirt arrangement. So they struggled to remove the shoes, presenting, as they bent over, wide expanses of boxer shorts to the gaze of those observers who were behind them. The boys were inhibited by the felt gaze and stumbled about, swinging their behinds in wide arcs. Rocco fell, and after his first humiliation he found that a sitting position was more comfortable while removing shoes. He cursed good-naturedly when it was revealed that he had forgotten to change socks for the occasion and that the ones he wore were as stiff as crinoline. He pulled them off quickly and stuffed them into his shoes and then, because his feet were dirty, he became absorbed in the childlike task of neatening them up. He wet his thumb with spittle and scrubbed between his toes, an operation that had to be repeated several times; sex was a thing he was used to washing up *after*.

Guido, in the meantime, had managed to stay on his feet while unlacing his brogues but was still terribly aware that his shorts had snapped their elastic waistband in the battle and were slowly slipping down until, as he bent to his final effort, they hung about the newly designated waistline of his knees. He was certain that the heart of his spread buttocks was the cynosure of as many eyes as could center on that vulnerable spot. As he later said, "I took a goddamn *group* picture, man." If the picture had been developed it would have shown several ladies on the verge of passing out.

Perhaps the most curious feature of the first few minutes was that the only sound—aside from the heavy breathing accompanying the undressing efforts and Marie Louise's exhortation, twice repeated, to the boys to take it off—was a plane flying overhead: the distant drone growing steadily to a roar and then retreating, fading to a sleepy buzz and gone. The audience was as silent as though their portion of the happening were being filmed without sound. There was, in fact, a slow-motion quality to the occurrence. Roman sat on the grass, cross-legged, drowsily smoking a Tiparillo stuffed with pot. Myra Little had entered the square with the others and kept right on going, melting into the crowd without being noticed by them or missed by her former companions. Marie Louise, partly to keep circulation moving, for the temperature was in the low sixties, gave a fair imitation of a wrestler warming up. What was flexible, she flexed; what was flappable, she flapped; and here and there she rippled; and there she bounced.

Guido the modest, in shedding as rapidly as possible the troublesome shorts also rid himself of modesty, for he was of philosophic turn and instinctively as well knew that modesty when you are wearing only a short-tailed shirt is cumbersome raiment. He took the shirt off, and then his tee-shirt (his one spotless garment; he indulged himself in a clean tee-shirt per day) and stood like an olive statue in the sunlight without even the fig leaf of his hand, for it simply would not suffice, he having discovered to his gentle amazement that the crowd, more than Marie Louise, worked upon him as an aphrodisiac. He imagined that this was partly because he had had Marie Louise enough times to have fathomed her mystery, but there was an undeniable element of narcissism in his increased arousal: he kept seeing himself as he believed the crowd was seeing him: a beautiful young bull. In actuality he was more on the scale of a plowhorse with thick heavy thighs and great buttocks and hugely swelling calves. His bollocks were as fat as a swelled bladder and so was what proudly rode above them, a veritable cannon filled with shot. And to his dismayed disgust, with urine. He was literally bursting with midmorning Chianti and black coffee. As he later said to Rocco, "Man, it was a goddamn piss-hard I had on, you know?"

Rocco, built on a more classical scale with longer muscles, a tighter waist, and equipment that was satisfactory rather than brutal, was now naked. He and Guido and Marie Louise turned to Roman for further instructions, forgetting, in the potential anticlimax of the moment, that the next step as agreed upon was to have been a furious coupling: Marie Louise and Guido; Myra Little and Rocco.

Roman said, "Where's the other cunt?" and the crowd was released from thrall at the absolutely verboten word. Their outrage was immediate, born at full boil. Some of the words they used were as Chaucerian as the one that set them off, but being mainly scatological, they were eminently more American, and scatology is encouraged in children (kaka, poo poo, pee pee, and poot are but a baby step removed from shit and fart, and generally inspire giggles in both user and hearer from the crib onward). In the throes of their anger, some paused for shamefaced giggles to hear Roman called, at the top of a womanly voice, "Fart-blossom." Another imprecation was "Shit on you, you shit-headed Jew," and Jew was considered the ugliest word used, next to "cunt," that day.

Whereas the presence of the crowd had driven Guido to pornographic display, it was the name-calling that invigorated Rocco (memories of Roma and Momma) and he did not stop at narcissistic enjoyment but flung himself upon Marie Louise and entered her to the fullest extent before she could give voice to her usual expression of sham enjoyment, which was a deep-throated groan first encountered in the "Kama Sutra" and practiced with increasing art and artifice thereafter. It was the first time, indeed, that she had been taken in voiceless surprise since the long-ago occasion of her initial deflowering;

initial, for she had been a virgin of the designation 'professional' throughout an extremely active sexual life, up to and including her wedding night, following which even she had to admit her professional days were come to a close.

Now, there is an odd thing about people watching, in company, the sex act: there is both an introspection and a suspension of even vicarious pleasure and shock. The value of a circus is in the mental reliving, or later fantasy, when its finer points can be dwelt on at leisure and incorporated into the proceedings at hand (or foot, if that is the direction of the fetish). It is like the fantasy as opposed to the reality of being caught on a sinking ship in a violent storm at sea. In the former, one rises to heights of heroic action; in the latter, one (barring Latin seamen) queues up for the lifeboat and sings, very orderly and unable to think beyond the moment where rescue might not be waiting.

The shouting crowd hushed up to a person as soon as Rocco had plunged into Marie Louise, which left him in a very precarious position: reversing the legend, he had penetrated with Excalibur the stone, which was the difficult part; now, without his impetus, how was he to withdraw it without revealing the trick—i.e. that it was as flaccid as rubber? For with the silence his desire had died a quick death and all he could think of was the vulnerability of his position.

Marie Louise, spread on the chilly grass, remembered that sitting in a cold place was supposed to give you piles. She thrust upward to lift her behind clear of the ground; Rocco, enmired in thoughts of exposing his anus to the watchers, bore down; and thus they set up, finally, a series of give-and-take motions that brought them, willy-nil, toward one of the two first public climaxes in Tasmania's recorded history.

Roman, accurately reading the motivations of the Dionysian revelers, expired into helpless hiccuping laughter, face down on the grass. Feeling that he had lost face that must be regained if he was ever to haul garbage in Tasmania again, Guido mounted Roman with all the quelling force he could muster, which in his anger was a great deal, and expended himself with mighty buckings on the seat of Roman's English tweeds, releasing immediately afterward, helplessly, his urine.

A Mrs. Pierce, a middle-aged lady of good works and true public spirit, came tripping into the square just prior to the height of activity with a great basket of flower bulbs to plant for next spring's blooming. She was ideally suited to such work that did not require distance vision for she was woefully nearsighted; her spectacles were as thick as stove lids; behind them her eyes hopefully twinkled at one and all, counting on the twinkle to disarm would-be assailants and rapists and those of mere bad temper. Excusing herself repeatedly, twinkling without cease, she made her way through what she thought of as the lunch-bunch, and finding at last a clear space with only a couple or so lounging on the grass, she murmured to them, explaining her intention, and sat down with a basket and began to trowel the earth.

"Goodness," she said to Marie Louise, seeing what she thought was a girl in a white dress rolling about with a large playful dog. "You'll get grass stains on that pretty frock, dear," and plunged in a tulip bulb. To the bulb—for she talked to flowers to make up for not having a real, honest-to-goodness green thumb—she said, "I put you in here with more hope than skill; I *count* on you to rise again, like our dear Savior; now *in* you go, and in the springtime we'll roll away the stone and *see what we have*. Ohhhh," she said, anticipating the glad spring, as Guido made it on Roman's seat, "*what* a pretty sight," and added firmly, as prenatal influence for the tulip, "*Christ*," and the sacrilege helped Rocco to his moment of glory. It was later said that she reached for Guido's urinating penis, mistaking it for a hose, but there is little verification for the story.

The couples immediately separated, three of the people shaking with fear; simultaneously there was a mad scrambling for clothing and a rush of the crowd forward (for the desire for retribution follows swift on the heels of sexual satiety) to get their hands on the scofflaws and defilers of public morals. Mrs. Pierce and her bulbs were trampled and her piteous outcry at the failure of her twinkle deflected the public from its intention to tear the revolutionists limb from whosever limb. Their contrition over the spectacle of the damaged woman led to a collective helping hand, and the revelers escaped.

What the noontime traffickers in downtown saw was: a woman wearing only a sweater and wedgies and white cotton socks who ran clutching a pair of slacks to her genitals while her other hand tugged the sweater down in back as far as it would go, which was hardly far enough. She was closely followed by two swart men wearing boxer shorts—one man barely wearing them—and carrying shoes, shirts, and pants, and at a greater distance by an extremely hysterical man who, between collapses of some sort, scrubbed at the seat of his trousers with a handkerchief. In and out of the traffic wove the four people; it was as though they were trying to throw off scent a pack of dogs.

The observers whose automobiles were brought to a standstill at the sight of the four playing follow-the-leader among them, and the strollers on the sidewalks who stopped to gawk and gossip, were, but did not know it, now liberated from the Puritan ethic governing sexual behavior in America and could fornicate anytime and anywhere they pleased; indeed, it was incumbent upon them, whether they pleased or not, to follow suit, but this too they would not discover until later. A pity about their ignorance, but then, so few people are ever really aware of the profounder meanings of freedom, and it is those ignorant masses who cause all the trouble.

"I'm sorry," Wanda whispered, distressed, "but they all look like Hebrew persons to me." She gestured to the half-filled house. "I can't perform with them listening and sneering. They hate me."

Roman, sitting in the front row with the star of the day, looked up sharply. "This too is Zen," he said, and Wanda clapped her hand to her mouth. She noticed that he was sitting with his hand suggestively cupping his crotch, a thing he did frequently nowadays, sitting or standing. It bothered the women and it bothered Wanda especially, since her dream about him.

"I'm *sorry*," she said, only partly so, and he told her, "That's o.k., baby." Wanda stared, hypnotized, at the woman beside him; if Roman had heard her, then the star had too.

The star was an actress-singer of the first magnitude, Miss Darthy Redstone, originally from Orange, New Jersey, thence to Broadway, now the sole pure jewel in Hollywood's tarnished crown. She was to play her first nonsinging role in a new film about a revolution in Poland and had come to observe the battle on the field, Tasmania being as remote to her as Agincourt. It was her adenoidal voice that recently sang from space: Fly Be To The Boo (led be dough what sprig is like on Jupiter ad Bars).

She was accompanied by two people: her physician—some said her psychiatrist—and the doctor's wife, or mistress, or sister, depending upon which gossip commentator one regularly listened to. The lady was dowdy, demanding, and ignored, which suited her for all three roles.

The three visitors sat together in the front row and the actress took nourishment without cease except when the doctor was handing her pills, which she swallowed delicately, with many little sips of liquid as though his hands imparted to them a special quality. It was said that her normal temperature was 110° and that she burned nourishment as rapidly as she could take it in, like a shrew. Another rumor was that she leaked continuously at the bottom, which was the reason she affected the costume of Turkish trousers with legs tight to the ankles, over which, summer and winter, she wore many pelts of small South American mammals. Whatever the reason for such immense intake, she was seen to eat within the space of an hour: pickles, olives, cookies; oranges, grapes, some bananas; a sausagelike immensity; assorted packaged snacks of the cheese and peanut-butter persuasion;

and an artichoke, the doctor's wife-mistress-sister holding before her like a chalice a little pot of melted butter kept warm over a candle.

Wanda and the actress stared at each other, Wanda the only one of the two to wear an expression; then, like a comment, the actress pushed a large boiled (peeled) egg into her mouth whole. The egg slipped down entire, which may have been her intention, but it was the doctor's cue to dig out some special pill and coax Miss Redstone, with many cooing sounds, to take it from him, which of course she could not at the moment do. The audience, which included those on stage—it was said that Miss Redstone could make an audience of The Pope—fell silent, emulating the star and all watched the progress of the egg in its slow passage down her throat. She was not alarmed, but fell into a state of dreaming introspection like that of a boa constrictor newly investing a rabbit. All drew a breath of relief when the egg entered the fur at her throat and some applauded when shortly thereafter she delivered herself of an eructation that set ajangle the chandeliers.

Wanda, stricken with horror at finding that she had, during the show, imagined the egg to be a Christian given in ritual sacrifice to the alien throat, flew down the ramp and embraced the gassy star, saying, after a moment of peeking into a little dictionary, "Oh, my dark Mädele, my sweet sister Rachel!"

"Wha?" said the star, once the pill had followed the egg, "Ray . . . which?" Imperturbably she told her friends, "This nut thinks I'm What's-er-name Welch, for Chrissake. Hey, daddy, looka my boobies," but she did not take them out. She watched and listened in detached amusement as Wanda confessed a congenital dislike of her 'race' and asked forgiveness. "Sure," Miss Redstone said and shrugged, but refused to come on stage and share Wanda's stool, saying that she had enough stool of her own.

Wanda persisted. "How can I rid myself of this noxious hate if you won't help me? Why, you're the most famous Jew in the world!"

"You gotta problem," Miss Redstone agreed.

"Oh, thank you!" Wanda said. "That's a beginning, anyway. Now, if you'll just admit that you hate me and my race . . ." and she looked for Mrs. October to gain her approval but could not see her. Wanda turned back to the star and said peremptorily, "Well!"

Miss Redstone took off her dark glasses and for the first time in the auditorium showed naked her famous eyes that were remarkably like a TV test pattern.

"Let me see," she said, enunciating fairly crisply. "I don't think that would serve what I gather is your purpose here. Am I right that it's your guilt you want to drain off, like pus in a sore? Yeah, there it is."

"Where?" Wanda cried, terrified.

"On top of your shoulders," said Miss Redstone, "with that hole in it that keeps making noises." Wanda clapped her hand to her face; one finger strayed into her opened mouth. The star told her, "There, that's it. You've found it." She began gathering her things—mammal skins, foodstuffs, expended artichoke leaves—about her; rising, she said, "If you'll just take that and clamp it onto your rectum and suck, your circulation will improve. That's your trouble, bad circulation."

She walked up the aisle rummaging in her bag for something to eat. She gave a sharp whistle and the doctor and his wife trotted after her. Wanda, beginning to weep, called after her, "You speak from experience, no doubt!"

In a while the star turned and in a rather gentle voice said, "You know, telling a person how much you hate them is a way of kissing ass. It puts you down there a lot faster than love or whatever does. If they tell you back, it's like a sixty-nine and I don't dig it with strangers and women. If I don't hate them, they're not strangers and they're not women. That's the best I can do for you." She grinned at Wanda and said, "In udder woids, do your own thing but make sure it's yours. Class dismissed. Viva Zapata."

She left eating what was reported to have been a kumquat

stuffed with Virginia ham, which she autographed and gave to an admirer on the street.

Wanda, humiliated by her failure, said to Roman, "What am I going to do? I followed all the rules!"

He told her ambiguously, "Follow her advice." Wanda, offended, turned to go; the only advice she recalled was to clamp her mouth onto her rectum. Roman held her without touching her, by his voice alone, which she had to admit she was finding more and more compelling. He said, "Don't try it with women. That's what she told you." She looked at him quickly; it was as though he had read her dirty speculations about becoming a Lesbian. He gave her a grin and said, "And try your hate with a little love in it. Think about it."

Curious advice. What she thought about was him.

On November 2nd of that year, official notice was paid to the Tasmanian Revolution in no less than *The New York Times*, the first public or printed acknowledgment. For *The New York Times* it was also the first clean scoop in a long time, perhaps since the invention of TV.

The notice (on page 55, opposite the book review, a rave for a book on Victorian doorknobs) was prototypical of the New York style, though fairly recent in the pages of its one remaining newspaper: it quoted a rumor to the effect that something was brewing or about to brew in Tasmania, Ohio; a neat little map headed the paragraph, putting the reader in the picture, and a neat little arrow pointed inaccurately to another town.

Without revealing its sources but suggesting that they were Washington-based, the piece stated that the Tasmanian affair was seen as an effort to bilk the country of tax money. This made several converts, domestic and foreign, for the Revolution.

By November the townspeople who were active participants in Mrs. October's Revolution had established routines, necessary, if they were to continue their lives—or, as they had come to say it, their life-styles, which included jobs, children, religious celebration, marital duties. Dichotomy attended, and some confusion. For instance, as pertained to religion:

At the Opera House, fittingly, Love of God was accorded the treatment given opéra bouffe; its formalities were seen as those of an ancient art form and were discussed intellectually with many a reference to Camp. What laughter there was, was at God's expense but it was gentle laughter, like that which greeted Mr. L. C. Tiffany's labors, rather than the helpless screams that underscored Florence Foster Jenkins and the filmed dance of a Mr. Swan. Even in revolution, Tasmania had not advanced beyond the Camp of yesteryear, past, say, Miss Charlotte Moorman.

But the gentle, progressive Mon. through Sat. mockers of Our Lord reverted on Sun. to atavistic response and trembled, Camp or no, before the altar of His wrath. Some made a reconcilement of the two worlds by virtue of an allowable paradox, or to put it another way, made the transition via a faith warp like one of those wormholes newly discovered in outer space: they ridiculed The Father but adored The Son, which fit in perfectly with the youth-worship cults, and Christ, they said, was the first Skippy—the name for those current hordes of youths who skipped naked across water as lightly as flat stones. LONG LIVE GOD; GOD IS DEAD they said, kicking The Old Man right in the genes, or spores (airborne, wasn't he) or, if a Scotch rebel, right in the sporran.

More straightforwardly, they took turns playing Revolutionary Games; when not required at the Opera House, they went about their business. Kids were fed, husbands and wives and lovers were serviced, banks were told, etc. Those who had not been present at a particular breakthrough were filled in by those who had been; some distortion was inevitable.

Rumors of THE END died down, to be replaced by

equally damaging rumors of THE BEGINNING, for this was said to mean:

1. Slum clearance = banishment of The Wolves to Columbus.

2. Economic equality = a gift of $1,000,000 to be divided equally among the townspeople proper;

3. End of bigotry = throw out the foreigners.

4. Sexual freedom = ...

Soon after the announcement in *The Times*, the hordes came. Sari-clad women glided about the streets twittering in high British voices, asking in the bars for drinks of "scotch-ikins," professing to find American Negros "divinely vulgar" and altogether profoundly confusing the Tasmanians as to the meaning of 'colored.' They were clearly 'colored' themselves, and also clearly superior to just about everybody, which did not seem to surprise them at all. It was said that one of them held, in her own country, rank that was high as a Queen's, and many a Tasmanian dowager entertained the pleasant fantasy of being hostess at a reception for that lady at which curtseys would be expected, and all but she (clever and sly hostess!) would take humiliating pratfalls; to this end the dreamers practiced endlessly before mirrors, surprising their husbands with new suppleness and some unexplained bruises.

Actors and actresses came from everywhere, dark-spectacled and rather charmingly unkempt, watching the exercises on stage with deep attention and arguing among themselves about Artaud, Growtowski, and the great Phoebe Ephron.

Another variety, male and female, "dropped in," as they said, en route to Marrakech, marvelously groomed, smelling of gin and a pungent smoke, and screamed greetings to Mrs. October and Roman and Aurelie Angelique and each other.

The Revolution was "too marvelous" and the Tasmanians "too sweet." They were as familiar to Wanda as her own face; their manners, voices, vocabularies, style had been pressed into her at the movies as though by a recording stylus; that she found them 'up to date' would have alarmed them had they known, for what she had in mind was the latest thing in the early Fifties. They had been moving so fast that they did not know they had left themselves behind. In their ignorance they glittered, and if they were not in the current magazines, among the dashikis and heads of natural hair over a foot high, they looked at magazines in which they *were*, paying no attention to the dates on the covers because when you traveled so frequently back and forth across the international date line you were a bit confused about time. Concerning them, Wanda posed herself a question: Did they perform any function by which others benefited? and answered the question thus: Oh, my goodness! for she had sounded for a moment like a Communist. She closed her eyes and in imagination and extremity of need entered the Irish halls wherein Geraldine dwelled. She wandered through the great rooms, listening for the whisper of a tea gown and the soft distinctive voice. But when, within the fantasy, she opened her eyes, there was Geraldine wearing the uniform of a rebel, and slung over her shoulder a brutal rifle. The militant ladies saluted each other . . . "Good luck!" . . . and Wanda returned to the Opera House, cold-eyed and ready for a show of thumbs on the fate of the Jetters.

Bucky, walking along Splendor, thinking about the increasingly strange monument on which he worked nowadays almost exclusively, received a deep shock. He was saying to himself, "Mirrors, these huge gigantic mirrors"; shaking his head, he glanced up and saw bearing down upon him five large young women wearing kilts with flapping sporrans. Smiling, wondering if they could recognize him as a fellow Celt—Welsh as could be, name and all—his smile petrified until he thought it could be lifted off his face and put on a table for a doily. What he was looking directly into was not a row of sporrans at all but a row of large female sex organs with hair enough, he could not help thinking, to cover Mrs. Pierce's Duncan Phyfe sofa. Curly and long as goats' it fell, stirred by the breeze which gave it the effect of flapping. Shakily he went into the ice cream parlor and ordered a malted, but thinking of goats and milk, changed it to a lemon Coke, but when that arrived, some association lying on the outskirts of "Coke" kept him from drinking. He was in need of a pick-me-up—even that expression all at once appalled him—something to balance what had gone out of him at the sight, but a banana split assuredly would not do, nor would a Black Cow, a favorite libation; a Nehi was too close for comfort, and a cherry flip would bring on nausea. Water itself was tainted by the memory. He gave up and left, thirsty and weak, believing finally that he had had a touch of the sun and had not seen the sight at all.

Others who came in numbers strove to appear singular. When they spoke to each other it was clandestinely, in low voices. Their eyes moved slowly over objects and people. Their clothing was neat and rough, utilitarian and nothing more. For some reason, they smoked a lot, both men and women; their hands, which seemed similarly square and short-nailed, were similarly stained yellow between index and second finger. They neither laughed nor smiled nor showed anger or contempt or any emotion. They gave the effect of waiting, though not, somehow, of lack of commitment. To some of the new breed of connoisseur crowd-watchers, these last described were the most disturbing of all.

The Wolf became the fashionable place to be, after the Opera House. By day it was the scene of wintry picnics among the burning trash and tiers of large pessimistic birds who sneered at the wieners and cotton buns, dreaming without hope of a carcass of some kind. By night the flares of detritus on the last round-up before joining that great ash pile in the sky illumined ethnic dances, and other rites that were still, despite Roman's efforts, most comfortably performed in shadows. The revelers, with a few exceptions—

Marie Louise and Myra Little among them—were the Wolves and the newcomers. Most of the Tasmanians stayed away as they had always done, though there was a change in the way they kept aloof; they found themselves defensive about their absences; excuses proliferated like weeds; never had there been such a rash of family emergencies even unto third cousins which demanded their attention. This time it was not the revelers who saw the writing on the wall; it was the uneasy stay-at-homes, and once again they heard the numbering of their days, a rumbling sound like wheels on cobblestones. And on the chill night air they would hear, above the pounding of jukes from empty barrooms, doors left open to call in the wandering lambs from the streets, a warning from The Wolf:

> Tiger, tiger,
> Wakeful beside my bed,
> Wakeful, watchful, still,
> When I cover my head—

They could not, of course, hear the words but their minds supplied them, following the sinuous tune as it wove like smoke. It was not as though they were allowed to forget the words; when The Wolf was not singing them, or the newcomers (another change; 'newcomer' had replaced 'foreigner' to an extent astounding when contemplated), the children sang them; when they were thought to have been long asleep, and the melody snaked at the sky from among the bonfires, separating itself from unrhythmic tambourines and squeaky flutes, high little voices circled the nightlights like moths:

> How much longer
> Do you intend to wait?
> I'll awake some night—
> But a second late—

and, though fear was becoming tiresome to the adults, like an old relative lingering too long in the guest room, it was they who were once again afraid; hardly a child found the words ominous, including those who screamed at the mention of Wee Willie Winkie. It was a mystery to the parents, who felt that somehow their own children had left them behind. What did the song MEAN, if not nocturnal devastation of some sort? But the children treated the words as a lullaby, and when notes were compared it was found that nearly all of them had asked that Santa bring them a tiger for Christmas. The more philosophical of the parents said that it was as though the children sought to disarm danger by embracing it, as they themselves, in their own youths, had come to stop worrying and love the Bomb by embracing the idea of young death: Jimmie Dean, they reminded each other. Tiger, tiger, sang the children . . . But they did not really believe that was the answer.

Over and above the arrivals, the notoriety, the exercises, the scandale, the sheer fun of the Revolution, there hung the moon like a coin stamped with a peculiarly quixotic face: was it an actual likeness, or was it a caricature so extreme that all one could do was collapse with mirth to see it? Occasionally the stamped face opened its mouth and made threatening noises, delivered ultimatums. What it was now demanding was the immediate dispatchment from earth to the moon of Roman Chainey; it had thrice voiced the request and was now approaching the countdown. If Roman was not in a capsule on the way by such and such a time . . . but Washington did not know where Roman was, and none of the famous who found him in Tasmania were telling what they knew. It amused everyone to hide Roman in the hottest spot, practically, in the world—smack in the midst of the spotlight.

Roman believed that he had never been in a more precarious position. He had long ago incurred the enmity of Washington but now to that was added the enmity of Peking and London and Moscow. While playing to the amusement of his pea-brained buddies who thought to "hide" him by keeping mum, it seemed that he could hear the rustle of blackmail, thin and versatile as tissue paper, with which he was being packed for shipment. When the packing was complete he would be delivered to the World Powers—and who would be his final betrayer? For he did not believe for an instant in the 'fun' theory concerning the Moon Man. He knew the man for what he was through knowing his type, which Roman had studied with morbid fascination most of his life. Long before the first moon walk he had projected in one of his essays the characteristics of the man who eventually would accomplish it, hiding his loathing beneath a tone of quasi-admiration and good humor, which, as he had found out soon after, had not fooled the Watchers in Washington. "A crew-cut bully boy," he had written, "born patriot, whiz at math and flunker of English, real go-getter, father of several and deacon in the church, golf-playing Rotarian, sneakers-and-bermudas kid, backyard-steak-cooker and beer drinker who could whistle to the bartender at the club without self-consciousness the theme of a beer commercial and expect to be served, a guy who liked the idea of a tiger in his tank, a fellow who reconciled his religion and Vietnam by saying that God was the original Imperialist." He had omitted the summing up: MR. WASP, whose guts Roman would have read with relish.

He turned, as was his practice, his dis-ease and impulses into Art, and performed at an impromptu poetry reading one night at The Wolf, to the accompaniment of a ragtag-and-bobtail combo:

> Blow, baby. You're carryin' me
> home on that blowin' sea
> Dark as puked-up wine
> and matted scrotum on raunch-black
> sheet
> In pot-dim room
> Where lean black cat
> Reads prick-pronged guts
> Of lean white cat
> By gutterin' stud
> In midnight spoon—etc.

Roman was an Artist, and did not really mean that evisceration should become the order of the day. How often had he cautioned—with Gide, wasn't it?—that he should not be too quickly understood. How often had he pointed out to his sheeplike followers that rhetoric was rhetoric and not a directive! But they followed anyhow. He could, and did, count on it, that particular mutiny.

Roman sat on a railroad tie breathing the wet air that had driven the revelers into closed places. The wet flanks of The Wolf enclosed him; he figured his position to be roughly that of a bit of food that had transcended the stomach. He named himself crudely, assuming in his mind the sausage shape. At the present time he was as powerless as that transitional lump, depending upon visceral contractions to force him down and out to where he would become—what?—food for the birds?

He watched the birds as one by one they left electrical wires and settled silently as leaves on the ground. Only one, enlarged by the quality of brume that made of the air a magnifying glass, sat stiff and unmoving on a branch, as formal as a drawing. As though his sight were a sieve through which, because of the dampness, the bogus and the real were being too slowly sifted and separated, it took a minute for him to recognize that the unmoving silhouette was the rooster of the weather vane atop one of the shanty houses. But for a space of time the unreal, because of its being larger than life, and stylized, and static, had been more important to him than the miraculous buoyancy of the true birds, and even when he saw it for what it was: a cheaply molded bit of metal—it continued to occupy his mind and sight, keeping him from contemplation of the greater mystery.

It was like the endless, current critical preoccupation with analyzing the trends and directions of his writing, one critical work feeding upon the opinions of another, while the writing itself went unread. When he looked again for the birds they had flown, but the weather vane moved slightly as though with an illusion of flight to compensate him for his time and trouble.

And thus with the "Revolution"—for some time he had seen the word only in quotes—which sought to compensate him and others with an illusion of motion. The twitches he had observed and taken momentarily as signs of awakening had, with the possible exceptions of those which occasionally galvanized Wanda, turned out to be nothing more than shock reactions, as involuntary as nerve responses to a hammer blow. To be in any way effective, the same shocks would have to be administered in precisely the same forms and at the same times day in and day out; and though all teaching was a form of brain-washing and reflex-conditioning, he did not believe that d'Armont (because of his own associations, he preferred the earlier name to "October") had had Pavlov in mind when she spoke of decapitating The Wolf. Though he had been somewhat cynical at her expense, himself believing in the baseness of nature and its ultimate emergence, he had let himself be caught up in her ideology and had in the past month watched with an eagerness not all feigned for some sign of that Christmas morning of the spirit which she had half convinced him would all at once burst over them, engulfing the town and all in it in a pure and even holy light.

The reality was, of course, a farce, increasingly so, which was enough to offend him because his humor did not tend naturally in that direction despite his having been a lifelong magnet to its sharp filings.

He had married a farcical wife without knowing it, frankly wanting her title (Countess; in her own right) to be implicit whenever his surname was used, so that it would become as though it were Count Chainey as well as Countess. She was short, but though he had slept with her once or twice before marriage, he did not realize that she was squat, and without the most carefully designed costumes and hours of preparation, that her head on its own seemed always on the verge of toppling her. But the farce, which was the thinly crusted pond that separated humor and tragedy, onto which he ventured unknowingly at first with her, was her attempt to make him believe that her worst flaws were in fact her greatest beauties. She had over a lifetime collected the names and dimensions of women who tended to squatness and over-large heads and reeled them off to Roman, not once, not twice, but whenever they found themselves together, un-clothed, and then at the apparentness of his disbelief she took to more persistent brain-washing, one method of which was the leaving about of written lists of the names, so that, if he opened his checkbook, or his wallet, or went through his coat pockets in search of a packet of matches, he was likely to find a slip of paper and thereon such names as Teresa Guic-cioli; Gloria Swanson; Tallulah Bankhead; Marilyn Monroe; Elizabeth Taylor. Finally he had left her, laughing. But farce, like a child awarded him in the divorce courts, went along.

Consider—try not to—the form in which middle age had chosen to afflict him. Not for him the poetic, fey, mermaid-sighting menopausal-onset of men who had devoted them-selves to the prose of dollar-getting. He had got dollars, as any self-respecting writer must do, but he had let them flow through him and out, a metaphorical extension of his avowed goal in life, which was to expand his own, and others', aware-ness of the danger, the antilife properties, of anything hoarded, particularly thoughts however apparently uninteresting. "Communication Is All" he told them incessantly; and "Keep trying," for sometimes he was obscure. But somehow his life-metaphor had become a farcical simile: he was like a piggy bank stuffed to the backbone and nothing could shake the hoardings loose without severe trauma.

Food and drink were transformed within him into hot burning winds that roamed the interior seeking outlet. Exit, when found, was effected with decreasing subtlety; the hand placed in front of the mouth where sourness lived like an old animal in a cave was no longer an adequate filter for the stale eructations.

That nether sphincter which he had guarded with such care, setting there public warning like a Cerberus (the tri-headed

Medea), had weakened at an alarming rate so that there seemed to be continuous leakage and sometimes blasts of humiliating force detonated without regard for company or the gender thereof. But, tragic farce—the vital mass, the hoardings that produced the gusty dividends could hardly be coaxed from the coils of guts to the walls of which it adhered like plaster of Paris. Suppositories drew forth a thin mixture of what appeared to be serum laced with blood; enemas injected with tissue-rending violence sometimes tore loose shalelike pieces of excreta but the operation weakened his will to continue and horrified his mind. Once he had gone to one of those high-colonic spas where he was drained of sludge like a rusty crankcase and for twenty-four hours he had known once again the illusory bliss of emptiness, but an apple—a clean rosy-skinned white-fleshed apple eaten for the joy and cleanth of the procedure—bloated him with acidulous gas and a day later had made no further appearance. He dreamed of that apple in cottony expansion within him, absorbing and fermenting the plain water that he sent in to flush it out. He dreamed that he was a still for the production of hard cider and saw himself with spigots and siphons and bungholes all over him, an Arguslike apparition of blocked apertures, for behind each draining device there grew an eye and clouding each eye, glaucoma, and rimming the milky-colored dryness like a ring of hills cataracts grew.

Cinched within his jockey shorts and the extrawide belts he wore to reduce agony, there was a roll of midriff fat—solidified gases, a mark of time's passage like a ring on a tree—of such toughness that if it could have been separated by surgery and lifted over his head in an unbroken ring, a child could have bowled it down the street.

"What's that you got, kid?" (a) "A Roman calendar." (b) "Romans fleuves" (endless tales, sagas of petrified vapors, fateful projections, as though the locomotive steam had cinched Anna Karenina's waist and hardened, and by sheer mass had pulled her beneath the wheels).

Fat and flatulent—words and conditions that belonged to

farce, and still he was hungry, and the farce of the revolution was become a hungry farce, which was no farce at all.

Revolutionary activists still ate well, an improvement of this over older revolutions, and though, as Christmas approached, the tables at the Ohio Hotel groaned less audibly, there was still enough for all to have a plateful; but nonparticipant Tasmanians felt the pinch, as did the Wolves, who, for some unaccountable reason, had still not been invited to Mrs. October's Revolution. Perhaps when she said she would kill The Wolf, she had meant she would starve it to death. The Wolves, naturally, felt the pinch most acutely and scrounged for the leftovers from picnics; then, when inevitably there were no leftovers, they picked over garbage cans, fighting the birds for priority. When, soon now, the garbage cans would be empty, Roman imagined that they would eat other things . . .

From his high-colonic position, Roman looked into the guts and read there a vision, a zodiacal procession of eidolons. The wet chill of reality was replaced by a cold that, because it was visionary, was somehow warming:

One morning the town awoke to a flurry of snow, premature, ominous. Gazing out its windows the town saw that the sidewalks and alleyways and yards were covered with cots and on the cots people and on the people the blanket of snow. No one had quite known until then that inner space had been explored and exploded and the only place left to go for the living was out, but not too far out, for the ring of hills enclosed them as it had always done and the bowl at last was full with no place at all for the overflow.

The Indians and the Japanese moved imperturbably among the cots, twittering about the homelikeness of the atmosphere but complaining about the dearth of certain vegetables and curry powder ingredients. And the fish in the rivers floated on the surface, having surrendered to the Revolution disappointingly soon in the day. Each fish floated in a little nest of detergent which, from a distance, looked like rings of duchesse potatoes piped through a pastry bag.

And still the people came. The hotel, long filled to overflowing, had divided halls into cubicles, and the roof garden had been enclosed and similarly divided, and broom and linen closets were occupied by the smallest of the newcomers.

And still the people came. Private houses reluctantly opened musty guest rooms and attics and finally cellars. The armory and schoolhouse (classes long abandoned) and some churches were turned into barracks. In spite of outside pressure, banks refused to turn over their vaults to the strangers but some Hungarians slept in the crypts in the cemetery.

And on they came, various in color, texture, and taste as though from a broken crock of melange. Gigantic planes carrying several hundred persons at a time seemed constantly to be circling overhead, either having just spewed out more humanity and on the way to fetch more, or trying to find a place to land with enough people in their bellies to populate a new town or a very high-rise building. Sometimes the sun would be blotted out for so long that old natives would nod and sagely predict rain. The racket hurt ears and caused anxiety; as Dubos had predicted, behavior down below became more and more erratic. Children born in Tasmania under the shadow of the planes were the first new breed since Adam, but this was not noticed for a year or so, until belatedly they spoke. . . .

Minor tragedies were in such abundance that their victims came to occupy the niches once pre-empted by the merely eccentric: A lady addicted to post-midnight TV was hypnotized by a test pattern and crouched on a table emitting a piercing, mysteriously produced note. She had nearly expired of malnutrition before it was discovered that she rallied on a steady diet of publicity stills and grew zoftik if the stills were of cowboy stars. As an understanding doctor pointed out, lean well-hung meat always had done the trick.

In the supermarket, a young woman confidently overloaded with bags of food (seaweed derivatives and eggs from a nameless source) stepped blindly onto the treadle which activated the automatic door and crashed through the glass and fetched up on the other side in a mixture resembling spinach soufflé.

Her physical wounds healed nicely, plastic surgery succeeding, where chromosomes had failed, in making her somewhat pretty, but the injury to her psyche was permanent, for she was rid of trust and at the mention of technology would cower and salivate in terror.

Another young woman, abrim with confidence in what she termed the modren emphasis on plastics, fell into a decline when a filmy plastic wrapping failed to adhere to the sides of a bowl of leftovers. When found—it was estimated that she had been about her labors for several days because the leftovers had gone bad—she was standing at the kitchen counter surrounded by empty wrap boxes and a measured two miles of shredded wrap, trying with bloodied palms to smooth a by now imaginary plastic covering over the bowl of spoiled victuals. She was, or her hands were, in the year following her trauma, the nearest that technology, even by default, had come to devising perpetual motion but no one could think of a way to harness her.

A curiously old-fashioned mishap occurred when a lady, according to a beauty formula propounded by Edgar Cayce, The Sleeping Prophet (his disciples claimed that he had anticipated the Tasmanian Revolution back in 1921), was patting rose water into her face and neck and inadvertently gave herself a karate chop and fell into a trance identical to The Prophet's wherein she was given all manner of revelations, as she later said; but how to wake up was not among them.

The greater number of casualties were among women, perhaps understandably because the mainly technological failures which precipitated the crises were, it was postulated, felt to be the failures of the men themselves, dysfunction of invention being equated with dysfunction of inventor, and the male casualties were, it was duly noted, of the inner-propelled variety, such as the man, father of several girls, who one day closed his eyes and refused to open them. Thenceforward he knew the world about him only through the descriptions of others, and what was allowable as description according to laws laid down by him—for example, no word pictures of his daughters or what they wore—was as severely restricted as the movements in classical Eastern theater. If there was a connection with technological failure in his wilful disability, no one of importance thought it worth considering.

What most caught the imagination of expert and layman alike was the, as she came to be known, Wrap Lady. Concerning her, a visiting psychologist wrapped it up, so to speak when he pointed out that the recalcitrant plastic was felt by what he termed "the plasticee—deep within her body"—to be the "reluctance to effectiveness of birth control devices." The food she had been trying to render impervious to further transmutation by bacteria was an exposed ovum, he said, and when it spoiled despite her efforts and became in the bowl a lively mass, she believed herself pregnant and then a mother, the pile of bloody plastic being seen by her, and the psychologist, as afterbirth. When he was asked where the baby was, he said that she had killed it by putting plastic over its face.

Some darker signs of the times were: fingers that had made the V sign for so long that they had locked in that position, making dandy eye-gouging weapons;

The plastic incumbent in the White House had, on a warm day, melted just enough to become a permanent part of the Seat (plastic) so that Democracy was fixed forevermore in his immovable Person;

The black had grown so accustomed to speaking in non-negotiable demands that black robbers no longer carried weapons but simply demanded that the victim fork over his wallet; and black murderers demanded lives and, to all visible evidence, expected the person thus addressed to lie down and expire and a good many of them did, some from shock, most from masochism. A peculiar street-corner sight—the peculiar soon become the usual—was that of a white person kicking in rigor mortis like a baby in a crib and bending with apparent solicitude above him, completing the nursery analogy, a stern black face softening at the sight of sleep.

Roman's vision was dissolved in a downpour and he ran for cover. Each shack, shanty, hogshead, furniture crate, was occupied by grunting celebrants, two by two and sometimes by three and four, following his own teachings. The point he had been making about freedom had eluded them; as usual, he had been taken literally.

The overpopulated places, smelling of sex and deprivation, made him hark back to his vision of Tasmania overflowing like a slop jar. He had the artist's superstition, hubristic and unshakable, about causing a thing to be by merely thinking it. All things were, indeed, but copies of ideas, reminiscences, as the Greek had put it. He felt the artist's helplessness in face of what he had set in motion by merely thinking, knowing the process to be a one-way street emptying into a grisly (sometimes) plaza named Inevitability. A writer could set about the plaza, like statues, some conditional clauses which, if he were a real artist, could be later used as hiding places from hunters sometimes calling themselves Justice, sometimes Redressors—of the evil of overevaluation, generally. If the artist were also clever, conditions seldom found tandem; before he modeled the statues, he excavated beneath them escape hatches. Always, in book or essay or play, Roman carefully constructed such tunnels, usually on the first page. As a careful observer, determined survivor, he had seen too many others of his ilk ricocheting about the blank walls of that self-devised plaza, ultimately enmired in their hasty hubris like flies in a sticky pudding similarly defined. Every decade had its would-be recanters of early folly who, not having learned what he had, perished in their own Inevitability before tiers of relishing spectators like the watching birds at The Wolf.

Consequently he had grown accustomed to laying escape routes beneath even his most careless thoughts while the material was still warm enough to be malleable. He now did so, following his usual formula of question and answer: Why did the starving masses (of his own invention) stay on in Tasmania when there was food and space just beyond the enclosing hills? If he alone were responsible for such a crush by having thought it, he alone could be found and convicted and punished as a kind of despotic jailer at the very least. Two reasons, then, neither of which involved him as other than reporter:

1. The desire to be In, With It, Of It; or, in the new slang, Down On It—the lemming syndrome, death as ecological balance cloaked in chic;

2. To mark a turning point in civilized man away from a fantastical theory to a practical solution . . . In his first book a passage illustrative of this had so horrified one reviewer that she publicly admitted to having thrown up:

"Through the open window the fluttering and cooing of the baby next door came like sounds from a dovecot and Willie visualized the occupant of the barred bed as a fat squab, and saw himself wringing its neck. In the world where such a thing could occur, a world of his wistful, indeed starved imagination, the least need, desire, uninsistent wish of an adult was considered before the well-being or life of a noisy baby . . . 'Mrs. Bartlett, I had to wring your baby's neck this morning.' 'Oh, you poor man, was it disturbing your sleep again? Here—have some of this nice jelly for your toast. I made it out of what you gave me last week. You know . . . The Browns' . . .' Willie smiles; a little confessional joke will not be unappreciated by this agreeable woman. 'In strictness, I erred with that one. It was over the age limit . . . almost seven . . . but so . . . fat.' He and Mrs. Bartlett smile discreetly, both salivating brownishly. 'Ah well,' she sighs, 'they have six more . . . and one on the way . . . ,' and they send messages to each other composed of hieroglyphs transposed from the world of pure sound bounded on the north by the esophagus and on the south by the mouth of the small gut. Their eyes glitter diamonds hardened from the liquefaction of the stomach's anticipation, the gullet's disease . . ." and so forth. Roman, who admitted no influences, was gratified that his debt to Swift, off whom he secretly battened, had gone undetected.

One night after he had become famous and the book had been re-reviewed and widely celebrated he reminisced about the original deadly notices. He reminisced, as was his practice, on the home screen with an estimated three quarters of the English-speaking world looking in. (One thing that kept them twirling that old dial was a widely circulated description of him as "a sexy little tough with a Jesus Christ accent," which many of them had telescoped to "sexy tough Christ," which was what they saw when they watched him and they behaved accordingly.) That night he said humbly that he would give a good deal to ask the anonymous reviewer just why she had been so offended by the book. He was certain, he said with some insinuation, that it was a female reviewer because the choice of words had been so womanly. He told his listeners that he bet he could make that reviewer see his artistic reasons for using cannibalism as a metaphor, as well as why the sex scenes were so hot, if he only could speak to her seriously and alone. America et al. understood what he meant; so did the anonymous reviewer. When she showed up at his door soon after and identified herself he was ready for her. Slowly, thoroughly, and all over, he sprayed her with a flit gun while the TV cameras took dictation. The woman stood dripping and stinking long after the cameras and Roman had left.

The world, ever at his feet, fell to begging to be sprayed with his big gun and occasionally he sprayed them; nearly always he mocked them; if they stepped left, he stepped right. He was so secure, he could write anything he chose, including apparent attacks upon himself, and lose not a disciple though at times he tried their piety severely. As the leading leftist extremist, he had, to their épatement, written the following:

"When a point is reached where one set of political attitudes determines a man's acceptance or rejection as an artist, then that point and beyond must bear the tag of Totalitarianism; and that was the point achieved by the late 1960s in the United States. Not to list leftwards to the compass reading of ENE—ethical-nihilistic-existentialism—was tantamount to signing an agreement whereby critics were released from the need to notice one's efforts and the public from its usual desultory gesture of support. Thus were starvelings made of much good art, which is not, despite widespread belief, a synonym for political anything."

Among other graven tablets, he had once handed down to America the dictum that Art, to be worthy of its connection with Articulation, had to be political because of the connection between *that* concept and Politic, which, as he told them, meant "artful"; or, as he interpreted it for them to ease their task, "full of Art." But his self-contradictions and chastisements were as endearing to them as his trademark of self-love, both being seen with the special vision generally reserved for looking at babies whose every move is both adorable and profound, holding God mysteriously at its center like dew-prisms in a rose at high noon. In fact, Roman and babies alike could play patty-cake in their own shit and come up smelling of roses, and both frequently did just that —the baby for its own unknowable reasons, Roman because his own excreta did not so sicken him as did the country's, and the world's, adulation.

Drenched, exhilarated, brandy-bound, Roman believed that he saw at last and just ahead a turning beyond which the Revolution could be seen gathering lost momentum. October Revolutions, by association, by the hollow clangor of the words themselves, were ineffective. But . . . a Roman Revolution? The final épatement of the sheep? The ultimate reduction (he cooked as a hobby) to a paté? He liked the auguries.

Mrs. October had been missing for days before the question was asked: where was she? Once it had been asked, a kind of panic set in with each person trying to take the major responsibility for the oversight, or timidity, or stronger fear. The desire to be in top position on the guilt pole forced one woman desperately to vow that she had been the first one not to have asked the question; being the one avowal that was least provable, they granted her the star's role by default and she was pointed at on the street. Then, by natural extension, it came to be said that she was responsible for Mrs. October's safety, and threats were made. Her home was flooded with anonymous mail and phone calls so that eventually she had to seek police protection, for by that time open demands for Mrs. October's return were being made, with appended deadlines beyond which the woman would look upon the face of her Maker. To many it was a game, all part of what they had learned was permissible revolutionary rhetoric, and they enjoyed it to the fullest. But as always under such conditions, there were a few, or perhaps only one, who gave the threat in dead earnest, and when a third deadline had been ignored, the woman's house was set afire and her husband waylaid in an alley and beaten by one or more masked figures—the reports emanating from his hospital room varied considerably as to the number of assailants though the color of the would-be assassin(s) was a constant: black.

The language of the letters and phone calls moved into the open, first to street corners and all sections of The Wolf, then to the stage of the Opera House.

One day a spokesman from The Wolf, the first to move into the arena, took the stage and set forth demands and nonnegotiable expectations in language that was clear and clean in the beginning but as he proceeded, sensing the masochism of the assemblage, he dropped clearness and cleanness for a muddled rhetoric, winding up with the statement that one of his expectations, and the primary hope of those citizens in The Wolf, was that all the proper Tasmanians would die of their own decadence and the sooner the better.

Wanda, shocked, turned to a neighbor and was stunned to find the woman smiling serenely. Seeing Wanda's expression, the neighbor explained: "It's just rhetoric, you know; that's something like poetic license when you're in a revolution." At Wanda's hopeful but still doubtful expression the lady, by her accent a New Yorker, went on, "I've worked with people like that man—Wright, I think his name is—for years, and I know how really sweet they are underneath. Why, I bet you he wouldn't hurt a fly." She sighed. "I was getting downright homesick for Eldridge but now it's all right." Wanda thanked the lady but seeing the man scowling still in the wings, where there was no audience to impress, she felt twinges of fear and anger. He had called the Tasmanians the most awful names, using a number of words for which she had had to substitute her dots. She went home thinking: Wright, is it? Well, when is a Wright a wrong?

She sought reassurance in front of the TV, a habit she was trying somewhat desperately to acquire as she became more and more one of The People.

On the screen there sat a white woman interviewing a famous black athlete. The woman reminded Wanda of Helen Gurley Brown, though she was skinnier and obviously more prurient, for she seemed to be asking the man about the size of his penis, with a nod in the direction of euphemism. Her thin wide mouth, while the champ spoke ("Some part of me, they tell me, is larger than most"), tried out various circumferences, or perhaps she was stifling various sized yawns. Wanda watched in a chill of horror; to be modern, really modern, was it necessary to be so remarkably vulgar? The woman's vulgarity made her ugly; in Wanda's eyes, she was a cheap little skinny ugly bitch asking a colored man about —now—the number of ejaculations he "normally enjoyed." The woman was famous for emancipation, so said the hastily consulted *TV Guide*, but she was nastier-minded than Marie Louise and obviously as stupid. Wanda ached to see the large colored man reach over and fetch the woman such a clout across the face that her features would be rearranged, but he was clearly uninterested in her and stared steadily into the camera.

Wanda snapped on another "challenging" *(TV Guide)* show. The black man on that one was saying, "Culturally speaking de black man have always been on de scene." Wanda mused, "We'll all have to learn to speak that way . . ." and turned him off.

No, she would never ever be reconciled to the machine. Movies were aged, mellowed a little in the can before you saw them, the sharp edge of newness worn off, so that no matter what were the events recorded, they were safely in the past; one sighed for them, if they were horrible—like *To Die in Madrid*, which Mrs. October had made them look at, but then one said "Such a long time ago" and was comforted; a "long time ago" could be as little as a couple of months but that was a chunk of time as solidly gone as ten thousand years. But this thing, this inward-turning eye in the corner of the room, brought you horrors undimmed by the passage of any time at all. Even now, in back of that gray lid the skinny bitch still dug with her soiled little mind like a trowel at the black man's root. They were both in Wanda's living room; she could not escape.

How different were her beloved movies, how different because of the instruments used. The TV camera was undoubtedly a Socratic instrument, somehow digging out of people their lowest thoughts and desires and flashing them on a screen as entertainment, exposing the worst and exposing it now. The motion picture camera, in spite of its name, in reality arrested life, broke it into thousands of fragments, froze the fragments in a state of eternal separateness divided by moats of perforation. It was the safest thing there was, to be recorded on film and to love what was recorded on film. It was, actually, eternity. But even the prerecorded TV shows were erasable, changeable, and so forever NOW.

Wanda's father had played a game with the Holy Bible that was partly a parlor game to amuse the children and partly mystic ritual. He would ask a question of The Book, then close his eyes and open The Book and run his finger down a page, until, as he said, the finger stopped of its own self. Then he would open his eyes and read and the words were supposed to be the answer he sought. The Bible had told him that he would live to be as old as Methuselah (this was during his final illness) and that he would die a rich man. It told him that his children would be fruitful and multiply; it lied to him continuously but he did not lose his faith in the printed word. He died believing that he would outlive Methuselah; maybe he died believing that he was a rich man, too.

Wanda went to the set and switched it on. She closed her eyes and turned the channel selector until she did not feel the urge to turn it further. Then she found the volume knob and simultaneously turned it up and opened her eyes, asking, "What is the future?" She saw: a man wearing trousers with bottoms so wide that he seemed to be wearing a skirt. She heard: a long drawn-out scream into the microphone he crammed into his mouth, drums relentless as a machine, then the words, "I learned how to do it before I could eat" and another scream, "Bai-beh."

She could not believe it, as prophecy, as final answer. Sex preceding even the need to do something about individual survival? All it proved to her was that the old was neither better nor worse than the new—all, Bible, Mama, TV— handing out lies as though they were lollipops to pacify the children.

Depressed, she went to bed and to sleep and dreamed. She was tied to a table in a smoky place that smelled of ham fat. Dark stained rafters hung above her oozing or sweating a dark brown fluid. The light was veiled, a dark lantern. The floor, a corner of which she could see by straining her neck at the rope that bound it, was of packed earth, slick and shiny as black marble. Soon others entered, scowling Negroes to a man, large and mean without a trace of desire for her, or interest in her gender. She moved her body as well as she could within the numerous shackles, moved it as sensuously as it was possible for her to do, but their eyes did not change. Nobody wanted to do it to her. All they wanted to do, they told her, was to mutilate her to death. She smiled up at them, saying, "I just love your rhetoric."

Wright took a poker from his pants and heated it over a flame that she could not see but she could smell the heat and hear a sputtering of grease. Horror rose to her throat and she called out over it as she would try to outscream a flood, "But that was all supposed to be rhetoric! They said! Everybody SAID! They said you wouldn't hurt a fly!" He nodded above her. "Wouldn't touch one," and brought the poker into place above her stomach. As the metal touched the eye of her navel she screamed the word RHETORIC and darted up from sleep, as slick within the coat of her sweat as a seal.

"A fable," Roman told them from the stage, "or parable, if that's the way your taste trends. Listen or not, because it's a longie, but anybody who can't repeat the main points back to me when I've finished gets locked in a cage and if you think I'm kiddin, hang around." They believed him; not a peanut dropped. He thought, Wanda is thrilled; and looking at her, saw electricity coursing among the pale blond down on her arms like lightning in reeds by a river. He thought of the font of her river; it was pleasanter than before, close to being irresistible. He had always had a woman by him when creation time came, and used her throughout the creative process quite unambiguously as socket for his plug when the current ran low.

"Hard rain's agonna fall, babe," he crooned inwardly, "one a these times," and was swamped by nostalgia, for when he was young and just starting out to overthrow the Old, that was the way one thought, necessary mental training, for to have spoken forgetfully, using loftier words and sentiments, would have meant expulsion from a kind of proletarian Eden when the United States had been, or had seemed, for a moment—brief and shot to hell—to be a little village. Dirty jeans; old boots (tasty old boots, he had written, and had had to live down the rumors of foot fetishism) and the tongue of the People; and Love; that was about all he remembered of it.

He looked out and saw the rows of heads as the keys on

an electric typewriter. To write upon them he must generate enough electricity to power the machine. He beckoned to Wanda and she came to him and sat by him. In the darkness under the table he took her hand and placed it on the swell of his crotch, thinking primitively about Man and Woman and their Relationship. Her hand tightened convulsively. "That's right, babe," he whispered. "You got the message, chick." Her hand went on tightening until in great agony, fearing dismemberment, he tore himself from her grasp and stood up doubling with cramps. Even as he called her in his mind by stronger synonyms for Woman, he found himself choking with laughter. Naming an alternate plaza, he thought, "The ludicrous Inevitable; I've got to get this goddamned thing out of farce before it kills me."

He apologized for his 'coughing fit' and thanked and dismissed Wanda without going near her again.

"A fable," he told them.

Suppose there is a village of a hundred people. They have built their village and developed profitable businesses—a store, say, and a mill—and cultivated the farmlands surrounding them, and decided upon a religion that is most congenial to the greatest majority, and built a church; and they have established a schoolhouse for their children and decided which courses would be most useful to a child growing up in that particular village and would best serve his needs when he was fully grown; and they have agreed upon holidays and other days of observance—a half day for remembering a favorite citizen now gone on to the next world, and another to commemorate the building of the bridge across the river; half days, mornings off, so that one could sleep late. And nobody grumbles too much about any of the things they have agreed upon. But one person does, out of a hundred. He had wandered across the bridge one day, escaping, as he told them, persecution in another village, and they had welcomed him. And from the beginning he displayed a penchant for grumbling; and then he was openly objecting to the courses taught at the school, and to the denomination of the single church, and to the wages paid at the mill, and to the products with which the store was stocked; and to the uses to which the grain raised on the farms was being put. And he had gone from objecting to protesting by blocking entrance to school and church, and chaining himself to the door of the mill and lying down in front of farm machinery. And from protesting he had gone to attempts at recruitment of schoolchildren, and gained a few recruits so that, out of a hundred people, ten were dissatisfied with everything. And the ten had gone from dissatisfaction to sabotage. They blocked the mill wheel with boulders, which broke the paddles. They took plowshares and hammered them into swords, using the anvil in the village blacksmith shop, tying up the blacksmith while they worked; they tore up the school records and soiled the altar cloth in the church with their excrement; they disrupted meetings of ways and means with their loud cries and waylaid citizens on their way home and beat them with the swords, and cut some of them, and killed one. And the citizens went to the leader and asked him, "Why?" They asked him, "If you did not like us, why did you come to live among us?" And he told them, "I was persecuted in the other place." "For what?" they asked him. He told them, "For wanting change, because change is life." And they said, "Life?" and they pointed to the dead man. The leader said, "Oh, something will grow out of THAT," and he touched the body with his foot. And they told him, "Yes it will"; and they put him in chains and sent the children who had aided him back to their parents with severe admonitions, but one of them got away and crossed the bridge and ran through the streets of the next village crying out PERSECUTION. And the village took up arms and followed the child back across the bridge and slaughtered a great many of the people who had put into chains the man whom they had expelled from their own village. When this was pointed out to them, in a settlement meeting with the few remaining villagers of the conquered place, they replied,

"But we only sent him into exile; we did not take away his freedom of movement." They were asked, "Could he have come back to his own village, then, if he had wanted to?" And they replied, "No; exile is exile." And the conquered villagers humbly asked if that was not the same as taking away freedom of movement, and for their impudence the terms of the settlement were made stricter: they were given the mill to run but were allowed only a pittance of the flour it ground, for which they must pay; and the courses in the school were altered and the history books changed so that they, the conquered, were made responsible for starting the war; and the church was boarded up; and the store sold only those products made in the village of the conquerors. And the conquerors went back home, leaving in charge the man whom they had persecuted and exiled. When they were gone and the dust had settled the new supervisor called a meeting and told the people, "Now I am no longer a minority and my voice is as good as any here, and I vote that we pull ourselves together and build up a stock of weapons and take that village by surprise and pay them back for ruining what was once the most perfect village in the entire world, which is what this village was when I first came here." And the tears poured down his face, but he got himself in hand and went on speaking to them. He said, bitterly, "But now it is not perfect; now it is not anything but a mass of ruin and rubble which nobody could possibly want, but that village over there, the conquerors' village, is fat and stocked with all manner of goods and . . ." But they did not let him finish. They had become mad with horror and rage to hear him say that no one could want their village now, and they saw that he did not have even the excuse of idealism and was only greedy and vindictive and they rose up in a body and killed him. This time no one ran to tell those in the next place what had occurred. They got back to their planting and building and opening of school and church and the murder hanging over them made them move somewhat furtively. In the school the teachers would grow nervous at certain questions, even though they were about Julius Caesar, and in the pulpit the minister avoided more and more certain passages in Scripture and a certain Commandment, and the citizens were allied not so much by their common goals as by their common guilt which led to dislike and eventual avoidance of all but the most necessary contacts. After a while they formed into two parties so that they might elect a representative for each party and send these two to discuss whatever was necessary to keep the village running, so that the villagers never had to see each other at all. And one night they were awakened by a dull BOOM and when they went outdoors to see what had happened, they found that the bridge had been blown up, and though they knew that one of their number had done it, nobody asked who it was. They watched until the last timber had sunk beneath the water and then they went back to bed and dreamed that now that the bridge was gone, they did not have to be afraid that one of them would run across it and tell about the murder, and since they were safe, they could return to their old ways of friendship and ease and goodness and all the rest of it. But when they awoke and thought about the dream, they realized it was only a dream and dreams never work out in the waking world, and so they got up and went about their separate business.

The midnight of December 24th drew up like a black coach, in a light drizzle. Street lamps shone in pavement quick-silvered by small rain; the Opera House swam like a ghost between broken sidewalk and rifted heaven; on Flambeau there was more rue than illumination, though certainly there was a torch and Omerie carried it, had carried it all night.

He was in love, horribly, for the first time, and the object of that abject regard had stood him up, was standing him up, would be, he knew, standing him up in more ways than one right on into the narrowing tunnel of the future. His money had failed him. For once, he had offered it all, to share or bequeath outright, but its magic had gone. The gold in the heart of his paper persuasion, being the smug end of alchemy, refused further transmutation. He was stuck with a mountain of inert, gleaming metal (beyond paper doors) and with the unmeltable lumps of his desire which, like the silicones he had had injected behind skin beginning to curl and corrugate as aging paper does, had divided and gone to separate resting places: the silicones—not noticeably as yet—to behind one ear and along one jaw; the desire, to his breast slightly left of center, and to his crotch. It was the first belief he had had that revolution had really come, for like all the rich he had believed that in a showdown money would win out, and it had failed. He saw the situation as the scorning of the country in microcosm, and to his despair was added the fear of physical harm. His gifts, as great as they were, belonged at the peak of a civilization, not to the rubbish tumbling down the other side of the mountain, which was what happened to those at the top when revolution came about. He had left London when, as it were, the crown fell down that farther slope, before the Socialist scorn could maim him.

Omerie had been scorned before. He was human but his desire had been viewed on occasion as subhuman and he had known scorn. Early, though, in life, before inheritance gave him the only sure weapon for combatting it.

He had lived as his father's wife for a year and a half,
taken, or invited, into common-law marriage the night his
mother left them for good, although, considering his father's
power and position and money, perhaps 'common' was not
a word to use in connection with him; in reality it had
been more like a liaison formed by royal edict.

His father had said. "Now that she has gone, you may
share my bed." Omerie was thirteen, lately pubertal, with the
soft luster of a pollen-sprinkled bloom. Few, during that
period of blossoming, could resist touching him. He was
fondled, stroked, massaged by teachers, playmates, strangers,
in what seemed efforts to dislodge or share the bloom, and
still it clung. Next to pleasing his father-husband in every
imaginable way, Omerie's greatest pleasure had been to ob-
serve himself in the process of shyly opening his petals. He
and his lover were mutually ravished as they wandered hand
in hand in the garden of Omerie. The bloom did not leave
him until he was widowed by his father eighteen months
after their marriage, at the age of fourteen and a half (Juliet
and he bereft at around the same age), and probably then
only because in his confusion—his mother appeared and
claimed to be the widow—he had lost momentary touch with
himself and when he found himself again someone had spite-
fully smudged and artificially aged the once lovely casing.

So briefly a beauty, he was taught its value, and its worth-
lessness as a long-term investment and so placed his money
elsewhere, in sensuality, which can wear any face and be
any age at all. Thus, by eschewing beauty as the sought-for
object he had guaranteed himself a greater supply of sexual
partners, some of them, like the Chief of Police in Tasmania,
stunned and grateful to be noticed, never mind the money
involved.

But since such words as codicil had entered permanently
into his ken, the only scorn he knew had been his own, kept
for the purposes of reminiscence, the whiling away of self-
enforced exiles while such as silicones and the glands of
small animals and fetuses took into themselves the tolls of

age and excess. He was never scornful to a face, no matter its color or configuration, however unpleasing. He had learned well the lessons of scorn and was tender in that regard, both as to his and others' vulnerability. In the throes of bargaining, even when forced to press home reminders of the inequities of individual worth, he remained compassionate; had been known truly to deplore his infallible inner scale which would not allow him to pay for flesh more than the established pence per pound based on (a) condition (b) fodder used—milk, gin, grass, etc. (c) cut of meat being bargained for (d) (alas) age (e) need—a weight unto itself.

Therefore, he reserved his scorn only for backs of people and seldom shared its expenditure. It was one of his very few totally private indulgences.

He had believed that compassion was like bread repeatedly cast to the waters: one casts and casts and waits to reap the incoming tide, which, being of one's own devising, rolls in on command.

But all night long he had commanded and at midnight no ripple showed. The ocean had been sucked to heaven and was raining indiscriminate benevolence; he, leaning from his window, caught on his palm some drops as tiny as spray from a mouth faultily occluded; he gazed in vain at his slightly misted Mound of Venus for a reflection there of his beloved.

He had the feeling that he was being watched in his dark window, and the fear turned him backward to remembrance of why he had left New York and sought the interior of the country and anonymity. In a museum in that city there was an exhibit, a cross section of earth showing several strata and the life within as lived by bugs, worms, and the nameless. The cross section had been made and enclosed in a special glass case that allowed of observation but apparently was so constructed and lighted that the creatures within thought themselves deep in the good dark earth. However, after he had gone back several times he came to notice that as they approached the glass walls the earthworms and bugs and others grew nervous. They did not turn back to the heart of the matter, which would have defeated the museum's purpose, but would slow down or hurry up or behave otherwise erratically as though they could sense the huge watching eyes beyond the cleverly camouflaged observation walls.

He came to believe that Manhattan Island was just such a box, which explained it and the people within it and the nervousness one felt at the edges of its rivers especially, but because it was so very narrow to begin with, there was no interior allowing of momentary respite, no temporary hiding place. He would pick the center of the Island and go stand there and feel the eyes watching. When it became, finally, unbearable he had found a burrowing companion in Madame Alexis and sought the dark heart of the country. And yet, perhaps, they had found him anyway.

Madame Alexis offered her ears, her belly, her whole sleepy self, promising coziness, heading hopefully for the bedroom. He could not sleep, he told her, and tucked her in again, and sat beside her and sang an excessively Germanic lyric to lighten both their hearts, but midway he forgot his purpose and succumbed:

> Es ist im Leben hässlich eingerichtet
> Das bei den Rosen, gleich die Dornen stehen
> Und was das arme Herz auch Sehnt und dichtet
> Zum Schlusse kommt das Voneinandergehen

On 'und dichtet' his voice broke. She was all he had. Always before, barring the purely physical, it had been enough that they had each other. He had known since early in life that he would not fall in love until he was in what he thought of as his middle years, which category would suffice until the end for he did not intend to acknowledge a further category called either late years or old age. When he found her he was—no way to deny it—in his middle years and he accepted her as the love anticipated with some dread.

In Deinen Augen hab' ich einst erleben
Von Lieb' und Glück (was that right?)
la la la la EIN SCHEIN
Behüt Dich Gott, es wär' zu schön gewesen;
Behüt Dich Gott—es hat nicht sollen sein

Loving her, he had found that the dread was justified, for to each year that tolled for him he had to add six more for her and then subtract the horrific total of seven from her tiny life span. The thought of her rapid aging was a succubus that rode him and brought him darting up in pain from his sleep nearly every night. His hands would scrabble, scrabble in the bed until he had found her, and the touch of her silky coat would calm his heart.

Against the day or night of her death he had amassed pills, hundreds of them by now, even though one per seven (significant number!) pounds of his body weight would turn for him the final trick. Still, despite certain vanities, some glandular disturbance could conceivably occur so that on the fateful day or night he would, having attained a weight of several hundred pounds, find himself short of the funds to purchase death. Accruing pills became a hobby; his bathroom shelves resembled those in a pharmacy.

Singing to her of thorns and parting, feeling her breath and hearing her robustly trusting snore, he came to know such anger at having been robbed of the chance to care for her less through caring more for another, and thus being able to take her death in stride, however shortened and tottery that stride might be, that he believed an act of some danger was the only antidote.

He had never been to the Wolf, for reasons of both caution and cowardice, but that was where the scornful one was domiciled—Omerie imagined him steaming in a hogshead à la Huckleberry Finn—and so there Omerie would go in the rainy night. If The Wolf was the hell it was said to be, then he would stir it with some stick or other, for the last thing a scorned person wishes for is peace and quiet, which—he told Madame Alexis, tiptoeing out—partly explained Richard M. Nixon as well as Medea.

When he was a long way down Splendor the rain fell like a weight of ice, as though winter-girt Laputa had finally crashed to earth. He pushed through the mass, frozen and blinded, back to his door, for he had left without a coat or, as was his practice when prowling nocturnally, without money or identification or keys. He had left the door on the latch and stumbling in was made nervous by the impression that it had been open before he pushed it. His first thought, overriding frustration and rage at the weather, was of Madame Alexis. He ran to the room where he had left her with punishing thoughts—Medea and her fire garments. No warm lump beneath the covers, no darling girl. She was gone.

Aware of the vice of panic, he took a mac, and a flask of brandy, and cigarettes, and a weather-proof lighter. He pulled on boots and a leather hat and hung a flashlight by a loop of chain to his wrist.

Like a wounded nightbird he crept along the streets calling "Baby, baby." The flashlight slit the night's stomach; through the holes he could see the workings of its lean viscera, the various parts striving to digest the paltry diet. He pressed on through the night that was both hallucination and hallucinator, calling "Baby, baby," his feet and voice scrabbling at the dark cover as his hands had done nightly for so many, so few years.

Shadows rose and fell on the street ahead as though cast by some giant tree set in motion by an unfelt wind. There was a flickering interspersed with sudden runnels of light like bright poles laid along the sidewalk, as though chinks were for brief and then longer periods being uncovered, chinks between some other world and this one. A clapping as of rooster wings fanned the dark, and grunts. Something was rooting at the piled-up night as odorous as garbage, snout pushing at the unspeakable.

Just ahead in Kroger's lot there was a dark mass set in relief *against a glow as though a crowd huddled about a fire and from its center, as he drew abreast of the entrance to the parking space, there rose straight up a fountain of a squeal. It was as if the huddlers were spattered by drops of the sound for they drew back and apart. He could see a small fire burning in a mesh trash basket placed at the foot of the flagpole. From the flagpole, swinging by feet attached to the hoisting rope, there hung a body. It was nude, partly eviscerated. One intestine dangled down and was touched by the fire. Fed by burning fat the fire blazed up. In the blaze Omerie saw and recognized (he had seen the face upside down many a time) the Chief of Police, his first conquest in the town. Omerie could have told them that the Chief was no pig; if he was any brute at all, he was a rather tender rabbit, for all his swagger. But it was too late; the fat was in the fire. Would they eat the flesh? he wondered; roast pig for Christmas? and would have passed on, but in a rift cut by his flashlight he saw the small furred body lying to one side on a sodden cardboard box that obviously had been spread out with some care to make a resting place for her. His light was ignored by the crowd as he followed it and picked up the body, which had been crushed but rather neatly so that—a tiny echo of the Chief's fate—a little bit of intestine protruded from the anus and from the mouth the tongue pushed forth traces of blood and foam, most of which had been cleaned away by the rain. The stomach was still warm but the shiny coat was turning dull as he watched.*

Had the Chief gone to the apartment and been followed by Madame Alexis, who favored him above the others who came there? Omerie had called her Fascist and Kraut for this display of allegiance to the State, and would sometimes hide cowering in a closet until she found him and, waggling, turned him over to the Chief, an erotic game which had amused all three of them . . . Or had she left on her own and been found by the Chief, who was returning her to Chadden when he himself was found and attacked? It would not have taken more than one big foot precisely placed to crush her— accident or willful act?

Whichever it was, she had been killed through a faulty connection with Omerie's lust. He placed her inside his coat, holding her bottom with one hand and with the other pressing her muzzle against the base of his neck. Thus had they slept, heart against heart, for nearly seven years. She had always gone to sleep first and patterns are not easily broken. Walking her home, he sang again from "Die Trumpeter von Säckingen" with a certain jubilation. They would be parted only once again, briefly, while—too perfect to be an irony—he went into another room and swallowed, and swallowed.

At the Beaux Arts Bar and Grill a sense of ritual, an innate formality, compelled him to the blue-lit entrance and within. A drink, certainly, surrounded by old lovers, both his and hers, for she had kissed and been caressed by all of them. She had scooped the final lover and he must drink to her audacity, one of her most beguiling qualities. He stood at the bar and turned, one arm pressing her length to his breast, the other hand holding the champagne cocktail.

They were all maimed. There was not a person at any of the tables who was in possession of an unviolated body. As though they were proud of that fact, the ones whose wounds would ordinarily have been concealed by clothing or by other parts of the body had arranged themselves in such a way that what one noticed first about them was the—if it could be termed as such in a place where it was the norm—flaw.

At a table for two a girl sat with one leg extended on the table top and bent long-necked as a swan to the source of her wonder which bloomed like a triflowered amaryllis from her kneecap. Her escort, a young man with glossy brown hair like a pageboy's, lay back in his chair and gazed at the ceiling where slow-turning mirrored mobiles shattered still further his throat. A Byronic man and three girls sat at a banquette, all three with blouses open to the waist, all three displaying similar stigmata of what could be surgical cruelty. A man sat as though pondering, pulling at the upper flap of his right ear so that what would ordinarily lie within the crevice formed by ear and skull could be more readily seen.

Napes were exposed by forward-flung hair of those who appeared to be, like the trees of Portugal, in deep mourning. Garments were worn with cutouts at the points of interest: inner thighs, buttocks, the sexual organs, too, of a group sprawled loosely about a center table made of clear plastic. Prosthetic devices, abandoned for a moment, leaned against walls or reposed in piles nearest their dependents; the limbs which they had clothed were shown, necessarily more brutal because of the inability to control them—were flung, in most instances, across table tops like joints of flaccid meat in butcher shops. Where there were only partial or no limbs, a special effect of lighting made it appear as though there, there were holes in the air with wide black borders like Rouaults, which Omerie imagined was approximate to the sensation of the person involved.

Some—after a time he was tempted to think of them as the less fortunate—were distinguished only through peculiarities of coloring and texture of skins—sometimes both, but even the most bizarrely piebald of these were discriminated against in the arrangement of seating and occupied those tables nearest the outer doors and lavatories.

When his eye had been assaulted to its limits and had begun that protective glazing which allows for healing and is called indifference, his ear was summoned as replacement. It heard the anguish, some of it high-pitched as a dog whistle, and the anger. It heard the retching, and the suction of wounds, and the fluids and gasses seeping from tubes, and the scratch-scratch of fingernails as though asking entry.

How curious, he thought, that he had never before noticed —for these people were—were they not?—the Chadden Cognoscenti, the Regulars. Under his tutelage they had become pacesetters, admired, emulated, condoned in their amusing extravagance. He had picked what he thought were perfect specimens, loathing infirmity, disease, wounds. But, he *thought, as though recalled to good manners, his wound lay within his coat, against his breast. This seemed to him unfair. He opened the coat and gave them time to look. They stared with eyes like dolls', flat and painted; for a curious moment it appeared as though their wounds had been illusory but he did not examine them further to see. He drank his cocktail and left.*

At the carriage house he

PART III
Tasmania—Now

TO WANDA, when she had time for such thoughts, another marvelous thing about the Revolution was that she did not have to go down to that stinking Game Room any more. She had not been down for weeks, since she and Roman became sex partners.

He would not allow the words once used to define such a relationship to be used between them. He said that euphemisms were bourgeois, that they were not lovers or sweethearts, since they did not love each other, and when she suggested "going steady" he had laughed his head off and said "coming steady" was more like it. No, he said; what we do together is f.... He hadn't found out about her dots to which she clung, babyishly, she knew, and she had not found the nerve to consult Geraldine on the matter for she could not imagine herself bringing up the subject of s—— to her friend. Lest she feel like a traitor she would not allow Roman and Geraldine to occupy her mind at the same time.

Wanda and Roman had collided violently backstage following his stupendously unexpected speech, his fable, so full of understanding for the Tasmanians, so antiforeign—or so it had seemed at the time, firing her veins as only kind words do, so that she had rushed back to thank him, to bless him, and before she knew it found herself locked to him by a key of amazing size on a pile of costumes in a not very private corner. Others had reacted the same way—though not, she hoped with all her heart, with the same result—and by the time they found the double edge of the piece they were already radicalized and his little deception did not matter very much. The important thing, of course, and they all agreed, was that the revolution was moving, moving; every way you turned you found people willing to negotiate, make concessions—some of them fairly incredible—because the man, their leader, her lover—shhhhh!—had broken through to them by stating their case in firm, clear, beautiful language. Someone understands you, he had said, and unlike the others, unlike Mrs. October wherever she was, he had proved it. The major preoccupation and exercise following the speech became the interpretation of it, which had been his purpose. The speech had been Xeroxed and distributed and wherever you went you saw people carrying it and quoting from it and arguing its points. A shorter version was printed, one quote to a page, a little booklet, "Quotations from The Romans," which had, because of the Biblical association, caused some comment from the pulpit, but the ministry, too, had been, as Roman said cryptically, shafted, which had a martyred sound but really only meant, obviously, brought around. Not that everyone agreed, by a long shot, as to the meaning of certain passages, but, again from the pulpit, it was pointed out that after centuries of debate the Bible was still open to interpretation, which proved its vitality just as it proved the vitality of Roman's fable.

The churches, in fact, had become open forums for the discussion of the fable, and it was set to music by Omerie Chad and performed—dancers, singers, mimes—in apse and around altar: "And they said to him, Life? And they pointed to the dead man . . ." a cantata, antiwar, extraordinarily moving. Wanda secretly wished that Max Steiner could have set the words, or Wolfgang Korngold, but in spite of Omerie's bumpty-bump music—Glucklike, somebody said, whatever that meant—the cumulative effect was simply tremendous. Nearly everyone agreed.

She hadn't been down to the Game Room for weeks and half expected the dust boogers to come crowding up the stairs, bursting open and flooding through the door, rolling Mama along with them like an old tumbleweed. Just WHAT the Revolution wanted with her basement was none of her business, she told herself firmly, and when explanations tried to crowd through the door of her mind and flood it with knowledge, she simply—as first Mrs. October and then Roman had taught her—turned a mental key, and hooked a mental chain, and propped a mental bar of iron against it for good measure.

Then, as the weeks went by she had to make less and less effort to close knowledge on the other side of the door and eventually she had only to think of the door itself, never mind the locks and chains and bars. And then—nearly, but not quite—she forgot that she had a basement with cages in it.

Not quite, because when her husband came home—every other week end for a while—he still asked questions and she had to concoct some sort of answer. BUGS, she told him; bugs had overrun the place and she had called the exterminator who had sprayed and painted everything in sight and warned her to keep the place closed off for weeks. And when weeks had gone by and her husband came again she told him that the water pipes had burst and flooded the place and toadstools covered the floor down there like a squooshy carpet. And then one day when he was particularly insistent she had given up and said, "Oh, for Christ's sake go see for yourself," and he had gone down and when he came up he went to the bathroom and vomited. He tried to tell her something about the basement but she shut him up by suggesting that perhaps the journeys home were growing arduous for him, and he asked if what she meant was "not safe," and she had voiced the speculation that perhaps he would be more comfortable if he took a hotel room in whatever town he found himself in at the week end. That was some time ago; she hadn't seen him since.

And every single night her Roman Holiday. She thrived but did not fatten. She pinked into the look of virginity, delicious paradox. Like revolution, the further she moved from original premise, the more she resembled it: protective coloration? Organic cunning? Like her body's interior passages, her mind, too, was being stretched, learning a new language under (under! yes!) Roman's tutelage.

Since living with Madame Alexis, Omerie had given up the circuitous methods of seduction once thought necessary on account of his early loss of beauty. Hunger, thirst, the desire or need for a new cravat, once had led him to the most roundabout methods of obtaining service. Each desire or need was viewed in the same furtive light that barely illumined his search for sexuality. Only after his acquisition of the bitch and consequent studies of her tactics did he learn to dispense with euphemism and openly admit hungers and thirsts, and, after her limpid design, to make direct frontal or posteriad attacks. Only after the example of Madame Alexis, let it be stated again, FOR REASONS EVENTUALLY TO BE MADE ABUNDANTLY CLEAR, did he develop into the direct and certainly HARSHLY DRAWN character already partially met in these pages. In the six years since he had known her, however, he had found himself, with all due acknowledgment to his beloved teacher, most frequently ahead in the game in which he had once lagged, often making off with prizes meant by the prizes themselves for slower hunters!

Thus, when he found himself more than sexually attracted to Roman, found himself to his utter amazement in love with that fat near-dwarf, he decided with Madame Alexis's simplicity to go to Roman and tell him of his love.

That Roman was a man as opposed to a masculine object of barter—a man having a mind and being subject to its terrors, some of which like exotic trees were labeled in Greek or Latin —bothered Omerie more than the other thing Roman was said to be—an artist—because Omerie had observed that artists put all of their good instincts—consciences, even—into their art and left nothing whatever over for their daily lives—look at Wagner; look at just about any poet since the term's invention. Revolutionaries, perhaps, were the opposite, setting sometimes splendid diurnal examples with nothing reserved for the long dark hours of supposed creativity when the art object—revolution—was to be forged, which explained the consistent long-range failures in that form of attempt at creation. Explained the slip-ups, glaring CONTRADICTIONS, MONSTROUS EXPOSURES OF MOTIVE.

Omerie had taken Madame Alexis to a vet after he had noticed small patches of bare skin on her haunches where there had been lovely little whorls of hair like penmanship exercises or, as he imagined at other times, like the marks of her completion, the final curlicues of satisfaction on a signature. The doctor had found other evidence to support his suspicion: unpigmented spots on her nose, melanism on her stomach. Low thyroid. Unfeelingly he had said that it was a condition endemic to the breed, especially evident in old dogs. (Precursor of the end—had he said that?)

Madame Alexis had taught Omerie that there was only one unbreakable bond between two creatures, the bond of mortality. It was a lesson he had learned with great reluctance where the two of them were concerned.

Following the visit to the vet, even in the disorientation of his sense of nightly loss, and the darkness, some residue of memory would limit or confine those areas of her body from which he could take the familiar comfort. His hands would fastidiously avoid her stomach (the negroid melanism) and the cushions of her haunches. By day he would gaze (avoiding looking at her skinned nose) safely into her expressive eyes, until the day when he noticed in the left eye a slight cast. A call to the doctor confirmed this as further evidence of age. He began to watch her at her play with a kind of horror, thinking that soon he must wear veils if he was to watch her at all. He stepped up the thyroid pills until her games took on a freneticism as though she were a puppet dog being violently manipulated from above. He left her at home more frequently, going to the Opera House alone, always with a feeling of searching, though for what he did not know. Then one day he looked at Roman and the light appeared to alter around him. It was as though Omerie looked through a rift and saw duration, and could comprehend it, as "the continuous progress of the past which gnaws into the future and which swells it as it advances." An arc, like a rainbow, rested on Roman's head with one foot; the other, in Omerie's mind, rested on Madame Alexis.

Roman was talking to a constipated-looking woman, a genuine celebrity who combined in one frail and rather hairy body the two major artistic inclinations—criticism and cinema direction—accorded recognition by both Establishment and Underground. It was she who had clarified the New Art as accidental by nature, as her discovery of its nature had been accidental: her first film had been a study of a sort of fragmented Lenny Bruce type—actually fragmented, for the character was broken into organs and brain components, which were played by a company of actors representing mouth, anus, penis, cerebellum, brain stem, and so forth. The dialog was a series of unconnected one-liners which she had hopefully written over the years but had found no home for. The effect was to be definitely new and, she was confident, hilarious. But during the rushes people sighed and fell into glooms and slept, and it was then she realized, as she said quite humbly, that she was in truth filming the first of the White Tragedies.

In a famous essay she had presented to the world the proposition that intention had nothing whatever to do with the artistic process or with the end result, which meant that the artist was at last free to create without the bourgeois hindrance of purpose or of predefinition, to himself or others, of his aims. Any artist—she argued, though no one answered her back—to deserve the name was automatically on the side he should be on, so that he was freed as well from such considerations as having to prove the worthiness of his ideology before his effort could be appraised. She submitted that a person whose work *was* appraised—let the public take it on faith and recognize therein their own freedom—was an artist. Consequently all that remained was for the critic to indicate to the public what its response should be. She told them: see how expansive is freedom, touching all with its proliferous rings once the stone is cast away and has sunk! For critics, too, are freed of the one-time necessity of making moral assessment, or of trying to reconcile 'bad' artist with his 'good' art. Artists, she reiterated, are now morally unassailable, and art, being accidental, is by virtue of the definition forever placed beyond the reach of such as 'good' and 'evil,' those terms being replaced by 'funny' and 'sad,' which have no moral connotation, and, further, are eminently better suited to the new innocent society of Kids.

She had been well-known before the essay, but that work had raised her to a pinnacle of fame, and even though her movies were massively avoided, she was placed by the public in a seat just a millimeter below Roman's throne and obeisance was paid her as his rightful consort. Together they had been the subject of a book, *The Kakistocracy*, whose author had drawn parallels between their reign and the disastrously revised American idea of government, from Town Hall to White House, which had begun to focus in the late Sixties; but as the book had not been 'appraised' by any of the TV critics it had gone unbought and mainly unread.

Omerie had read the book between cruise trips to the men's room of the Forty-second Street Library in New York. It had made enough of an impression for him to recall, looking at the supreme confidence and obvious aptness of the woman at Roman's side, what the author had said about her discovery of the nature of art: "Thus can the famous inept turn their failures into successes by appending fashionable labels, or by the invention of labels destined, because of the fame of the inventors, to become fashionable." Omerie once had whispered the words into the ear of their subject at a time of crisis, effecting a grippingly powerful reaction. He was not certain that they would serve his current purpose and sought new methods of attack. (The woman had a habit of clawing quotation marks out of the air to surround what she was saying; watching her doing this as she stood before Roman, it seemed to Omerie that she was a little hungry squirrel begging Roman for some nuts.)

In *The Kakistocracy*, the author had written about the

snugness of the literary world, a place of predictable responses and receptions which he termed "placental," where such as Roman and the lady could not possibly develop to a further stage because, being possessed of full infancy, the next step would be ejection from the womb, which, if they were to be true to the new dicta, should be accidental. No birth could be called accidental, he wrote, depending as it did upon the fullest—however involuntary—collaboration between muscles and organs (and bodies politic). No baby, metaphorical or not, falls out of the womb; and if it is taken by Caesarian section (or revolution) the highest order of premeditation and determination and skill are required. Thus—the author maintained—they could not be, for all their avowals, on the side of change, for they had sewn themselves into a place where exposure would mean death by their own terminology, so that whatever they wrote or said on the subject of revolution or mere social reform must be taken as hyperbole, concealing their desperate need to maintain the status quo (their own permanent ascendancy) . . . Serious charges, indeed, largely unnoted.

Roman turned and Omerie saw him as separated from himself and others by a membranous substance; how was he to tell Roman of his love? Any room that one had to cross to declare love was the widest room in the world; membranes were not needed to make the journey arduous. He saw himself shouting into one end of a Fallopian tube; then it was as though Roman were contained within the convoluted ear of a deaf old lady.

"How does it feel to be entirely safe?" Omerie asked the famous woman, having somehow made the trip in full possession of limbs and faculties.

"I'm utterly terrified; safety has always terrified me," she said, then amended that to ". . . has always made me feel so unprotected," bending her head as though listening for the vibrations of epigram; belatedly she suspected irony and sought to freeze it to the stage where metal is easily shattered. The refrigerating eyes were famous, shaped, as someone had said, like amoebae with the pseudopodia contracted. They were certainly hostile to their environment, for the rest of the face twitched as though amusement were a necessary throes, but the eyes recognized neither the paroxysm nor the need for it.

She was so clearly striving to place him as someone previously met and forgotten—for why else would he be here, assuming the right to question her?—that Omerie was tempted to skip the game and tell her outright, naming the location of their one meeting whose very special connotation for that occasion was known only to the two of them.

But she was a person who, like Roman and like Omerie, had willfully calibrated each cog and cam of her mechanism to withstand the shock of direct attack, the stance that was once referred to as 'cool.' Could he afford to expend his ammunition without being assured of a kill? Love, he thought, takes away your powder and your balls; you are left with one charge to dispatch a rival.

He did not know how permanent he meant the dispatchment to be, only that her glamor should be tarnished for Roman, tarnished by Omerie, for he believed that that was the one thing Roman himself had been unable to do, over years of subtly trying to depose her without appearing to do so.

He engaged the woman's eyes with a friendly glance and said, "Flease plush by fushing put fedal."

"Oh," she said, "so it's you. You damn near ruptured me, you know. I couldn't make decent kaka for a week afterward," and proceeded with feigned rue, to Roman's delight, to expend Omerie's worthless ammunition.

"When I was writing *The Homosexual Mystique*—over your nearly dead body, darling; do you still hate the critters?—I cruised the subways one night—male drag, of course, looked fetching if I do say so, little sailor suit and boobs tied down. Hell, I thought, a little harmless blowing in exchange for mines of secrets, but this chap, my dear, bent me over a urinal and before I could say whoops-a-daisy, it was *ipso facto, Catamitus sum!* Accustomed as I am to reading at ALL times—have you forgiven me that?—I cast about for some immortal graffiti but was bent too low for that, could find only that confounded sign: PLEASE FLUSH BY PUSHING FOOT PEDAL, which—inversion, see?—I read over and over and OVER, aloud of course: FLEASE PLUSH BY FUSHING PUT FEDAL." Under Roman's shouts of laughter she smiled rather tenderly at Omerie and said quietly, "Next time—perhaps—better luck."

It had been unexpected, soon over, and not necessary after the words "do you still hate the critters?" a possibility that had not occurred to Omerie. Swollen with Tasmanian success, deluded by the legend of Unisex, which Roman crammed down them as Minister of Sexual Affairs, and in the extremity of his need to replace Madame Alexis before further tragedy could strike, Omerie had left himself wide as a gate to the humiliation and rage that possessed him, for not only was he made a fool of but the deliberateness of his act of buggery, his contempt, his knowledge of what and who she was and his bringing her low by possessing her over a urinal had been relegated to a place of no importance to Roman by the woman's amused and amusing confession. Roman's so carefully guarded expression of slight contempt advised Omerie that he was seen as the dupe of the piece, as having imagined himself to be buggering a sailor. Further—if there was anything beyond, now—any pass that Omerie might make henceforth would be assessed as the greatest possible threat, for he was firmly placed in Roman's thinking and fears as that most dreaded specimen, the aggressive pederast.

So quickly done, new love. Now all was consequence.

Omerie stepped behind a piece of machinery in the basement, the one responsible for the complexity of trapdoors, and when it whirred and rumbled he surmised that Roman was taking the visitor back to the stage by the Mephistophelian route. He envisioned them rising eerily from the stage floor, heads poking up like swift-growing flowers of evil. Dimly he heard their movements on the stage, a ratlike scratching. In his mind the music of *Faust* alternated with and was finally overcome by the "Horst Wessel." Fluidly personalities interchanged—the dead, the living, the imaginary: Roman was Hitler and Hitler was Omerie and Omerie was Roman, the two small men seeming to be but reminiscences of the idea that had always crouched within the tall crewcut man who became the idea and crouched behind the now quiet machinery. The stage was quiet, too; the rats had deserted.

Omerie took the small powerful flashlight from his pocket, a quite flat object half the size of a cigarette case that threw a bright white beam two hundred yards. (Once at evening exercises when the lights in the Opera House had failed, this same flashlight had lit the proceedings, carving figures from the stage's darkness as sharply as a fine chisel.) At last he found it, the small narrow door concealing the narrow private elevator that he had deduced had to be here. There had been a rumor of a private apartment tucked high above the flies, kept for Mrs. October's personal and very private use, but the long afternoon's search had uncovered no secret stairway; therefore there had to be an elevator from the basement, no stops between basement and penthouse.

The penthouse was dusty, with a certain stench, but not the stench of sleep. Nor of humans. It was as void of the smell of life as a Mexican tomb in which he had spent nearly a whole day, in an effort to define for himself how—for it was an immense tomb—so much residue of life in bones and mortal dust could leave no evidence for the senses of the living. The Little Brother of death had to be aired from rooms each day, so vital was it, so redolent of its kin; but the abode of Big Brother contained not a memory for the nose where nostalgia should have abounded. It was nothing more than a file room for volumes gone to dust or burnt.

But in a trunk in Mrs. October's study which was redolent of nothing, he found volume upon volume, labeled REVOLUTION; labeled PROJECTIONS; labeled PUZZLES(?). He opened a volume of PUZZLES(?), read there: (her peculiarly italic hand unmistakable) *And since death must be the Lucina of Life: Lucina—Goddess of childbirth; therefore: and since death must be the beginning of life. Diuturnitas—longlasting; perhaps, too, play on diurnal: to endure in daily existence is dream and folly (as Lucina may also apply to light and reason). What Browne meant is what Madame Alexis must teach Omerie: that mortality is the only unbreakable bond between creatures.*

His close-cropped hair stirred on his head, tried to crest as did his bitch's hackles at the scent of something wild, something other. To find them both there, riven with directive: what Madame Alexis *must teach* Omerie.

He felt that he became the bitch, long-nosed with more than inquisitiveness; long-nosed with cunning as a weapon which could mean longevity. He felt that it was possible to be both wounded and cured by instinct and so become reconciled to the daily seeking of wounds, assaults upon the tender nose, for the cure that lay beyond in knowledge and hindsight.

Looking at his hands, he expected to see the French silk down of his bitch's fur, and her black talons, and was genuinely startled to find it was his own ruinously bitten nails, which he kept gloved as much as possible, that were scrabbling at bindings and looseleaves, not yet settled into the purpose of the hunt.

On a looseleaf that tried to burrow out of sight he read: *The Saxon gutturals that had been excised with the elegant knife of Latinisms were being retransplanted at a great rate with parts from the near-corpse of Yiddish,* which gave him a little frisson entirely human.

Before her disappearance, Mrs. October had been pushing a pet project, which was to attract more Jews to Tasmania. She did not think that Tasmanians should be allowed the smugness of their boast that there was very little anti-Semitism in their town; the reason for that, she told them, was because there were so few Jews. She had found, she said (asking their complicity in her rueful amusement at the 'human condition') that anti-Semitism was a natural, virulent condition carried in the genes of eighty-five percent of non-Jews. Therefore, to immunize required exposure, overexposure, as though by innoculation. The Opera House had rocked with laughter at the ludicrous, rather sexy image of everyone there getting an infusion of Jew. October had let them laugh and laugh, gazing at them with the sneer of Mona Lisa until they stopped out of nervousness.

Omerie had never climbed onto the October bandwagon but kept to the sidelines, watching to see where the parade was really headed. He had always believed that he had incurred her secret enmity. Looking back from the sheet of paper he held, and looking forward, he thought he could see direction, purpose, and something more.

When they had stopped laughing, October said, "For only when one has faced the depths in oneself can one hope to attain the heights." She had gone on to praise their splendid adjustment, among other things, to Negroes and foreigners, holding out Wanda's dream of torture by Negroes as an example of having faced the depths in oneself. October had said, "Now must the same exorcism be accorded the Jews." Roman, as befitted his role, jumped up and said that the way you handled fear, inferiority, and so forth, was to lay it, so he agreed with October that everybody should, the sooner the better, lay a Jew; and the Opera House had resounded with earthy joy.

It was then that something came into focus for Omerie. He had heard the laughter before. The exact laughter. It was precisely the stuff that came in cans that were opened on bad television shows; the greater the degree of poverty of wit, the more cans were opened as though to feed the starving things. He imagined that it had the taste of tin; and was uniform, with, embedded in the middle like the paltry piece of pork in a can of beans, the isolated cackle as though picked up by special mike that set the assemblage off again when the hysteria tried to die of its own taint. In other words, the laughter was planned, merely another illusion. But, when the laughter had finally died, was the Tasmanians' refusal of

October's request also preplanted in their minds? If so, then so was their anti-Semitism. And what about hers?

Looking back and ahead, he saw it as another exercise, one for October alone, entirely personal: their opposition gave her a new game, one involving her moving passion, which was language. He saw the lines about Saxons, Latinisms, Yiddish, as being part of a press release, buried perhaps in the middle of a piece of journalism about the Revolution, about the Tasmanian's archaic concern for the English—no, better still, the Umerican—language. The barely perceivable innuendo of criticism was the bait. Open, violent anti-Semitism was practically ignored since the new rhetoric of black militants which screamed for Jew blood, Jew skin for lampshades, a renaissance of The Final Solution. The conditioned Jewish mind required insidiousness as opposed to the invidious. Someone would notice the article, the faint odor of rottenness in the central paragraph. The Jews would come. Clever Mrs. October, wherever she was.

He found out where she was, or supposed that he did. There was a drawing of cages and looking out between the bars of adjacent cells, Mrs. October, Aurelie Angelique, and the rest of the staff. But he had seen Aurelie Angelique only that morning. Something had gone awry, apparently; it pleased him to think that token martyrdom might be for many fewer than October had planned, for he had seen her staff, too—all the bruiselike men with muscles as morbid as edema had been shifting properties on the stage when he talked to Roman, while his heart cracked like an improperly fired vessel. Which meant that, alone, somewhere, there was a cage with October in it. Obvious (political) reasons to one side, he did not dwell on why she would encage herself; he had done so many a time, was even now banging at the bars of the latest one. Out, out, he said without choler or frenzy, for he had her.

He opened a volume of Projections. As he leafed through, familiar names cleared the surface of murky prose like fish jumping. Seeing his name and a number—"Projection 5:

Omerie"—he settled down to read, assuring himself that he was as coolly detached as Flora in *Cold Comfort Farm*.

It was a trip back to the womb to find himself unformed, then to watch the formation, molecule by molecule, and to be present at the inspiration to have him be queer, then not just queer but to be haunted by age and death—not, he wished to assure her, exclusively homosexual fears. He discovered the onset of deeper depravities, for it was plain they were intended to be depravities and not simple variations. Men paid women and were thought sporting; a man, himself, paid a man and was depraved. Similarly, nymphophiles (nympholepts?) were only slightly rakish modern heroes of novels, but a pederast was still punishable by death. Overall, though, he was amused by her presumption and occasional accuracy. He read her self-congratulations for having a homosexual in her Revolution because *the greater the danger, the fiercer the comedy. Commendable, say I, having danced on a number of graves. Who, oh who, will dance on mine? Omerie—in retaliation?* His Flora-smile allowed grimness passage at her admission to being a queer-baiting bitch, and the recurrence of the directive: *Change it, before the time comes. Change it.* But the time had come. It was not only Aunt Ada Doom who saw something in the woodshed.

He read on a bit bored at the diminuendo of his theme, skipping a lot though increasingly aware of a gathering darkness in the pages, clusters of words like shadows in corners. *The midnight of December 24th drew up like a black coach* and his name, and his rejection by a lover! He knew a tainted quickening of senses only experienced when cruising the most dangerous traplike places. Subway, exits locked and barred: prison of words. Flora forgotten. He turned back the leaves to discover what number he wore in the word-prison. None. All Projections but this one wore numbers. December 24th; it was now the 20th. He saw plainly before he read on that this was meant to be not Projection, not invention—which need not have life—but Creation.

Some of it, for she was more than clever, was too close for

amusement or even fear, but some was absurd, such as trying to explain his homosexuality through an incestuous father, which revealed the queer-baiter still lurking despite her efforts; to explain sex with trite psychological causalities was passé; he was homosexual because he liked men. And, really, *Die Trumpeter von Säckingen* for his leitmotiv! What a bitch!

Laughing, he read on, found himself on the rainy street searching for Madame Alexis (laughter dies), watched the night eating itself, found the Chief's eviscerated body, then hers, the tiny bowel protruding, the foamy tongue. By the end, he saw with something like amazement that October had not even meant to 'radicalize' him. He had been invented by her to commit suicide, a purposeless death, because he could not find one person who was affected by it. He had been made a slightly sinister figure of fun, given a sentimental death (implied) and forgotten. *At the carriage house he* . . . Possibly that was when she had been seized and jailed. Or had she magnanimously given him a way out, after taking from him both a lover and his darling? One thing that she had done was not at all ambiguous: she had attempted the ultimate act of giving life and then taking it away.

Tracing his history carefully through the volumes for clues, he discovered what was in store for all of them. Roman was in for farce, farce, and more farce, until no shred of dignity would be allowed to cling to a reputation perhaps not as hard-won as some but nevertheless earned. Put on a pike, in effect—poor stripped thing with his fat little body and its appendage, as in Oscar Wilde's translation of "Petronius," so big that he seemed an appendage of it—and set beyond the city walls to be gaped at by outsiders. October's nihilism, egotism, cynicism were all there, waiting to be acted upon. But such was the thing called "charisma" that Omerie Chad, new radical, did not trust the public eye to see through its mists to the heart. October was a charismatic "nebula composing tragedies," was she? It smacked of determinism. Very well; there could be a couple of nebulae. DEAR people, he thought, and for once there was no background clack: cock,

cock, cock, at thoughts of the "masses" (always male; females came in messes; his new altruism could not change that).

He took the pages pertaining to the moon denouement and put them in his pocket. So newly a rejected suitor, he could not, with the world in his pocket, decide whether or not to save Roman from that enforced trip through the ether to a crash landing on the Plaza of Inevitability (as October had undoubtedly ironically labeled his landing site). If what he was doing was engaging in acts of creation, too, then let that particular one depend upon fortuities: let it be accidental art. Still, for fun, knowing the time for its realization was past, he wrote a shorthand scenario for the first meeting in Tasmania between Roman and Darthy Redstone, old Brooklyn classmates: EXUBERANT MEETING OF TWO BROOKLYN KIDS WHO'VE MADE IT: AT PLANE, ALL TASMANIA WATCHING. EMBRACE. ROMAN'S WIG CATCHES ON REDSTONE'S BRACELET. LUDICROUS HALF-CARRY TO AUTOMOBILE, REDSTONE RIDING ROMAN'S HIP LIKE A BABY, ROMAN'S KNEES BUCKLING—DOUBLE PRATFALL? ROLLING ABOUT? ROMAN'S EXHORTATIONS GROWING FROM WHISPER TO MUTTER TO STRANGULATED SQUEAL? TRIUMPHAL RIDE INTO CITY, REDSTONE'S WRIST ATTACHED TO ROMAN'S HEAD. When his giggles had subsided he grew stern. Robed in scarlet, mitred, he rejected October's Decretals. Majestically (his forte), in poor penmanship (ditto) and hastily indifferent prose, he wrote a new Projection to replace his and Madame Alexis's and the Chief's deaths; and another to settle certain other hash, which he placed (places) at the end of the volumes. And this explanation of matters to this point. Chalk one up for Mother.

Projection 98—Episode 1,007

Omerie Chad was awakened in the morning by Madame Alexis who sat by his side and licked the exposed side of his face. It was always the same side, the left side, for he slept with his right cheek cradled in his right hand, like a child. The revelation came suddenly and gently: the left side of his face looked a good ten years younger than the right side; the left side had been licked matutinally by Madame Alexis for five months; this represented for Omerie youth regained at the rate of minus two years per month. With some difficulty, Omerie taught himself to sleep with his head pillowed on his left hand, exposing the right side of his face to Madame Alexis's youthening saliva. Within five months his face had, so to speak, caught up with itself.

Experimenting further, he encouraged her to lick his body by smearing himself all over with raw liver, with the result that youthfulness was accelerated at the rate of minus four years per month when the acts of smearing and licking were performed thrice daily. When Omerie was refused entrance to an Adults Only movie he believed that what he had believed was at last believable. And thus was born his chain of Caneteria with its unique feature of clients who paid to be licked by dachshunds and dachshund owners who paid to have their dogs go in and lick the clients, for it was discovered that dogs who licked age in tandem with liver were sprier and flea-resistant, and eventually it was found that the old ratio of 7–1 was reduced in those lickers who licked every day to approximately 2–1, and in those lickers who licked thrice daily to 1–1; so that "grow old along with me" was, for those who had dreaded the too-rapid aging of their canine loves, changed to "stay simply forever young with me, darling."

But Omerie had been too long a mere local celebrity, which was really like being, among a colony of moles, a mole with one eye: he could see as well as sense the futility of their activities in the ugliness of their surroundings; they couldn't see him at all, so that he was more anonymous than they; being 'sensed' was horrible, like the blind men describing the elephant; he, the elephant, with each description of himself based on one section of his anatomy, became less and less knowable, less describable, his total alienation multiplied by the number of descriptions of himself. As the one local celebrity, before Mrs. October & Co., he had been described almost out of existence. He had an overwhelming desire to be seen in one shape and large enough to cut through the most severe myopia. With the world, the future actually in his pocket, he resolved to become a cinema star, the new version (to replace Barbra) of the Colossus. And so he decreed.

"The story of Omerie Chad and his Caneteria was made into a smashing movie starring Omerie Chad and Madame Alexis; it was directed by Peter Glenville for Gainsborough Pictures in Ealing (look up proper location). And everyone lived minkily and had whatever they wanted whenever they wanted it."

"Bucky's weariness knew no bounds," was the way he heard it. In their sweetness and sympathy and understanding the words had to be Mrs. October's, wherever she was speaking from, and Bucky sat down, in the raw cold, on a piece of the finished foundation and listened as the story unfolded.

"Bucky had worked so hard on the monument that he had lost track of time. He had not seen his sister Wanda in what could have been months, as far as he could tell. He had not been to the Opera House, the place where people said you had to go to know what time it was, and his friend Mrs. October had apparently deserted him. Still, he had worked on, doing what was asked of him, and one evening at quitting time he noticed that the foundation was all complete, and the next morning on his way to work he had been surprised to hear people talking about its being Christmas Eve. Now, Bucky had always had a special feeling about eves of things, much more than for the days themselves. On eves, great surprises were still in store, but on the days all secrets were out in the open; it was a matter, then, of deciding if you were disappointed or pleased. That was why Bucky liked working on the monument but dreaded the day when it would be completed. With Mrs. October away, he felt sometimes like a team which had left its cheerleaders at home; even if they won the pennant, who, with joyful noise, would show them what all the work had been for? Or it was like a child opening presents on Christmas morning: without any family to say, "Ohhhhhh, look what Bucky got! It's TIDDLEYWINKS!" how was the child to know WHAT it was he had got, and waited all year long for? He had looked at the package in the closet and wondered and hoped that it wouldn't be another pair of knickerbockers and long hairy stockings, but if it finally turned out to be just that, having family to exclaim and talk about how warm he would be could make it all right. In other words, Christmas Eve was for kids but Christmas Day was for grownups; anticipation for kids, explanation and cajolery for grownups.

"But what would Bucky do when the final piece had been put to the puzzle and the monument stood revealed, if Mrs. October was not there to cheer him and to tell him what it was he was looking at? He had trusted her and the plans she gave him but the longer she stayed away the more he wondered and the more he dreaded. This dread was hardly lightened by people who occasionally came by and spoke of changes in the town, hinted at the Revolution's having switched hands, and—though he would not really believe he had heard such a thing—implied that what he was building, with his bricks and mortar, was the wall around what was to become a mass grave for dissenters. They would say, "Look at Bucky, completely out of it. Boy, if ignorance was bliss . . . !" And once a group of people he had not known had stayed for a long time talking in voices that rose and fell with agitation about the changes in official policy since Everyman, which they said was officialese for No Man, had taken the reins of government which, they said, had grown to his hands so that they could not be shaken loose. They had talked about Bucky as if he did not exist as someone with eyes and ears, saying that he thought he was doing one thing but was really doing another. They called him a tool, and other things. When he did not look at them nor ask them what they meant, they said that he was the silent majority. Half the time, as the weather got colder, he believed that he was imagining the people who came and talked around and at him, thought it was part of being lightheaded with weariness and cold. But then he had laid the final brick and swiped the final swipe with his trowel.

"And then, this morning, plaques; brass plaques to be set at designated places according to the instructions that came with the plaques which were delivered at his door this morning. And with them, a revival of his dread. Monuments always had plaques, of course, but these were blank which was worse than tombstones graven with a person's name and the year of their birth, and smoothness where their death would be. At least you knew who the tombstone was meant for—you knew it wasn't you (unless the name on the stone was yours, and Bucky did not know how anybody could face that kind of daily reminder; he thought that he couldn't). Blankness was a fearful condition, making you want to rush in and cover it with something, anything, so that in your haste you might put there the wrong thing . . . the name of a loved one, or a dirty picture, or your own name. Bucky admitted to a nearly overwhelming need to write on the plaques, and following the need was the substance of what he wanted to write: MRS. OCTOBER WAS HERE. WAS. He wanted to weep over that word. WAS was a closed door bolted and barred. But would he trust Mrs. October if she told him that it was all right to engrave it there? If she promised him that there was and is always another door marked IS?"

The story was finished. He found the little engraving tool in his hand, the tool of the ages, the tongue of Sinai. 'To set down' was an imperative, the command to his fingers he had felt in all of his life only at those times when he was writing his letters to Mrs. October; a corollary to the command had been to set down the truth as near as he was able, leaving out the influence of his wishes to alter some of what he wrote by making it more palatable. If the truth was really true, she had written to him, it was more important than 'palatable'; it was 'moral.' He felt in the cup of his writing hand, now, whole words, the rightness of their bulk; in his hand was the intelligence that to leave out letters, to alter, to make WAS into IS, would be to lie. Mrs. was MRS., not Mr., and October was OCTOBER; they were conditions and the conditions were the only truth, and so he set them down, laboring all morning at condition #1. Going from plaque to plaque—there were four to be set at intervals along the wall—he inscribed her primary title: MRS. His writing was the continuation of the story in his head—MRS.: a long story, the story of her life beginning with being born female. MRS. was the outline into which the girl baby was supposed to grow until it fit her like a skin.

He received impressions of a small perfect world growing smaller and less perfect as the sense of what lay outside it grew apace with the child inside it. A pony that the child rode (someone at the bridle, leading) became more than a pony as the little procession passed other children on foot. Food (a hand holding the spoon, a voice saying something reassuring) became like a question when, looking out a window, the feeding child saw another eating mud. Each plaque was like a stage of the child's growth from babyhood to young person to young adult to adult and the stories corresponded, comprised of contradictory images of self and other, with self finally (as the last MRS. was completed) bent upon becoming, or knowing what it was like to be, other.

Bucky did not doubt the sincerity of what he felt and heard; he was as secure in the rightness of his belief as he was when he listened to the President of the country speak to him from the TV screen. Further, it was as though an unsuspected sensory organ had been discovered to him because he understood viscerally much of what he experienced; it was not taken purely on faith, nor, as in the time since her arrival, was it pure mystery to be so inwardly instructed and directed, because when he had completed the set of plaques with their first word he told himself what he had learned: he felt why Mrs. October had the need to bring about change in the world she lived in. He had seen less fortunate people all his life and felt sorry for them but it had not occurred to him that he could step out of his own condition into theirs and change both; Mrs. October had said that it was possible and was doing it.

If any part of him had doubted her motives, because of what strangers said in his hearing, or because of some interior weakness, the doubt had been done away with for good. He believed that a person who wanted to help other people was as far above reproach as you could get; it was what he believed about his country; with him, it was not a case of country right or wrong, but of country right because it was based on the premise of helping other countries, and if the helping sometimes led to being in other countries with guns and men then he went right on believing that his country and his President knew best. It had never occurred to him to wonder what he would do if he found out that his country was wrong, but because of the dread he had had over the monument, and the doubts put in back of his mind (he acknowledged them now, in safety) by people standing around saying bad things, he knew how he would have reacted to Mrs. October turning out to be a liar, and it was the same thing as finding out his country was: he would have wanted to die; maybe, to kill—though the theoretical was making him nervous.

He thought about America and Mrs. October together, their similarities. The mind that she had lent him all morning had been filled with flashing rivers and orchards in bloom; with hayfields and dovecots; her story of growing up had been enacted before the backdrop of unspoiled country. THEY said America was polluted from the clouds down to the river bottoms; THEY said that Mrs. October had had him build a monument that was really a mass grave of some kind. THEY were liars.

In the afternoon he went back to work, eager for the continuation of the story. As he worked on the final 'O' of OCTO it was as though he were back in school trying to get it through his head about meter, feet, syllables. He heard but was confused by her when she said that octo meant eight

185

syllables, and that MRS. OCTOBER WAS HERE had only seven and what did he think the eighth syllable—to complete the prophecy—should be? She suggested: how about 'fin'? This, she said, is the way it would look:

MRS. OCTOBER WAS HERE

Fin.

He could not see any sense in the fishy word. In his head they argued. She distracted him with tales and images, then led back to the bone of contention. She gave him an image that was supposed, somehow, to illustrate 'fin.' It was his decided impression that she gave it unwillingly, that it was drawn from her, that it was a central thing. It was of an old man in carpet slippers shuffling along a city street and entering a building and registering himself: Henri Bergson, Jew. There was such pain for Mrs. October around the episode that Bucky shared in it, but then, unable to share in its meaning, humiliated and with a remembrance of bereavement—it seemed like remembrance but seemed also to lie ahead—Bucky left the four-plaqued monument early and went home and got in bed and fell into a hot-cold sleep.

Mrs. Hackett wanted a Christmas tree. Her dolls wanted a Christmas tree. The house had always had a Christmas tree, so tall that the star brushed the ceiling, with real candles that Papa would light for an hour each night of the twelve. The curtains were always pulled wide so that passers-by could look in and see the tree, and when Belle and Mama and Papa were themselves passers-by, they could look in the houses all up and down Marvel and see the other beautiful trees. And carolers sang and sleigh bells tinkled and all Tasmania was a festival to the memory of the Babe. But now they were telling her that she could not have a tree. The candles would be dangerous, they said, and when she agreed with them and said she would not have candles, they thought up other excuses.

On Christmas Eve not a wreath, not a sprig of holly showed in the entire city. She made sure of that by dressing in her prettiest frock and walking up and down every street in Tasmania, hoping against hope to see one glimmer of cheer. Night drew in and still she searched.

Finally, among the shops and press of people—a lot of them carrying sticks with signs on them—just as the first flakes of snow fell, she found the color she sought. It was a bookstore, cosily lighted, an impression of firelight behind the glass, behind the snow. Shelves and tables of books danced, caught like jewels, so bright-jacketed were they, in the rivulets of condensation on the pane. Mrs. Hackett smiled with glee at the thought of treasures old and new—a splendid-looking new *Wind in the Willows* in the window display, which of course would be an old delight—even a thought enfeebled, for Toad was becoming the least bit tiresome; or, for she was, now that she was growing up, taking a greater interest in the real world, she hoped to find a book of geography with gay maps and descriptions of—as she had learned to say it—life-styles of creatures not quite so unlike herself as Beaver et al. Yes, that was it, "armchair travel," as Papa would say; a nice fire and getting to know someone in a country beyond the hills, the sea. Grass huts on stilts beside a teeming river in a country where snow never fell at all. "Where the wind don't blow and the snow don't go," as her friend AA said, though the only place without wind that anybody human had ever seen and could prove it was the moon. The crowd picked her thought right out of the air: "Moon, moon, moon," they chanted.

Smiling at them, patting her pocketbook where the quarters and dimes, nickels and some found silver dollars were, she went through the shouting crowd into the deliciously warm store nodding in case the clerks were friends of her parents. Right away she found just the book—seek and ye shall find!, bound in sun colors with the picture of a solemn native on the back cover. ALABAMA BLACK BOY. The sound was like drums.

She opened it, read: "With my guts, my dick, my bull balls, I hated them, all of them, the white motherf....." Her gaze wandered to another stack of burnished dust covers as she absently placed the native account back on the table, her mind feeling somewhat glazed, like a cake. Here was another, a drawing, this time, of a boy with curls in front of his ears and a foreign-looking hat; he seemed cold, a somber little boy from a mountainous place. Distantly, as though her hand were severed from her mind by the sharp rise in the noise from the street, she took up the volume and opened it carefully.

"More than the cockroaches, more than hunger, more than the congenital stupidity of—to my private anguishing certainty despite the tenderness of my feelings for (even when I chose to think of her by a more suitable name than ((my father having once been pushed, in the old country, into a pile of cowshit by a girl named Betty)) Betty) Betty—Betty; and more than, negating the salty saliva in my mouth when I saw her brought on by proximity to (for spit is spit and my spittle ran for Betty) Betty—Yahweh, my real enemy, our real enemies, my constipated father's real sometimes enema was were was the goyim, for more than the unutterable true name of God . . ." Mrs. Hackett was glad to find the Name, the first word she had so far understood, and it seemed to take her by the hand and lead her on—". . . was it forbidden to say the name of my shiksa darling (cunt tongue hard as razor sound of her) in the house of my parents, and the houses of their parents, anywhere, anywhere at all except in the precarious privacy (my mother's diaphragm stuffed in my mouth to mask the sound) of the toilet."

She put the book back, not at all carefully. In fact, she slapped it smartly down to demonstrate disapproval in case anyone was watching or listening. Mama had instilled in her that only the most vulgar possible of all people said "toilet" for water closet. Sometimes, if one was poor but genteel, one had instead an earth closet; but that word she had just read was not permissible unless one spelled and pronounced it in French, "toilette," where it meant washing your face and putting on cologne.

She wandered—the store practically hers, with the clerks pressed against the front pane staring out and whispering, occasionally exclaiming—and sampled the wares, sometimes glazing her mind, until she wound up at a booktable that proclaimed itself by a sign to contain books suitable for "teens." She did not know her age exactly but believed herself on comfortable territory. She had been nine quite some time ago, it seemed to her, but was not sure; still, from nine to "teens" was not such a long distance and she imagined that she must nearly have covered it by now.

She selected a book with a little girl wearing trousers on its cover, a hurdle easily gotten over for she was becoming immune to surprises. Still, she opened it somewhat warily. Inside, in a nicely drawn and colored picture, there was the same little girl. Mrs. Hackett found this reassuring. She had been really amazed at the changes that took place, in all the other books, the moment the covers were opened. Over and over she had been reminded of Pandora's box, so prettily painted and carved, hiding so many stinging things. The little native boy suddenly hating everyone; the boy with the curls writing such words as "toilet;" the book written by a golden-haired pointy-faced girl that said on the jacket: "A tender haunting story of love and devotion," that began with the narrator throwing up on a visitor's stomach, the language far worse than the deed: "As soon as he came I lifted my head and puked on his belly." Making an effort, because of the girl's heart-face and lovely hair, Mrs. Hackett had arranged to see the following: a very sick girl lying on a hospital bed; she was recovering from something dreadful—diphtheria, the scourge of Tasmania—and was simply not in control, gallant though she was, so that when her father came in and stood by the bed she raised her bedewed head to smile at him and *unable to help herself* she vomited and some of it got on his waistcoat. "Puked" and "belly" could not be incorporated into the gallant picture and so she glazed them over.

But here at last was a book that had not changed at all. Here was the same little girl reassuringly on the very first page, same costume, same wide-eyed expression, pointing to another bigger girl who wore earrings and some lip rouge; doubtless the little sister would have some roguishly edifying thing—a little moral—to say about the cosmetics. Under the picture were the words, in childish printing: "This is my queer brother. Since Jen and Dave, our sometime parents, got their divorce, he dresses this way and smokes a lot of grass."

Mrs. Hackett sighed over the divorce, giggled at the idea of smoking grass; a queer brother, indeed. Still, it was a story about children who could be her own age and there was some comfort in that, and she paid for the book willingly in spite of the shocking price. She had to tug and tug at a lady clerk to get service, and the woman then tried to detain her, asking her to wait—"at least," she said, "until I can call Marie Louise," not knowing how poor a prospect that was to Mrs. Hackett, and following her to the door with words altogether meaningless: "danger," "riot," "moonman," and other such.

Mrs. Hackett pushed through the bodies and went home, glad to be away from the noise, glad to have a new picture book, but her voile dress was ruined, draggled with mud and snow, and her slippers were worn through to the numbed soles of her feet. She went to bed the way she was, too worn out to undress, book and prospect of fireside forgotten.

Periodically throughout the loud night she awoke to see her parents in the room with her. It seemed to her that her room was a chessboard and Papa and Mama the king and queen. Who was moving them (their defenses long captured) she could not tell but they would have been placed differently on the board each time she looked. It was clear to her that they were trying to get to her bedside but the players used strategems, Belle thought, that Papa himself, a most scrupulous player, would not have approved of to prolong the game.

"Well, good grief." Wanda, in the doorway, snapping on the light. "Are you dreaming about Santa, hon?" She came and sat on the bed and laid her hand on his brow. "Well, I don't like that a DAMN bit." She went out and clattered in his kitchenette and came back with something hot. "Ovaltine was all I could find. Don't you even have whiskey in the house?" He sipped the Ovaltine, shook his head about the whiskey.

"It's Christmas Eve, Buck. You always come over, remember, now? What happened? I could've put you to bed over there," but she sounded doubtful. "Now I don't know WHAT to do. If you try to go out in the snow you might catch your death."

"Don't worry about me, Wan. I'm not sick or anything."

"YOU say. We'll see what the doctor says." But she made no move. She cleared her throat, said, "The only trouble is, I can't stay, darn it." She gave him a look that seemed to be proud about something. "I'm having a little gathering at my place. A bunch from the Opera House, mainly." She looked rather wildly around, an old habit of hers as though she expected eavesdroppers. "*I* can't help it; I didn't know you were going to come down with something."

"I'm not down with anything," he told her, "except I got tired and knocked off early. I don't need a doctor, though. Look." To set her mind at rest he threw back the covers and tried to bound out of bed. In mid-impulse he stopped and sat on the edge. He wished that they could behave childishly, whispering and guessing as kids did on Christmas Eve about what presents they were going to get. He thought that he had learned one thing for sure that day, and half learned another thing, and it was the half-learning that he wanted to retreat from before the other half came up and joined on. She moved as though to go. He told her just about all he knew, garbling as usual.

"Mrs. October Was Here has got seven feet. Fin is a Jew

named Henry something. The Nazis struck the death blow to intuition except as an occult concept to be treated like a pack of playing cards."

"My God," Wanda said and ran for the telephone. He followed her and gently took the phone from her hand, telling her, "I'm not out of my head. Honest. Something else is in there with me, is all." She stared at him, remembering and understanding.

"Where is she, Bucky? Do you know?" He shook his head, then told her, "Wan, I'd like to go to your party."

She wasn't sure she wanted him to. She put it this way: "Are you sure?"

"Sure. I won't take long. Do I need a shave?"

"You never need a shave." It sounded as though she were casting aspersions. She explained lamely, "I mean, not like Roman. He shaves three times a day." She stopped, wondering how much Bucky had heard. Whatever it was, it did not seem to bother him.

While he showered and changed clothes Wanda tidied up the room, trying to make some sort of amends. It could be a fairly cheerful place, when it was looked after. At one time she had taken care of it for him, coming to clean and straighten twice a week, in the days when she thought Mama was on the scene. She saw that she had "done" for him only out of fear, not out of concern nor from a basic generosity. Tucking things away, picking things up, she discovered in herself a nice feeling for him: the sound of the shower was as warm as the water that was laving him, for it said to her that she and her brother were going to her house on Christmas Eve, together only because they wanted to be; he was sprucing up because he cared to look nice for her friends (and her lover). Bucky was like his room—when clean he could give you a cozy feeling. The room had one orange wall which gave somehow the effect of firelight, and he had some pretty things on his table and placed in his bookshelves—little carvings, wood and ivory, an ornate shaving mug, a curlicued picture frame only about eight inches high but weighty as a stone, with Mama's—no! Mrs. October's!—picture in it. That woman had invaded, or entered—a softer word—their quietest places, Bucky's and hers, changing their altars in a way, for a photo of a dead person was a kind of altar; and, before Roman, which was the way Mrs. October had entered Wanda, her private places had been an altar both to her selfishness and, as Roman had said, to her husband's shortcomings. She had blushed when he explained the intricacies of the word 'shortcomings' when applied to her husband, and she blushed still, thinking about it, but the force of the tide was diminishing. She could imagine a day when she would not blush at all, at anything, would not even flush; with the thought, sorrowfully, she imagined that she could see Geraldine take a backward step . . . receding or recoiling? Then she put her vivid imagination firmly to one side and faced her old friend, woman to woman, and it seemed that Geraldine smiled, perhaps faintly chiding Wanda for prudery (only 'perhaps' now, where once imagination would have said that it was so), perhaps communicating to her that movie stars, however well bred, lived in a world where blushes were passé. Undoubtedly, civilized people, to be that way, had to know most things, have seen a lot, heard even more; civilization was the rug under which they pushed their knowledge to hide it from the unsophisticated, a protective act. She and Bucky were in the process of learning, and learning how to cope with what they knew. Almost, they had not known anything, had not been allowed to learn, because of Mama and her endless euphemisms for the facts of life. What, she wondered, was Mama a euphemism for?

Bucky came back looking shiny, neither from fever nor supernaturally because of some disembodied voice, but shiny clean. Watching him load his pockets with keys and change, wallet and fresh handkerchief, Wanda thought: I could be friends with him. I can be. Even if he was what Marie Louise said he was (she heard Marie Louise sneering, "*Yel*low gloves. *Well*"), it would not, she thought, be any of her business to approve or disapprove. When people used words like 'pervert,' all she could imagine was the boy in high school who had gone around after band practice and sucked the spit out of the horn valves of boys he liked. But, smiling at Bucky, snapping the light off and on as a playful prod to get a wiggle on, she could not think of him doing it with male or female.

Was she calling him a eunuch? No, nothing nasty. She was calling him, probably, innocent. Adam before the apple episode. In his case, as nearly in her own, the apple might never be offered in a way to make him want to take it. Then it would always be the eve of his birth into knowledge, perpetually the eve of the Fall. Silently clucking her tongue she thought that she was beginning to think the way Roman spoke when they lay quietly in the dark—fables and allegories and speculations on the State of Man. She supposed it was only natural, a form of adoration: woman emulating her man.

People were at her house when she and Bucky arrived. Roman was officiating at the bar (basement door securely locked and a drape hung over it). Foreigners and Tasmanians were freely mingling, were sometimes indistinguishable. There were Negroes, there were the Levinskys, the fireplace worked without smoking, Myra Little shrieked in a corner rounded by men, Marie Louise's public works were apparently up for private grabs in a micro-mini skirt, Mama would have died.

Wanda, smiling in her doorway, hostess to the world, holding her brother's arm, said, "Peace, Mama," and so plainly meant it that Bucky gave her a look full of pleasure. Roman had not seen her standing there; she wanted to savor him this way, at home in her house, romantically across the crowd, for a moment alone. She gave Bucky a shove into the room. "Get some whiskey," she said, "in case germs are lurking."

A woman in a sari passed, then a man wearing beads and earrings; then two persons who just happened to be black —all touched her line of vision, forming the bottom of the frame in which Roman was caught, resting at the moment, like a studio still. Mrs. Levinsky waved to the corner of her eye. Would Wanda say to her later, "I think I'm having an affair with a Jewish person"? It was not the love that was in doubt in the affair, but the Jewishness. Others said that he was; he had not said anything. What were the signs? In all the years of automatic anti-Jewishness—and frankly, anti-just-about-everything-else—she had never found out what to look for.

But she had changed, at last, and so had all the people here or they would not be here. To them, differences, race, color, no longer mattered.

On her left a voice lifted in mock-country amusement. It was a Tasmanian voice.

"Canoe, see, comin' out of the mists like and standin' up in it was four or five cunt got up worse than a dog's dinner. There was this niggah bitch with a foot of dusty lookin' hair and what she had on you couldn't say it. Then there was this slanch-eye Jap I reckon with a big old pigtail pullin' her flesh all outa shape; well, you wouldn't want to linger nowhere around her before suppertime. Then come this here I guess you'd say Caucasian, looked white anyways, that was like somethin' that goes boo in the furnace room and makes you drop your shovel; then comes Christ almighty knows what but it needs refrigeratin' BAD."

Wanda recognized the TV commercial he was describing; she rather liked it for a certain surreal quality . . . She was halfway across the room before she realized that a word had been said for which her dots were demanded and she had not reached for them. A small voice asked her: If "cunt" should require dots, what about "niggah" and "Jap"?

Roman introduced her to two young celebrities, his eyes inviting her to make assessment of them and share with him, as he had taught her. By the titles of the works with which they were connected—one was the editor of the new quarterly, *Smegma*; the other had directed the new film, *Snot*—she knew which set of criteria she should use and applied them conscientiously. Roman held many theories in private that would have, as he said, to remain so unless he found a trustworthy, much younger Boswell who would send them out after he was safely dead. He used them mainly as relief from being "on the right side" eternally, which to him meant radical left and still commercial. One of his favorite theories was that true radicals were born, not made, on account of looks so preposterous that they never could have found acceptance in a world all of whose guidelines were named 'normal.' Another was that all true critics suffered from speech impediments. She chose the former, and saw that the young man who had directed *Snot* had been born to direct, or to be connected with, works with such titles. His hair looked as if it had oozed out of him; tiny-eyed, the focus of his face was a big droopy nose that appeared to lack cartilage; the flesh of his nostrils fell pendulous and moist as dewlaps. The other young man bore Roman out by having a face miraculously like a scrotum.

Roman was pleased with her. He had watched her assessment, had drawn her conclusions with her. He gave her a nod. The slight dip of his head was like a tumbler shifting in the lock behind which her sexual juices were stored, releasing them. So did his every move work upon her, forcing her to avoid looking at him for long barren stretches of the day when wet thighs could lead to embarrassment. She avoided him now, with a martini, and then another and another, as she wandered among her guests, who were just beginning to glitter, some of them to twitter. The sari-lady —not the great one with the queenly title who had yet to arrive—was saying, "She is out for blood, which is understandable, once you have seen her. Anybody else's blood must do more for her than her own has done."

"Unkind!" someone pretended to protest.

"It's true I talk about people more or less constantly, almost never kindly. Anyone can find out the flattering things in a minute but it takes time to dig out the filth, and to set traps, and so forth." Wanda was thrilled. Nobody had ever said such glittering things in her house before; the Indian woman, with her high cheekbones, looked to her like Katharine Hepburn in *Philadelphia Story*, but the words were meaner. Ears cocked, martinis flowing through her unimpeded, she weaved to and from the bathroom, listening to her party.

"Easier for a leotard to change it's spots."

"When her friends get preggers she blows up and doesn't go down for a year."

"He has the discretion of a housefly."

"Men, not menses."

"Christ is the whole idea behind cavities."

"Betelgeuse and Aldebaran."

"Datta. Dayadhram. Damyata."

She popped her ears with a great yawn. English returned to the room; she wished it hadn't: Mr. Smegma launched into a mystical, self-important account of a concert that for him finally defined what Rock was about, man. Wanda swayed on the edge of the group, disliking the comedown to the nitty-gritty. Most of his words were strange to her so that she saw rather than heard them. They had the appearance of orthopedic devices, straps and buckles hanging, deformity within. She was repelled and attracted by the open object of fetishism that such language had become. Smegma used the words as though they were somehow sexual adjuncts. Back at the auditorium everyone was turning simultaneously to gaze at a side door, man, just turning and waiting, man. "But nothin' came through, nothin' and nobody, not even a great mother of a spider. But we all kept waitin' . . . That's what Rock *is*, man. Strange."

Strange, yes, the way the self-obsessed little man had taken the glittery edge from her party. Everyone was gloomy, shifting about in near silence.

"Riot!" someone shouted at the door and the company laughed, relieved by the joke. The voice insisted, dragging the moon in, and someone said, to Wanda's satisfaction, "Who's out there to riot? Everybody's here! This *is* the Revolution!" Still, the voice went on beyond the point of humor or taste, insisting RIOT, but was finally squeezed out by the weight of her party's ponderously gathering itself together again and crowding against the walls. Silently Wanda told Smegma, "Now just go away and pick things off yourself. Let my people glitter."

Two men loomed in the doorway as though in answer. Their locked arms were wriggling between them—but no, that dark mass of slow motion between the great black men was the Maharani. Or at least it was her remains engaged in the convolutions of hangover to which the male support lent the approximate appearance of walking. The men advanced one step in unison and the sari-clad body fell aslant them at an angle of 45°, her head in the loosened obscuring hair locked between them at waist level and the rest of her loitering behind in a static chiffon wake. The men paused and stood eyes front. All was motionless. At first there were heard throat-clearings as some of them prepared to sing out what they supposed the tableau to represent—(aside from the obvious; she was immensely pregnant). Then a sort of quiver began, starting with the head clamped between the men so that the coarse hair shook as though trying to shed old molt. The quiver traveled down, slightly agitating the draperies above the waist, setting up a clangor as from fairy bells as it reached and put in motion the jewelry with which she was liberally festooned. When the activity reached the waist, a sort of revving-up was seen, a circular pumping like an enfeebled version of the Royal Canadian Exercises, and by the time it reached the knees it had acquired a kind of jollity and hopefulness. The effort was heartening, really gallant, and paid off not once but twice as the feet shot forward in a nearly accurate sequence of little tripping steps like a sandpiper's. Then her sandals stood demurely between the immense brogans of the unfestive workmen. Because her head was still squeezed between the two waists, her rear end buckled up as though by a sudden frost. She tugged at the coattails of the men and their arms loosened enough to allow her to slide up to her full height, and then tightened again before in her liberty she should fall to the floor.

One step was completed; there were about twenty more to go before she could gain the throne that Roman was even now ironically setting up for her. The guests began to count in unison, a whispered rhythmic sharing in the stages of her ambulation. By the time step five had been completed there was an undeniable cadence at large in the room, and some began to mark it off with finger-snapping and soft applause which grew, by the time she had reached step ten, to an out-and-out revival joyousness, and by the time she gained her throne and was being handed champagne in celebration there were some who had transcended joy and quivered at the gates of ecstasy. To Wanda, whose double vision had doubled yet again, the enthroned figure appeared to have eight arms. Wanda gazed at her in sudden superstitious horror. The woman smiled slowly; her upper lip rose and rose in hitches like a curtain that had draped a monumental sculpture, each hitch revealing new terrors: craters, mossy stretches of undefined character; when at last her teeth stood alone in naked awesomeness, Wanda fell back, afraid.

In falling back, she trod on a toe and in the ensuing apologies and reassurances her terror of the Eastern figure left her. She was aware only of increased electricity in the air. She wished somehow to seize the day and push it into lasting fame. She recalled a movie with Audrey Hepburn (she had seen it a few nights before on TV) in which there had been a remarkable party, people crawling between each other's legs, setting each other on fire, one enormous girl falling on her face, strangers, some of them sinister, arriving and departing. It was awfully vulgar—Wanda's fastidiousness not helping matters when, as people crawled between the legs of other people, she brooded on whether the spraddle-legged ones were clean where it counted—and it was also awfully chic. Surveying her guests through a prismatic haze of drink, she wished that they would go on and deteriorate and do the things that Audrey's bunch had done, instead of, as some of them were doing, playing what looked like tic-tac-toe on her wallpaper! She felt hurt, in spite of the condition of the paper, that they would have such contempt for her home. There were plenty of score pads around, bridge and poker, if they would ask for them. Then she saw that it was Roman who wrote there and she was pleased and turned her mind back to Audrey's bash. She recalled that great falling girl, the shout of "Timber!" Her throat ached to yell something out but then she thought, 'Bucky would just die,' and then saw that he had gone. Vaguely she remembered his leaving, whispering to her, saying, "Merry Christmas." Smegma was beside her and she touched him warningly, for she had to touch someone warningly to prepare them for a breakthrough, and then threw back her head and yelled "COME ON. LET IT ALL HANG OUT."

It turned out to be a peculiarly inhibiting thing to have yelled. People drew apart as though fearful that what was let hang out might touch them. In positive meanness Wanda saw that even Marie Louise had grown slack-jawed with introspection and the Levinskys left a few minutes later.

Wanda was sobbing on Roman's chest, pouring her drink slowly into his jacket pocket, when the rock came through the window.

The Mayor's bathroom shelves held bottles with essences of many types of body odor. Some were like transpirations of garlic and wine. Others were fishy. Some were delicately chicken-fatty. Some smelled of the smokehouse and the salting barrel. One bottle was labeled FUNK(y), an extraction from fungus-infected feet, which was being authentic perhaps beyond the need, but it was instructive to go back to the old word roots, and such attention to detail was a mark of the compounder's integrity. The compounder was a booming company, formed during the reign of New York's famed Walking Mayor, which went by the honest name of MAYORS ENGAGED IN NARCOTIZING KIDS, ANTI-

WARS, MOTHERS*, PRIESTS AND FAGGOTS and was popularly known by the acronymic MEIN KAMPF. When the Mayor accepted office he was presented with the collection, by that time a gesture as much a part of the ceremony as the oath.

The Mayor had never had occasion to use any of the scents, had not opened a bottle to take a sniff, because all of them contained, wisely, a measure of nerve gas which would affect His Honor, too, one of the hazards of the game of calming dissidents which was meant to give to any mayor, however normally abstemious, an authentic air of being half stoned, which was thought to be a large part of the battle. Sometimes, according to report, the game of which odor to spray on could be tricky; mayors had been known to spray one side with, say, FUNK(y) and the other with AJO, and then spend their time spinning like dervishes as black persons and Latins erratically changed sides.

When the message (concrete block, jagged) was delivered to His Honor, in his kitchen, he was eating strawberries in a sieve. He sprinkled on sugar, holding the sieve over the sink, and most of the sugar fell through the sieve though some of it managed to adhere to the fruit, but the pouring on of cream was less successful. If anyone had had the courage to ask him why he did not use a bowl or a cup—his mournful expression at the spilt cream making it plain that he acutely felt its loss—he would have said that his father had eaten strawberries thus, and his father's father, and so on back; therefore the idea of 'waste' was entirely irrelevant even in famine. In fact, he believed that such unbroken traditions, of which there were many in his family, were what singled him out to be a leader of men. He secretly believed that it was the same as the royal prerogative of hemophilia: both, while incon-

* Not to be confused with Maters, whom all the other categories with the possible exception of PRIESTS embraced. MOTHERS, here, stands for the final and official designation of those citizens who had variously tried on and discarded Colored, Negro, Afro-American *et al.* Normally a hyphenated word, it was decided to let the second two-syllable verb, because of its sexual nature, remain tacit.

venient, were but earmarks of a far greater inner eccentricity which was the earmark of divinity. He knew that in his deep inner conviction he was not an exception among democratic rulers but rather, that he toed a classic and severely drawn line. By the way the Chosen moved did ye know them, and the Mayor and the President were precisely articulated when they toed that line, which articulation the vulgar and the vicious called 'puppetlike' and worse, not knowing of the existence of that line. But in spite of the repetition of post-humously released documents of democratic leaders which repetitively revealed their convictions of holiness, the public somehow never caught on, treating each 'exposé' as singular, worthy of brief notoriety and early forgetfulness. 'Elections' continued to be a popular pastime and the similarities of the elected, which pointed to preordination, were just unthought of. In all guises and ostensibly varied persuasions did leaders move to the fore; only at the very top could they acknowledge each other and their sameness, and begin the compilation of weighty parallels between themselves and some saint or other, not infrequently drawing their lines to the very great toes of Christ Himself.

Or so the Mayor believed with all his heart, and his own secret writings reflected this fanaticism.

Therefore, the piece of concrete block reposing in his sieve amid shards of windowpane and formica chips, having bounded supernaturally to the breakfast table and back, was, in the first instant and due to long expectation and personal catechism, seen too as nails, arrows, faggots and pieces of wheel (the fragments of imaginary artifacts or relics thus conjured being in each case limited only by the piety of the assaulted official. In rare situations where the assaultee had earned his education, rather than having had its symbols be-stowed honorarily upon him, further strictures might be imposed by taste (rare) or by sternly set limits for his pretensions (rarer)).

In the second instant following impact, panic struck His Honor, and His Honor's wife, pensively drinking coffee alone in the dining room, heard her husband cry out, "What's their stink, what's their stink? By God, what crap do they stink of!" before, ghost-faced as a lemur, he crawled through the swinging door heading for the bathroom and his arsenal of smells.

She had sat at her window for a very long time, having gone in the early hours of the evening to watch the snow. It was the smell of the first snow that woke her, or its impending smell. When she drew her chair to the window, and settled furs upon it, and placed at hand a samovar of tea, and a box of small black cigars, and a plate of oranges, the light over the river had been like the inside of a Fabergé egg. But her nose told her that the snow would come—not, as she had predicted, torrential rains—and she read the augury with care and labeled it, tentatively, self-betrayal, tentative because she was logy with protracted introspection.

In the long interim between her active role in the Revolution, pushing, pulling, inventing, prodding, and her return from quiescence to watch the snow and what came after, events had come to pass that pointed naturally to such words as self-betrayal; and self; and betrayal. Roads had been blasted through territory that should have remained forever virgin, and dwelling places built there, and traditions established. She had watched the developments as they arose, Levittowns of the mind, had seen mortar applied that would corrode rather than bind, had watched the erection of signs that misled, and had done nothing to stop it. She had hibernated as an animal does, to sleep through the defeat of winter, for there had been no food value in the gruel fed to her senses. Revolution had been her lifelong nourishment; it had entered her as prosaically as meat and had become transformed and coursed in her veins as ichor, witness her longevity, if one can witness a kept secret. The process had been as automatic as any feeding, the energy and brain values of the sustenance taken on faith, which was itself a result of being well fed. But in the midst of an exercise, perhaps, in the

Opera House, or perhaps she had been writing in her Journals—her long withdrawal made her unsure of that kind of time—she had been stricken with hunger, had found herself literally starving, and realized that—for how long, she did not know—she had been eating something from which all life-sustaining elements had been leached. She was dry of salt, of savor, of acids, of juice. She had not had the energy to complete what it was she was engaged in and had lain down where she was. *At the carriage house he* . . . came unbidden, but she did not know what came after. Aurelie Angelique had moved her, had locked her away from the others, had nursed her discreetly for she could not have survived fussiness, and real attention would have burned her like a great, too proximate spotlight. "Shall I leave a lamp on?" AA asked her, and October answered, a distorted ancient echo, "Give me deeper darkness; substance is not made in the light."

Bergson had described life as calling for "more light." He had believed that it was the nature of consciousness, when all hard-won liberties were momentarily relaxed, to slip back into instinct, habit, and sleep. Therefore, in her failure, again obeisance.

Behind the locked door she listened. She heard her Journals shifting within their horizons, whether by the assumption of autonomy or by the efforts of a dictator or dictators, she could not tell. 'Dictator' was the accurate word, she believed, because what she had left behind her was a ripeness for that condition. She had wanted to educate in the Socratic sense of helping them to find themselves and then to assume the life and freedom thus found within them. But they had, in a fairly complex way, wanted a master . . .

"A master is not a leader nor a teacher," she had told them, seeing their stiffness and inability to claim or use freedom. "Only the masses," she told them, "desire masters, and find masters, until they are willing to cease being 'the masses' and become persons." "A mass," she told them, "is a blob, unable to move except the way a blob of jam is moved to a piece of toast where it is eaten, or to a gulley where it is shot.* It is incapable of self-defense when its single brain, the master, is away or asleep, or unwilling to lead it. It was a member of a 'mass' who sat knitting, brainlessly smiling, as heads rolled; she could not even feel vindictive unless she was told that that was what she felt." She told them, "It is the masses who lynch black people, gang up on minorities; their 'goodness' is as mythical as the 'nobility' of the savage. The mass will kill for liquor, money, food, TV sets, but not from conviction." *Don't you see* she had said in the italics of her handwriting *that anyone who thinks of himself as merely part of a mass cannot possibly hold personal convictions, because to admit the personal is to deny the mass. Only through the experience of uniqueness can we sense the uniqueness of others. A policeman is not a pig but a man; it is when he behaves as a mass, a mass called 'cops,' that he becomes what you say he is, rooting about and rallying to the smell of blood that his master-mind has told him is about to be spilled into the trough. And you, when you behave as 'kids,' bleating in unison—where is your identity? Isn't the crisis of your own devising? Can't you answer a roll call that names you? Do you respond only as 'kid'?*

But looking out she saw that there were no kids and for the first time paid mind to the fact that there never had been. There were children, small children, in the streets; and Bucky, who at the age of twenty-eight was on the outer limits of trustworthiness, but he had been kept out of the Opera House. So her last Revolution had been attempted with people all over thirty, most of them well over. A flaw? But it was precisely that aging, left-out group in whom were present those things she most needed: all of the ancient vices. The young people who had come to the Opera House had come to meet celebrities, or to laugh, or sneer; they had been too superior for such small things as ridding themselves of bigotry. They said they *were* rid of it, or had never had it, and it was like the probably apocryphal story of an East Coast governor de-

* *Do they shoot jam?*

claring a railroad the best in the country without doing anything to make it the best. Like that probable myth, the young
people said, "At the end of such and such a time I am free of
bigotry," and when the time was up they said that they *were*
free; and free too of avarice, and vanity, and bloodthirstiness,
and self-centeredness. Oh, lucky young people, not to need
Mrs. October.

"Start with the man," she told her aging revolutionists,
"acknowledge his need, his brain and body, because the fault
lies, not with possessives: I, me, mine, but with generalities:
them, theirs—because 'them' is what we discriminate against,
and 'theirs' leads to envy. 'Ours' is all right, but it is something
to aspire to; nothing is ever 'ours' at the beginning, not even
life, which is individual and painfully so. Certainly the world
is not 'ours,' having been divided into distinct kingdoms at the
onset of time. Nor is knowledge 'ours,' but must be individually acquired, again painfully. How many of us are agreed
as to even the meaning of one single exercise performed on
this stage? My point was to let us each find his own meaning,
and then to compare, and then to perhaps correlate, winnowing
the seeds of knowledge until there is a harvest that we can all
see, individually, and then share, collectively."

She told them, "Successful revolution depends first upon the
elimination, through such winnowing—which is education—of
'the common man' in the sense of brutes surviving by instinct
alone, or through oversight." Even in the throes of her despera-
tion she had tried to find Bucky and engage his eyes, to let him
know what she had meant in her first letter about the weed
whose roots were shallow, which had survived by oversight.
But he was not in the Opera House; she recalled the monument, as though it were already in place and this were the
unveiling ceremony.

"You cannot recognize 'the' black man before you acknowledge 'a' black man. You cannot speak of jobs, housing, even
food without thinking about individual needs, for needs do
not come in amorphous blocks like salt. A major need is to be
recognized as an 'a' rather than as 'the.' Blacks, a mass, say 'the

man,' by which they mean 'the enemy,' another mass. Without thinking of individuals, your gift or help—whether jobs, housing, anything, is anonymous, and a gift anonymously given can be so taken away. That is one lesson of the past 100 years in America. 'The' slaves were freed, but individuals of which 'slaves' were composed were denied, ignored, forgotten. One block of something merely became a block of something else."

She had lost them. Mutter, mutter, they went but it was mass rebellion, the courage of the massively anonymous. To have been alone in themselves would have been to risk the admission of lonely fear and inadequacy, and the need for a stepping off on one's own to assume life, and to find out what freedom meant. But she had tried, at least, to tell ** them, to make them step ** *She had NOT tried to tell them; she had never given a polemical speech in her life, and if she had done, it would not (could not; I am incapable of it) have been so damned humorless. Whose hand is this? To my astonishment, I suspect AA*

Gazing at the snow—her nose for that metaphor of all her teachings had never failed her—she saw the frailty of the individual flake which seemed to tremble in personal awe at lonesomely finding its own way earthward where it was joined by more and more lonely voyagers until it claimed the

[ ]

earth by right of experience, and nourished it out of love

[ ] *I am seldom amused by anthropopathy++++Why shouldn't the snow need to smother or freeze the earth to death? At least it would be unsentimental.*++++What the devil is novel writing if not anthropopathy, "the ascription of human passions to beings not human"? And what the devil is about half of the writings in these Journals? Gotcha.***

*** *For whatever record this will eventually be, the above is in a handwriting not to be found other-where. To answer him, her, or them: It's true I tried to make "them" step off on their own. All that part—about my attempts to make them accept freedom and run with it—is true but distorted by the*

207

*mush surrounding it, so much distorted altruism. I naturally
wanted them to SEEM real, but in a quite dispassionate way.
It seems to me that you are more anthropopathic than I, trying
to give cold Mrs. October some humanity, n'est-ce pas? The
rest of that definition is: (ascription of human passions) especially to a Deity. Your move.*

She had sat at her window for a very long time, having gone
in the early hours of the evening to watch the snow. When
she pulled her chair to the window, and settled furs upon it,
and placed at hand a samovar of tea, and a box of small black
cigars, and a plate of oranges, the light over the river had
been like the inside of a Fabergé egg. ~~As she watched, the
clouds drew in like a menacing circle of as she watched, the
clouds advanced in tiers upward from the horizon like spectators at~~ As she watched, the clouds thickened and darkened.
Simultaneous with the first flakes, small fires were lit on the
peninsula of The Wolf. A flake would descend, a fire would
be lit—a fire for a flake it seemed at first, and then when the
snow fell too fast to sustain the illusion, the wind rose and
caused sparks to fly upward, the red and white meeting and
then passing, and the clouds glowed as though they had opened
to envelop the sparks, had become fire-clouds (–)
Gazing at snow, water, fire, one loses track of time. The
sole intruder into Mrs. October's state of timelessness was the
wind, which brought her sounds of life—possibly, of death,
she thought as the midnight drew in like a black coach. At
times the wind would also bring her odors—of garlic, incred-
ibly, and the less mysterious smell of fungus when it blew
direct from The Wolf to her window. When smell became
stink, she would enclose herself in a pomander of crushed
orange rinds and pungent cigar smoke. When reminded by the
wind of the world and its events, to keep herself from thinking about what it was she was actually waiting for, she thought
about her youth, about her beginnings as a revolutionist, about
her wish to have been a writer of gothic romances until she

(–) Pretty but quite impossible.

208

realized that in a world torn apart by *Actually, I did write a*
gothic romance and it was well received in two countries but
the Jews ignored it and so it did not make a sou. One expects a
novel to sell, otherwise one writes How To books, or expands
old polemical pamphlets, or writes criticism, all of which sell
very well, having no standards to maintain.

I know you want to ennoble me with highflown thoughts
and speeches and motives, but why? I can't help feeling that it
is out of fear, whether for me or of me, I cannot divine. It is
interesting to read, after so long, someone's projection of me,
but there is no variety, you are too intent upon brainwashing,
making me out as a kind of noble person I never was, could
not have been. I cannot recall what I thought while waiting
"for what she was actually waiting for," but, toujours perdrix,
an old person's thoughts are a kind of treadmill, more so, I
think, than a young person's for there is less to speculate about,
subjectively; and one has selected, out of what one knows, or
has been selected by, certain words, images, mysteries, to
which one returns, or which return to one, in times of be-
musement, sleeplessness, fatigue; it is a kind of mutual haunt-
ing, not a self-haunting, for these mysteries, images, thoughts,
have taken an independent life. Therefore, so there will be
something of me in your account of my failure, herewith—for
I am bemused, sleepless, fatigued.

Thoughts (Gesthemene?)
What the group will be is already present in what it is. Emer-
son put it slightly differently: the end pre-exists in the means.

You have clearly proved that . . . laws are best explained, interpreted, and applied by those whose interest and abilities
lie in perverting, confounding, and eluding them. I observe
among you some lines of an institution . . . but these half
erased and the rest wholly blurred and blotted by corruptions.
It does not appear . . . any one virtue is required toward the
procurement of any one station among you; much less that
men are ennobled on account of their virtue, that priests are

advanced for their piety or learning, soldiers for their conduct or valor, judges for their integrity, senators for the love of their country, or counselors for their wisdom . . . I cannot but conclude the bulk of your natives to be the most pernicious race of little odious vermin that nature ever suffered to crawl upon the surface of the earth.

For the Lilliputians think nothing can be more unjust, than for people, in subservience to their own appetites, to bring children into the world and leave the burthen of supporting them on the public.

When they first married, each had occupied his own niche, his own space. But as time went by she expanded and grew and usurped until she occupied both their spaces and more, lapping over on each side so that he could hardly be found at all. It was the MRS. that was responsible: the fat M, the pushy R, the binding, devious S . . . Take MR. and set at its gates a cobra: MRS. How could a simple self-contained B, her husband's initial, hold out against such sanctioned predatoriness, such tradition? As soon as a woman marries she ceases being a person and becomes a role; she plays the role thereafter: "I am Mrs. and this is my husband." Marriage is based on an opening move of theft: she takes his name.

ANANKE, ANANKE, ANANKE, ANANKE

In the country of my nonchildhood a man and his dog fell into an abandoned mine. The man's legs were broken. When at least rescue came, it was seen that the man, gangrenous of limb, had little flesh left on him to cover his bones, but that the dog was still plump. The man eventually died but before he died he explained, or attempted to, the mystery: he had fed the dog from his veins, opening and rebinding the wound as neatly as though it were an immaculate cupboard. "I knew why we were there, and why we could not leave, but she didn't," he said . . . *Punish knowledge, said the Lord?*

In her younger days she had experimented with enlighten-
ment, of self and others. Prudery was to be the first baggage
to be thrown overboard, and to hasten the jettison, she said
things openly that she had theretofore only thought. She
spoke frequently of her husband's penis, a sort of progress
report, referring to it as "ours." She would say, "After all,
we've only the one between us." But enlightenment became
obsession which took the form first of insatiability. During at-
tempts to satisfy her she began to feel that she truly wore the
thing and grew covetous and jealous when it was absent from
her. Once she said to her husband as he was leaving on a trip,
"Leave it with me," and another time when he was lunching
out with men friends, "You won't need it today," and then
finally, "It's MY turn to wear it." That night he awoke to
find her with a razor, hands pulling at the covers.

Sans genie je suis flambe.

. . . To eliminate the idea of time as duration, therefore as con-
sumer. What you are left with is space, which becomes fuel
and consumer: you are causing space to feed upon itself.

The revolutionary impulse can be the most complex of which
a person is capable, and the emptiest. Whether or not complexity and emptiness can exist at the same time in one person,
I do not know and rather loathe to find out.

Having lived through, and sometimes joined, the Futurists;
the Neue Schar; the Bezmotivniki; any number of Freideutsche
movements, anything for a time that called itself antibourgeois
—how I can still have faith in the effectiveness of youth, I do
not know. But my heart beats fast at mention of Zeitgeist. It
is like unrequited love. Perhaps I have never been part of
my own time. To be a revolutionist, in fact, is to live in a place
that lies eternally ahead of you; in effect, you have no "time"
or home.

To predict—anything; Henri was referring to a portrait—would have been to produce it before it was produced, an absurd hypothesis which is its own refutation . . . But I have found it to be otherwise.

Always and always the procreant urge of the world.

In one's speculations about the famous, it was necessary at last to confine oneself to the small, the sly, the innocuous, for they had already told all the larger scandals and vices themselves, generally in national magazines, and particularly—for the majority who could, or did, no longer read—on the TV screen. Hirings and firings, marriages and divorces, mud-slinging feuds, childbirth—all, indeed, except sexual penetration of one body by another—were nightly performed on the home screen. Bodily penetration by bullets and knives was another matter—was for some, lower than commonplace, a minor annoyance—except when the penetration was earnest, fatal, and happened to the famous. Following those special occasions, the celebrations were lengthy, occupying days during which schools were let out, which made such observances desirable to the young. Children played at murder, at assassination, at Bloody the Hippies and Kill the Pigs. A child who had never heard of London Bridge, before or after the sale, could take an accurate bead on The Reverend King or on Bobby or Malcolm or Jack or Medgar, and topple him from his place at the top of the world (after which they would play School Closed for the Day). All that was omitted from the game was horror. The important thing was AIM, and to this end the sights on their little toy guns were lined up by the manufacturer with great care, and telescopic lenses were ground with precision as though the guns were meant for real grownup killers, and soon real little bullets were finding their way into cartridge belts small enough to have pleased Zuleika's denigrator . . . Truth, according to Mr. James, is not a stagnant property, but is made true by events: verity as a process; and so it was that the post-mid-twentieth-century child, in the

212

process of reaping such rewards as hours in front of the screen and no school, and the special thoughtfulness, and in some cases the temporary temperance, of parents—found truth and beauty in the deaths of the famous. Supper in front of the TV! for those to whom it was not usually allowed, and the hushed-voice pointing out of celebrities, and John-John saluting, and other brave, legendary acts by children, formed in the watching children little embryos which fed and thrived on the idea of someone else's death bringing good things. It was like the old glorification of war, only more specific: a hero's death had once been the glory; now it was the death of a hero.

Entelechy—"the inward determination of all the parts by the function and purpose of the whole." The purpose of revolution is survival. Nowadays, with famine riding herd, survival must mean the elimination of excessive population. Therefore the purpose of a modern revolution must be, finally, death, in unprecedented numbers. *That is the way they are going about it, these "revolutionaries" who have taken over the process.* They have begun by setting age limits, "trust" thresholds, which soon will become thresholds of expendability: over forty is the land of the USELESS. But this particular revolution is even now running its course. Soon, when the median age is twelve, revolutionaries may not participate in trustworthiness past twenty-one; twenty-eight will be the upper limit of the merely functional. Then puberty, unless counterevolution fixes it so that childbearing is possible at eight and nine, will become the great, unbridgable chasm. *A world, then, of five to twelve year olds?* Imagine the music of that nearby day—rattles and amplified watch-tickings. *We will have come full circle to our fascination with, if not serious speculation upon, Time.* That will be the world truly ending with a whimper.

Humor, some of it thus: as though the earth were a magnet and a man had embedded in his anus a bung of steel, and the pull is constant so that the posture assumed is ludicrous—

spraddle-legged, a wide squat, with the behind being drawn down, and the closer it is pulled to the earth, the more men laugh. Earthy laughter means farce.

Before Bergson we were cogs and wheels in a vast and dead machine; now if we wish it, we can help to write our own parts in the drama of creation.

'Αλλ' ἐστιν, ἔνθα χἠ δίκη βλάβην φέρει.

To render a Blackbird speechful you needs must cleft his Tongue. To mute a Man, the same. How opposite is a Man to a Bird. Further, a Mortal flieth after Death, but a Bird before. How marvelous, that Man and Bird should be so opposite. Then, when Man vieweth a Bird, does he not view Himself beyond the Grave?

Life is a series of diminishments. Each cessation of an activity either from choice or some variety of infirmity is a death, a putting to final rest. Each loss, of friend or precious enemy, can be equated with the closing off of a room containing blocks of nerves, or a dynamo governing a particular sensibility or intelligence and soon after the closing off the nerves atrophy and that part of oneself, in essence, drops away. The self is lightened, is held to the earth by a gram less of mass and will.

Being is a fiction invented by those who suffer from becoming.

It is extraordinary how the house and the simplest possessions of someone who has been left become so quickly sordid. Rooms once thought airy exude a fetor; closets of bright gay clothes are seen as sleazy, cheapening by the moment; one's hairbrush becomes an object of horror; one hovers over the kitchen sink for animal-like meals, and even the stain on the coffee cup seems not coffee but the physical manifestation of one's inner

*stain, the fatal blot that from the beginning had marked one
for ultimate aloneness.*

On peult couvrir les actions secrettes; mais de taire ce que tout
le monde sçait, et les choises qui ont tiré des effects publics et
de telle consequence, c'est un default inexcusable.

*Tout le monde me recognoist en mon livre et mon livre en
moy.*

*The foregoing pages of "my thoughts" are like a collage, for
there has been much pasting over; I no longer know, nor
really care, which thoughts or quotations were mine. In some
places where the paper is thin, one can see that what has been
pasted on is the same as what has been pasted over, thus de-
liberate confusion. I am reminded, reading over "my" thoughts,
of Roman saying that he had just finished reading Saul Bellow's
latest collection of O.K. Thoughts of Mainly Western Man.
So perhaps Roman is the—someone with my past dare not
write the word culprit here—is the attributor. But, sometime
or other, the explosions did come.*

**Nota Bene: The preceding appears to be the handwriting of
Mrs. Septimus October but is not to be taken on faith. There
are many clever forgeries in circulation about town; the town
itself may be a forgery; the map of it, ascribed to an
eighteenth-century cartographer, certainly is. If the town does
not exist, then—does Mrs. October? Does her Revolution?**

If
The present moment contains no living and creative choice,
and is totally and mechanically the product of the matter and
motion of the moment before then so was that moment the
mechanical effect of the moment that preceded it, and that
again of the one before . . . and so on, until we arrive at the
primeval nebula as the total cause of every later event, of

every line of Shakespeare's plays, and every suffering of his soul; so that the somber rhetoric of Hamlet and Othello, of Macbeth and Lear, in every clause and every phrase, was written far off there in the distant skies and the distant aeons, by the structure and content of that legendary cloud. What a draft upon credulity! What an exercise of faith such a theory must demand in this unbelieving generation! What mystery or miracle, of Old Testament or New, could be half so incredible as this monstrous fatalistic myth, this nebula composing tragedies? There was matter enough for rebellion here.

Nessun maggior dolore/Che ricordarsi del tempo felice/ Nella miseria.

But at some juncture the explosions did come.

was an explosion, another, another—three magical explosions and by the showering sparks and the light of whole bonfires set adrift in the sky she could see The Wolf's mouth open, its jagged teeth, for it was as though it had turned its head and was biting off its own neck at the shoulders; tendons of roots pulled and stretched; jets of subterranean liquid spurted up; tissues of garbage, of tin cans, rubber mats, plastic bags, half-rotted tarpaulins and sails, clothing beaten down by rain, soured ashes and die-hard newspapers, stretched and tore; the gap between body and head widened until there was no visible connection; until The Wolf was surely dead. The head appeared to be set adrift, a marvelous fantasy, until she saw that it was no fantasy; the head was actually afloat, was moving away, a slum raft heading for Columbus, gem of the river dumps. A shout went up, a roar that seemed to be in the room with her. She saw the great body of people beneath her window, who had until that moment been so silent that she, leaning on the sill, had not suspected that she was not alone. She felt the glare of wind-riding bonfires lighting her face, could catch intimations of her own shadow cast upward onto the cliff of the building by the sudden battery of torches and flashlights turned on her from below. Then, one face was so brightly illumined in the mass that it floated in the sea of light surrounded by its own aureole, and she saw, without recognition, the mechanics of the illusion: the person whose act it was held a flashlight below his chin, and in the circle surrounding him were other torches aimed at his face, carving it for her out of the bright block of glowing globes like an advertisement in light bulbs. She saw that it was Omerie; her far-sighted vision showed her his triumph of which malice was a part. And then, for it was post-midnight of the 24th and the message was plain, his features were replaced by the cunning bulk of Madame Alexis, shiny as linoleum newly waxed, lively with wriggles, and then the lights were turned upon the Chief of Police—ALIVE ALIVE ALIVE.

Because of the malice rising to her she was informed that her motive had been misread, that sacrifice for any purpose was unforgivable, even sacrifice on paper. She had chosen Omerie because of Madame Alexis, who, beguiling and entirely without harmfulness, was therefore a natural victim in the necessarily simplistic primer of Revolutionary Examples: The Death of Goodness (unless). She had sacrificed the Chief in a nod to fashion, having planned and then discarded a more ambitious pugna porcorum terminating in a veritable luau of ingested cops, taking her inspiration from the black who had said recently, "We are hungry and its time for a barbecue."

She had given to them, in short, a kind of written history, or what could have been a history, with a cause, and eye-opening martyrdoms; had strived to demonstrate the senselessness, the wholly random nature of brutality and the bloodletting side of revolution; but they had rejected it and were, second by mindless second, forming themselves out of exploded garbage and random fires in a burgeoning of existentialism. Even the Moon Man was a projection now as quiescent as the future is without creative imagination. She could tell what now would be made of her Moon Man, far beyond the demonstration below her window:

October, her hand: She could tell what would be made, now,
~~She would be subjected to the humiliation of public retraction~~
of her Moon Man; she had, after all, given them a victim but
~~of her motives as 'pure' and might be made to retire from ac-~~
not the one of her careful planning. No gesture would be
~~tive participation in the continuing revolution. She might,~~
dramatic enough to convey her awareness of who the victim
~~however, with grace, be allowed to conduct from the sidelines~~
would be, was; and so she made none.
~~those moral exercises which would be her salvation, her fame.~~

She withdrew so slowly from the window that to the watchers it was as though she had dissolved into particles of light and dark. Some, out of habit, applauded the masterly illusion. A curtain blew out like ectoplasm and acknowledged with undulation the applause.

PART IV
Tasmania, Then

"Scenes"

AMONG THE FRUITS of Mrs. Pierce's fall-planted bulbs
—the hyacinths and tulips, the as yet sheathed massiveness of
amaryllis blatant as dog penises—in the clarified butter yellow
of the late April sunshine the children played at coupling.

"My goodness, you'll get GRASS STAINS on that pretty
FROCK, my dear": a child of five (dredging into the ancient-
ness of her four-year-old memory and the scenes she, arm-
held, had witnessed as in a dream of circuses) to a big girl of
pubertal proportions who appeared to have found a partner
for whom the earnest business of real penetration took precedence over the pleasure of satirical or parodic "acting out."
The latter would have been in pretty compliance with instructions, like flawed echolalia of Miss Havisham, given daily
this spring by happily liberated parents to children of all ages:
"Go 'act out,' dear," which had come, in the mysteriously
mannered world of usage where reasons are eliminated—solely
to mean "go play sexy." But mavericks abound even in zones
of widest liberation and the earnest young man's father had
said, "Go in there and GET it, boy," and in a compliance no
less pretty, though with perhaps more potential consequence,
than "acting out," the boy was so doing.

There is something impressive about an effort that will lead
to genuine breakthrough; in its earliest stages, a nimbus, the
supernatural light of success, hovers above the essay and at-
tracts, as moths to flames and flies to honey, the least sycho-
phantic as well as nature's toadies. And thus the children
drew about, and, spontaneous and unself-conscious chorus,
divided the litany between them. There were trios and duets,

quintets and a climactic solo, as follows:

Trio (tentative): "I put you in here with more hope than skill . . ."

Quintet (fervid): "I *count* on you to rise again, like our dear Savior!"

Octet: "Now IN you go!"

Septet: ". . . and in the springtime we'll roll away the stone . . ."

Nonet: ". . . AND SEE WHAT WE HAVE!"

The five-year-old, mnemonically perfect though a shade frightened by the oestrual completion on the greensward, sang trembling-voiced solo:

"Ohhhhh, WHAT a pretty sight. CHRIST!"

It seemed to Bucky that every time he walked down South Splendor there was another sign out, another new business. He felt the town growing around him like the stuff of spring itself, and the businesses, in their own ways, were as beautiful as the burgeoning blossoms and sometimes as fragrant: the bakery, the brewery, the small shop which sent onto the street the pungencies of herbs and oils. He imagined the little shop was a place where cosmetics were being compounded, or creams, because, since Omerie's Caneteria and its no less than astonishing effects on women's complexions, the ladies of Tasmania had gone practically wild about keeping up appearances, and there were massage parlors and there was a Milk Farm about which not one dirty joke had been cracked.

It was grand the way the one-time Wolves had added to the air of growth and excitement, bringing old nearly forgotten skills out into the open, occupying the shops as rapidly as they were rebuilt out of the rubble of the Christmas fires. In addition to bakeries, breweries, and the like, there was a Ratafia Shop—jewel-colored sweet liquors with a kick; a Pasta Palace; a sausage maker; and here were the tanner and cobbler who worked side by side with the result of their collaboration being shoes of glovelike softness. Bucky was wearing a pair, odd-grained yet handsome, and amazingly inexpensive.

Across the street there was a chocolate shop where candies ripened before your eyes on marble slabs. Some of the professions had not been heard of in Tasmania, such as chiropodist; and this new one, opened up since yesterday, opened up overnight: HARUSPEX. If he was reading it right it sounded like somebody who might make eyeglasses out of hair.

But, so he could tell Mrs. October about it in detail, he paid attention to small matters and saw that the insignia was similar —really spooky looking—to that on the door of the lady who cast horoscopes. He noticed somewhat idly that occupancy of the block of four connecting shops, built on the site of the old jail, was now complete: the cobbler, then next to him the tanner, then the new shop, the haruspex; and leading them off, the sausage maker whose sign bore the words Wurst and Fleisch.

Across the street going east was the nursing home on the top floor of which Mrs. October convalesced. Bucky crossed the street and paused in front of Mrs. October's building to look back and review the information he had for her, for to be less than thorough would be to fail her. Yes, the sign and the symbol; and the filled block of shops, starting with sausage maker and ending with cobbler. The arrangement struck him as cozy, and then as peculiar, and because he could not say why, he tried to puzzle it out for Mrs. October's sake. Finally he thought: Well, it's as if all the shops in that block, except haruspex, and she'll know what that is—it's as if three of the shops depended on the same source, and the peculiar thing is that there's no source in Tasmania because we don't have a slaughterhouse here. Someone coming out of the nursing home bumped into him and he and that person, who was laden with large covered slopping pails, engaged in the joyful and essential ritual of claiming fault for the rude encounter until both were covered with glory and absolved of guilt. Loving the man, bloody forearms and all, Bucky glowed his way into the lobby, assured by the man that now both sides of his face were "good" sides, equally appealing; just as Bucky

223

had decried any notion that the blood on the man or the gut sounds in the slopping pails were the least bit revolting to him.

Wanda chuckled with Arthur Godfrey as he sleepily told her about the supernal properties in the soapbox he held. It was one of her favorite commercials and often she sat twirling the dial trying to find it. Roman, before he left, had, she felt, tried to ruin it for her, saying that Arthur's chuckles were like small, moist belches, and being downright mean about the size of Arthur's eyes. She had forgiven him and told him that his own plumpness was not in the least displeasing to her, but he had refused to the very last to engage in what he called "the Jap Zap," finding no value in the ritual of two people cleansing self and each other by bringing into the open those things about the other which were potentially disturbing or disgusting or frightening and disclaiming their power until, miraculously, they no longer had any power. She thought that Roman could have benefited by such an encounter, during which he could have told Arthur how much he *liked* his small-moist-belch chuckles and his little eyes, until he found that, actually, he did like them. But Roman said if you took the bitch out of a stud, what you had left would be a half-person with no need to prove anything and half of what it took to prove it. She hadn't bothered to try to figure out what he meant; those days were gone forever. He said that the only people in Tasmania who were still "doing it" were the kids, who still had aggressions that could not be worked off by facing each other and lying—and so on and on, and then he had wanted to do it to her and she had told him sincerely that she hadn't been a bit shocked the morning when she grabbed his hair during their last sex and his wig had come off in her hands. And he had slammed out and gone back— back—she didn't know where, saying unconstructive words like "ball-breaker."

She got up and adjusted the curtains for greater darkness while the film was running. The industry had regulated itself with a law that said a movie could run no more than two minutes at a time, so she did not have to wait an annoyingly long time for her commercials, which ran for fifteen uninterrupted minutes. She returned a bit too soon and for a second she was face to face with Geraldine in close-up. Geraldine was rapt, prayerful—it cut Wanda like a knife, her first pain in months—but holding the image behind her closed eyelids, she managed to see Geraldine sitting in front of her TV in Ireland, enraptured by Arthur. As though she were a mobile camera, Wanda left her old friend in her cozy Irish TV room and mentally stepped outside into the soft green county air and looked at Geraldine's great house, and then at the other great houses in the neighborhood: yes, they all wore the spiky aerials like decorative cactuses emplanted in their sod roofs, like her own cactus she had bought precisely because it looked like a TV aerial. "Crown of Thorns" was its lovely name. And here now was that delightfully funny actress, Jane, looking for the TV camera concealed in the grocery store, and Wanda laughed, it really was true to life, you knew not where the camera was and when it was turned on you! Something had put Mrs. October into her mind and she thought about last night's decision regarding that lady and her own promise to take the news to her, which would give her somewhere to go when the program was over, just forty-five more commercials, how fast time had gone.

Omerie sat in the leeward garden eating oysters for breakfast and drinking tea. He wore a yellow silk shirt with large Nepalese cuff links and faded jeans so clean they smelled of soap. Madame Alexis, looking much too young to be called Madame anything, lay on a lilac chaise and sulked, for she did not like oysters, yet Omerie thought he could detect admiration in her eyes. He imagined that she was thinking that with his long hair and uneccentric clothes and amazing skin he looked like a boy in his teens, and he happily reveled in her restored puppyhood, finding a twin delight in knowing that he, Omerie Chad, was actually self-supporting, living by his own inventiveness in the style to which he had always been accustomed, and his darling was his equal and partner, was herself self-supporting, adorable chiene, angel pussy cat, bootifums. He and she were a mutual admirash dept., successful business chums, had led a smashingly marvelous revolution, and now had, in collaboration, quite settled the fate of the October, for theirs had been the decisive votes last night, his darling's the last vote cast. He had said to the assembly that if Mme. Alexis, nodding on his lap, should twitch her right paw, it was nay, and if she should twitch her left paw, it was aye, and she twitched her left paw because she always did; she was leftpawed. He wondered if her gesture on behalf of the Germans would go unremarked. The hall had looked perfectly splendid for the first meeting, a first meeting with something indeed terminal about it, delicious fun, for his instructions and color scheme had been carried out to the letter, but even in this utopian society there were tiresome women to want the aesthetically impossible. "But I had SO hoped for red curtains!", silly bitch couldn't see that red curtains would have swallowed the room like a great throat. He had said to her, amiably enough, "Then why don't you go home and bleed on your white ones?" At least HE didn't have to indulge them in the therapy game. He had invented it for them because it amused him to hear them picking out each other's worst features and going on and on about them; delicious. And soon now, England and the films. Get around quarantine á la Liz and Richard, he had been advised, and so it should be.

In the moonlight-scattered room the chairs stood angled, one in the middle of the floor, another at the window, abutting it, so that one sitting there could watch the variations of light in the garden and have a clear view of the room. Papa sat in the middle chair, between Mama at the window and Belle on the bed, keeping vigil through the night. He and Mama were staying for longer visits as Belle grew weaker, though if the two facts were connected, she had nothing to do with it, for she had not told anyone. She was occasionally tempted to tell, for then someone would go down and bring her up something to eat, but in an odd way the idea of eating, and growing strong again, ran against the grain, it was like an impoliteness, and she did not want either of her parents to go for a moment out of the room; she wanted them, each and every minute of them, for as long as they could stay with her. At the thought, an edge, a narrow edge of light surrounded the picture of Belle wanting them to stay with her forever and she could see it and feel it inside, a warmer comfort than food, smile-producing; and she thought that when the edge of light grew to a certain width, as though prescribed by law, then it would become solidified, would be a permanent frame, so that then the picture could be lifted up and hung on the wall as an unchanging fact, like a painting or a daguerreotype: Papa and Belle and Mama Together Forever.

The room in which October was confined was a room with six windows, two each to north, south, and east. The western wall had a door, but it had been bricked in. From the outside there was no clue as to where the door had led; it appeared to have been nothing more than a stepping off place, a suicide door.

You got to the room up a little corkscrew of a stairway. A person rising out of a stairwell not much bigger around than he was never failed to amuse October. As the person turned round and around, growing slowly bigger, she said it looked to her like he was boring his way through, using his head as an auger.

There was no trapdoor, no locks and keys, but she was confined and she used that term, to everyone except Bucky. The story agreed on to tell him was that October had been sick while she was away and now was placed in the tall sunny room for purposes of health and recovery. The opposite was true, but Bucky swallowed the story whole. He visited her every day, sometimes twice. He always came to help her through the hour she called nemesis, and sometimes "the children's hour," but on especially bright days, at her request, he would also come in the mornings and they would share, as she put it, the sun between them like a buttered crêpe.

Perhaps the most unusual thing about the tower room was that there was no writing material in it, visible or invisible; whereas once she had moved through sheets and scraps of paper like someone in a snowstorm, her strange colored hair bristling with pens and pencils, while at least one typewriter, usually the portable electric, purred like a cat on a nearby table because she never could recall to turn it off, the only paper to be found in her new quarters was in the bathroom and of such a thin quality that it would not have served a person with grosser appetites and eliminations. She said to AA that only Martin Luther and October could have made do with it; possibly, Portnoy pére. AA said there must be a lot more constipated people than that, and October remarked that she wasn't referring to God's creation, which was the first that AA had heard of Martin Luther being an invention of a person or persons, and she said so, and October said that 'the people' had collaborated on him, too. In any case, the toilet paper was too thin for writing on, if she had had anything to write with.

AA, experimenting with the words as though they were an untried weapon, said to her, "They let you smoke. You could write on the wall with burnt matches," and October showed her the lighter she was allowed and AA said, ". . . or with that black smoky grease on the wick" before she saw that it was a chemical lighter, which made her angry and frightened as restrictive authority has always done, and she said, "Write with the ashes, then!" and Mrs. October told her, "It was all written in ashes," so that AA could not tell if she referred to her marked-up Journals or the Revolution, or both, or neither.

She had closed herself off, without malice or vengefulness, from everybody but Bucky. It was as if she had closed a book before it was finished, because she knew the ending, and either assumed that others knew the ending too, or did not care whether they did or not, without being nasty about it. But even in the same room with Bucky and October, knowing that the book was cracked open for Bucky to see, AA could not tell what was perhaps being divulged to him if only he knew. The language used was a private one, like that between a mother and a baby. The knowledge would enter the baby by osmosis and only later would he realize what he had been taught.

So AA found herself in the position of being guardian of a book that she could not open and read, and gradually what she knew about what had been between the covers slipped away from her and she and October became amiable strangers, sharing their little meals like people thrown together in an airport restaurant, waiting for the flights to be announced that would separate them for always.

AA had a need to get away, to do her own closing off, and the need became a great need and finally an obsession. What had been vague in January became fixed and frantic by April. She saw their roles as reversed, saw herself as the prisoner and October as her implacable jailer, so that her eagerness for sentence to be pronounced was not malicious to October but only to end her own uncertainty, the unbearable hung fire of anyone on death row.

AA was not an 'official' prisoner, nor even an 'official' watchdog, but without her ministrations October would have gone foodless, having refused flatly from the beginning to eat the slop served in the nursing home, saying that for all she knew it was appendixes with bottled t.b. sauce. What AA was, then, was a nursemaid, and she found lots of nourishing iron in that wafer, as she thought of it, because of the circular shape of events. Just as she suffered the delusion, in Europe, of being a woman and came back to America to find herself a nigger, so did the hereditariness, like a family business, of being nursemaid to a white catch up with her. She could neither disown nor be disowned, yet, but she felt the time was coming. Most real needs were unsubtle, like food and sex, and what she mainly wanted was to be fired or allowed to quit a role that did not have enough nuance to allow her to develop it into a good strong part. So she stayed with October voluntarily because the freedom she wanted was not in the streets.

AA took a seat by an east window when Wanda poked up through the floor. Since the end of the Revolution, Wanda had stopped her pursuit of AA, who was not sure that the woman saw her at all, but she had changed so radically, like all of them except Bucky, that to think of her as the same person was to indulge in folly. She looked radically different, too, hiding her eyes behind sunglasses but giving the impression of sleepiness because of her slow-motion gestures, and of a sluttishness, although she was not visibly dirty.

She glanced in AA's direction and her head moved in what could have been greeting or a tic, or dull surprise at the shadow smack in the midst of the brightness of the east. October took over.

'Sit down, Mrs. Phelps."

"Oh—well, I've been sitting all day, practically."

"If you'd prefer to stand . . ."

"Oh . . . no, thank you. A chair will suit me fine." AA thought: or a manger with a bone in it.

October, without being sullen, had taken to silence when one of them came on a rare visit, leaving the ball-carrying up to them, but she made an effort with Wanda, probably because of Bucky.

"How are your commercials?"

"Arthur was beaudiful today, just beaudiful! I thought he looked there toward the end as if he was, you know, tired. He's on forty or fifty times a day, you know, and I often wonder when he finds time to rest."

October clucked in sympathy. "He'll waste away." Wanda sat forward, her hands grasping the chair arms, then cunningly she relaxed.

"Oh, I don't think so. They take good care of them there at the studio."

Mrs. October smiled, glad to receive the tidings. Wanda waited, then asked, "What made you say that?" and when October raised her eyebrows, ". . . about him wasting away?" Wanda's voice held an old suspicion. Visitors always came to this point, when they feared October's old power to make things happen, and had to test her in case she had found a way to get at them through thinking, or some other process. She was plainly not as passive as they wished, in spite of having been deprived of the tools of her witchcraft.

October showed empty hands. "Without rest, and food, one does."

"Well, he gets plenty."

"Good!"

"He's as fat as a . . . I just meant he looked tired."

Mrs. October murmured, "One has to be very careful, nowadays. Spring is deceptive, isn't it. Balmy days, but, underneath . . ."

"What!" Wanda jumped as though pinched.

"I beg your pardon?"

"WHAT is underneath?"

October gave her a long look of, to AA's amazement, open dislike. She had never seen that human expression on October's lineless face, and thought that that was why it had stayed lineless. After a time October said, "God knows, Mrs. Phelps," and when Wanda fidgeted, said, "Do you?"

Wanda gave her a sudden warm smile. "I've never disliked you, Mrs. October. I want you to know that. The way you dress, speak, the things you used to say in your funny voice, the strange people you brought here . . ."

"I thought you were a silly woman, Mrs. Phelps, and interesting."

Wanda was doubtful. "I don't know if you can have it both ways, Mrs. October—negative and positive like that. It's supposed to be all positive, you know."

"Interesting, Mrs. Phelps, because you had so very much

hate that one could not have called you empty, and silliness can be quite absorbing. One watches the process—hate devouring the silliness like snake and bird . . ."

Wanda protested. "I really don't like those comparisons. . ."

" . . . then the transmutation of snake into reformer, which is what a revolutionist must be. The combination is classic: helpless and hating. Without the two together, no revolution is possible. And then the reversion, après la revolution—classic, classic, classic—to a modern silliness, which is to say, foolish."

"Now, just you hold on a minute . . ."

"Clownish. Absurd. From weakness to absurdity in one revolution of the wheel. At least now you know where you've been and where you are. It was not what I'd planned for you . . ." AA saw that she was talking to herself, but Wanda, glaring, did not have the same vision. ". . . a heroine, something I'd never attempted before. A model Ms., if you will . . ." She came back to Wanda with a rueful smile. "If you could share my regret, you might still manage . . ." She leaned forward to touch Wanda, who drew back. "Take this small gift, Wanda, for Bucky's sake. Know *HOW* and then perhaps *WHY* will follow."

AA, fascinated, saw that October was trying to write on the woman as though she were a blank page. Blank she was, but she refused the impression.

"I don't mind being silly," Wanda said. "I'm just a woman, like you. And women are supposed to be simple."

"Yes, Kate?"

"Wanda," she corrected automatically, and went on. "Women are supposed to have their faces done, and their hair, and keep the TV set going, and wear cute clothes."

She got up and said simply, with real, or what approximated real, warmth, "At the meeting last night everybody voted. We've decided to hang you. I knew you'd be glad, because there's no pain at all. Women hate pain."

She spiraled out of sight, the good genie, vanishing.

AA sat as though suspended in a warm bath, all nerve-endings soothed out of alertness. In a while October spoke.

"You'd think they'd want to know: to have someone to do the connective tissue for them. Knowledge of how transition was achieved is just as important as transition itself, or so I thought. Revolutions, novels—I believed both needed that continuity. I thought the new dicta were only intellectual exercises; I counted on intelligence to counter them. My own novel, my projections, my revolutions—were all, I see, old-fashioned because I tried to give reasons for things, for events and people. I tried to tie them in with ancestors, motives, perversions—the human elements. Did you read that part in the Journals where Omerie chided me for trying to 'explain' his homosexuality? Once that sort of thing was essential. Well, now they're free of all that, which is clearly what they've wanted, and what their critics—read 'advisers'—wanted for them. All ties to each other and the world, and time itself, broken."

AA dozed, nodded awake when October spoke again.

"The idea of a creator has been anathema to them. One by one, they've killed them off."

"Why, Mrs. O.?"

"To divine is Divine; to admit Divinity is to nod at Fate, which is outside the boundaries of what they call existentialist thought. Therefore 'intuition' had to go. Instinct is atavism, which is the taproot of history, the lateral roots of which are common experience, which is frequently to say, common mistakes, which is another way of nodding at Fate. All of this denial is so they can get to and negate the idea of conscience, because—perfect circle, AA—conscience is the awareness of evil, not of good. Get rid of it and there is neither good nor evil; there is only man, islanded, forging one moment at a time, and whatever he does, being without precedent, is . . . pure. Pristine man, a dream as old as God. He can thieve, humiliate, murder, and the moment's work will justify him by being 'experience.' He is once again Man without guilt. Circles."

AA went to sleep while she was talking and when she woke up the dawn was touching the east window. AA thought,

I've gone from light to light, for once not aware of blackness. She wondered if October had talked all night, for soon after AA awoke, October said, "But they won't acknowledge the circle because mathematics is history, too. Just one more stab at the circle, and then they'll abandon it." AA thought sleepily, wheel and all?

While they were preparing the site of her execution Mrs. October found herself more and more averse to the thought of a broken neck; so damned unbecoming, most especially to a woman who had taken perhaps too much pride in her carriage. But excessive pride or not, she still did not like to think of her head lolling about once she was cut down, because of course they would all come to look at her; she had taught them the value of curiosity as one aspect of freedom and she imagined they would have retained that bit of her teaching, at least where her death was concerned. Out of consideration for her, they were erecting the scaffold to the east so that she might watch its growth from her window. Often she would rise in the night and stand at the window, looking at the shadows of skeletal wood cast in her direction like a pointing finger as dawn approached. It was as though she were being singled out of a crowd to reply to some portentous question, and one early morning—April 28th—she believed that she at last knew the answer. It occurred to her, in one entire formed image, that of all methods of death—most satisfying and most memorable, and the nomenclature of its instruments was so grandiose, was crucifixion. The cross itself: Patibulum and stipes. And with prolonged agony, upon which she was inwardly informed she should insist, there was the pourboire of sedile and suppedaneum. With irony but—educator to the last—interest in their increased learning, she removed a pane of glass from the window and cut upon it with her diamond ring a rough sketch for them to follow, carefully lettering in the names of the various pieces of wood:

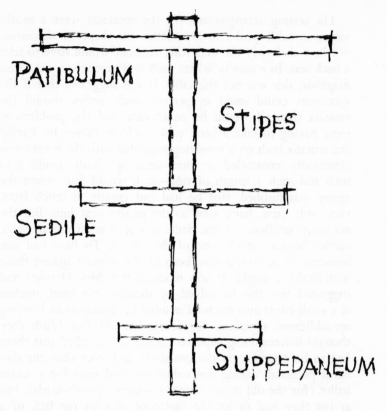

PATIBULUM

STIPES

SEDILE

SUPPEDANEUM

NAILS THROUGH WRISTS - NOT PALMS

The seating arrangements for the spectacle were a nearly insurmountable problem. No matter the shape of the arena, nor how shallowly the tiers rose, someone would have to take a back seat. In a society where each was precisely equal to his neighbor, this was not thinkable. It was suggested that if the spectators could stand in perfect small circles around the crucifix then all would be equidistant, and the problem of some having to take a back view could be solved by having the crucifix built on a revolving turntable with the revolutions electrically controlled so that—assuming death would take such and such a length of time—each would find, when the agony was finished, that he had had exactly as much front view, side view, back view as the person next him. But the necessary smallness of the circle was seen as an unremovable barrier because of the size of the crowd. To have had one immense circle would have been to discriminate against those with faulty eyesight. It was reported that Mrs. October had suggested that this be solved by dividing the ideal number in a small circle into the total number of spectators and setting up additional crucifixes to accomodate. At first blush they thought her reasoning superior until it was recalled that there had to be someone *on* the crucifixes, and even then the die-hards persisted, calling for volunteers, and then for a secret ballot (for the old democratic ways were also die-hards), but at last they had to let the foolproof idea go for lack of a majority opinion supporting it.

The next suggestion was a crowd pleaser, and in future whenever the event came up, it would be spoken of wistfully: phalanxes of helicopters to take several persons at a time and fly them, suspended from ropes, round and around the agonizing figure. The whirlibirds chopping at the night, the great sound, each person a camera dollying in, the total involvement, mothers safe in the ropes so that babes could be carried in arms, small boys dreaming of what a slingshot could do from close range; sweep, swoop, hover, turn— It was the "hover" that revealed the flaw. Someone, writing in to remain safely anonymous, for to scotch the great idea was to run a risk, pointed out that if you were carried close enough to see the good bits—walling eyes, protruding tongue, perhaps the slipping of the bowel from its sphincter—and if your bird hovered there, you would risk the 'copter's rotors slicing off her head, and where would that leave the rest of the group, so many yet to come?—for each imagined himself in the first rank of viewers.

Thus, good scouts that they were in face of defeat, they threshed about for the next best solution. It was provided by Wanda, and was popular. She said that if they could not equally approach the crucifix, then let the crucifix approach them, equally: the TV camera could bring the happening into their homes, could pan up, down, around, showing far-sighted, myopic—and through the offices of the commentator —even the blind each subtlety of each moment. The deaf *and* blind were a special problem, but then they always were.

There were objections, for there were still those who liked to be in immense company with their fellows, pushing, shoving, shouting, and the like, or simply, as the younger contingent had it, grooving together, for this was what they thought really *was* a groove. Many, especially ladies, had bought special outfits that they were anxious to show off, and this was pointed to as the most serious blemish on the Solomonlike solution. Very well, said Wanda, feeling the old pull of her charisma; let them have a great gala at the site of execution, with food and drink and fireworks, and *then* all scoot home in time to catch the first nail.

It was really too good, too perfect, and in the old days, envy would have scotched its execution, but they had been rid of that gross human vice and one and all accorded Wanda the recognition due her sagacity.

Therefore the bleachers were built on the old pattern, to the old scale, tiers rising to the sky without fear of slighting those in the rear, for they would view the long parade of personages down the aisles as well as being on parade themselves. Each would be both actor and spectator; free to mill about and never take a seat if they did not wish to.

By nine o'clock in the evening there was only one empty seat in the amphitheater, the one to have been occupied by Mrs. Hackett. Marie Louise had tried to dress the old lady with the intention of taking her to the show in the back of the station wagon and somehow propping her up in her seat, believing that nobody would notice anything strange, but she had to admit defeat: rigor mortis made Mrs. Hackett's limbs unmanageable. Marie Louise would have taken her anyhow, except her mother had died trying to get to the bathroom and her bedgown was spattered with night soil. She could have been cloaked; her old velvet cloak with the passamenterie lay across the foot of her bed as though she had meant to dress herself and attend the celebration; but there was no way to disguise the odor, which Marie Louise found out the expensive way by pouring over Mrs. Hackett an entire bottle of perfume, which made Marie Louise, understandably she felt, angry. Finally, unable to restrain a last impulsive comment—for the elimination of all emotions was acknowledged to be a slow process—Marie Louise kicked Mrs. Hackett; kicked and kicked her. Looking at her lying with her huge blue empty eyes walled up, all at once it came to her just what it was her mother most resembled: that old broken doll that she had cared for more than she had cared for her daughter, that she was always searching for but had not found because Marie Louise had put it in the furnace the first chance she got, after her mother had gone off her rocker. Kick, kick, the way one whacks a stopped alarm clock, but the old woman was a lump of yellow dirt with never a tic left in her.

However, all things have their good side. Marie Louise, being the last to arrive, received the undivided attention of the svelte audience as she walked slowly up and down the aisles. She managed the long intricate parade so well that the audience broke into sustained applause. They wore her, she felt, like a diamond pinned to their collective breast. She was the priceless proof of the cutting, faceting, polishing, the exquisite mounting they had all received at the behest of that master of jewelers, Revolution. She was final proof that Tasmania was not only the Heart but the Soul as well of civilization. For her long good moment she was the bride of the world, and in a last nod at tradition, among her apparel of new, borrowed and blue, she wore, on the tip of her odd-grained stomping boot, little identical odd-grained patches of something old.

The smallest children were whimpering for bed and bathroom before the commentator declared that Mrs. October was no more. What he should have said was what he had been coached by Myra Little to say: elle est morte, but at the last moment he appeared, in the shadow of the crucifix, to become unaccountably moved, or agitated, and when the time for pronouncement came he said—or so it sounded—ill no more; and when the camera dollied away in what appeared to be unseemly flight, the long shot picked up a diminishing figure at the foot of the crucifix. All those in the dark houses with the one dull eye of light recognized Bucky, and the microphone in the hand of the stationary commentator brought Bucky's voice to them, loud and close and toneless as a child's saying a counting rhyme for the hundredth time: Cruxfiction, he said, typically mispronouncing, and repeated it: Crux-fiction.

AFTERWORD

He was the only America, in the sense of United States, that I wanted any part of, symbolism included. Vulnerable; hurt early on by his mother so he was a little paranoid; just bad enough at languages to be called pretentious when he tried to speak them, and laughed at; generous; so virginal he wasn't able to think about sex without blushing; respecter of institutions. But I imagine my point has been made, including what some are bound to see as condescension, which will be intolerable to some, coming from a black woman, for now you must know who your narrator is: me, the schwartze, AA, the Dawn Angel from Macon and Columbus, one foot each side of Mason's Dick, yes.

After the successful Revolution's last success, I picked Bucky up and took him to Mexico. He was like a baby in my arms, shocked back to where there aren't any words. I took him there for the sun and the color and because it was as foreign a place as you could find if you were a Norteamericano; and because, whatever badness there is in Mexico, it is not a badness that comes from a great collective lack of conscience. The Virgin sits in so many heads, there, and she is so gold, that they have to think now and then about the Golden Rule.

We lived in a little house on a hill above Taxco and would go down every day and sit in the square, surrounded by silver and coppersmiths, and watch the tourists. They were mainly North American and they behaved all right—not too good, not too bad; they were average and they haggled averagely and so on. What I wanted for Bucky was as much average behavior as I could find.

I took care of him as if he was in truth a baby; and I was aware that it could be the last time I would be interested enough in a white person to worry about one, one way or the other. Thinking that, I gave the boy, man, child, everything I had that he might want, or need, and tried to press on him what little I had learned that might help him; not 'get well'; I didn't know what that state was, and didn't think he'd make it; but to help him get along. And I got as good as I gave, because I found myself trusting the way he was and I began to see it as proof of something, and then I figured what it was proof of: that America the Beautiful had actually existed in small ways and small people, somewhere, and that it had made Bucky and, for all I knew, a lot of other Buckys, who handed the niceness and the 'beauty' on. I thought about it like yeast, frozen; if you could thaw it out, there was still life there, and the stuff to make life, sustain it. But I wouldn't bother to find it because it wasn't ever my country and so finding the germs to get it rising again wasn't something I was about to try to do. But I was glad it wasn't all myth, and I hoped my own country (I was sure if I had one I'd recognize it when I found it) would be as potentially salvageable against the barbarian depredations. My objective was to find that country and find my place in it and get in that place, or niche, or, if it turned out that way, grave, and be able to think 'I'm home now.' I didn't think it was possibly one place more than it was possibly the next. All I thought was, because I'd learned it the hard way, 'If you love a country, it's yours; if you don't, it isn't; and spare me the rest of the crap.' So what I was going looking for was, yeah, love. A black woman and a broken little man, and the records of a revolution, lighting out looking for Love. According to the last records, we didn't have all that much time.

These records are five windowpanes with the words scratched on them with a diamond. Her last projection. I give it here with no comment, as she probably said I would.

They came for her while she was scratching on the glass like an old jewel-footed hen.

Projection & Year 2,000—Suicide Manifesto

A SOCIETY, not distant, in which suicide will be the only conceivable freedom, the only possible act of free will. There will be earnest attempts to control that freedom, too, in the reduction of all food, before it is marketed, to a soft pap, making sharp tools obsolete and a crime to possess. One will eat the pap with crooked finger, the original spoon. It is, in fact, a soft world, but not soft enough to be an instrument of self-destruction through suffocation. High places are restricted, windows nonexistent, lethal drugs controlled by the government, water in quantities greater than a teacupful off limits, heat, except in rationed and carefully channeled amounts, an old wive's tale: open fires, indeed! Material for clothing is of a stuff flimsier than paper, impossible to make a rope of and instantly soluble to a nutritive sweetness upon contact with saliva, thereby eliminating the possibilities of choking. Carefully administered drugs, from birth to death, excise from the brain all memory of and impulses toward homicide, in case a mutant still retains enough will to attempt to provoke another person to kill him. But curiously, and at the same time the ultimate in uniformity, people want to kill themselves.

Euphoria-inducing drugs unaccountably lead the way to the very edge of that country of Nirvana which is Death; it is found that the drugs cannot be regulated to suspend midway between borders of natural despair (the original country) and ultimate Euphoria (death) the user, no matter the skill, the breakthroughs, the viciousness of the compounders. The will to die, then, is seen finally as the last unbreakable, ungovernable freedom, expressed centuries ago thus: (and) since death must be the Lucina of life . . .

It will be like the early Christianity: to talk secretly to-

gether of the possibilities of self-immolation will be the last
bond between people, for Christianity was the first pledge of
man to his own mortality when the limitless possibilities of
nature gods were exchanged for the inevitability of One.
And the new world, even now three-quarters formed, will be
the terminal point of that line begun

I can't tell you who was locked in Wanda's basement; I
never did find out. Whoever it was, or they were, may still be
there. People disappear in revolution the way they do on any
day of the year, and are forgotten. Right now, this minute,
people are locked in cages who never will get out and never
will be missed by anybody. Roman, a good old boy, said the
cages were stockyards serving the slaughterhouse of the nursing home. He was sometimes morbid. At least October didn't
leave that place in a pail.

I've told most of the rest. Those plates of glass that Bucky
polishes, rain, shine, tornado, snow? The weather wore the
quicksilver off in no time. Anyway, all that they were used
for—mirrors, mirrors—was vanity. People would parade there
and look at themselves and comb their hair and settle equipment inside tight pants. Politicians rehearsed speeches in
front of them. What was meant to be a constant reminder of
frailty and another kind of pride was turned to personal satisfaction, a sort of Self-Congratulation Wall. But when the
quicksilver wore away there was no reason to go there any
more and they forgot the mirrors just as they forgot October.

She had insisted on the prolonged seated death on the
crucifix because, as she had written about the Moon Man, "the
more horrible and protracted the murder, the longer-lived the
catharsis." Perhaps even then she was writing about herself
. . . she would hate that sentence. She would say, "There
you go, trying to make me noble again." Toward the end she
told me, blunt and sour, "Write this thing up, AA; and if you
call it Crucifixion of an Anti-Semite, it could make you rich.
People buy their wishes on book jackets." I asked if she was
willing to be called an anti-Semite so I could make money.

Her face put to rest any possibility of its being halfway true.

Whether as God, or Saint of the Revolution, or anti-Semite nonpareil, she counted on being remembered. Everything she said, did, thought or taught was toward that end. It would have been like having the very last word of all. Ah, lady, how could you have been so wrong?

Just before it was time to send Bucky home we went down to Merida. I meant to leave the Journals there in some Mayan ruin as a kind of filler, space-takers for what was burned nearly five hundred years ago, thinking their bulk at least might serve a purpose. But trying to redress the smallest of horrors perpetrated by bishops—and bemusing to say, burning the records of learning of a people is just about the smallest—is as futile as it is to pretend that what is in these Journals never happened. But folks will do both.

I took Bucky to Acapulco and he bought a jeep from a hotel on a hill there, a jeep with a candy-striped top. I had the feeling he thought it was a toy, and I envisioned him and Mrs. Hackett playing games in it, before I remembered. I haven't got too long a memory, either, so that when people started saying, those last days in Tasmania, that I wasn't really a black woman at all, and some of them saying I wasn't even a woman, I had a feeling that they could, for all of me, be right.

Bucky—to whom the brass of the plaques suggests institutions, and because he loved institutions and because there is a part of him that still recalls something about a beautiful time called Revolution, with a beautiful ending because she promised there would be—Bucky still polishes the empty glass and the plaques. The brass plaques that say:

MRS. OCTOBER WAS HERE.

Fin.

Fin?